Rosemary for remembrance

It looked to Detective Chief Inspector Jack Finch like a classic case of the blunt instrument wielded with considerable force and deadly intention. Murder in other words. But why the sprig of rosemary clenched firmly in the dead man's right hand in a final cadaveric spasm? What cryptic significance was contained in such a powerful symbol?

In an atmosphere of peace and privilege, a summer course in creative writing was in progress at Morton Grange Girls' School, an eighteenth-century mansion set among cedar trees and tended lawns.

Its organising genius, Bernard Livesey, urbane poet and influential literary critic, was having difficulties with his volatile staff of three: Ron Arnott, former bestselling novelist now facing declining sales; Harriet Wade, attractive, single tutor of the 'Aspects of Novel Writing' course; Jake Nolan, drama teacher, whose physical and emotional energy, like an electric charge, attracted anyone who came close to its field.

And some of the thirty students at Morton Grange were no less explosive elements in a drama that was to claim three lives.

While the grounds swarm with uniformed men, Finch and his Sergeant pursue their patient interrogations. A visit to a fringe theatre in north London, the search for an incriminating letter, a reacquaintance with the text of *Hamlet*, are all inexorable steps towards the culmination of a tragedy inspired by pride, vengeance and ambition.

June Thomson's increasing command of a wide range of social types, together with her subtle handling of a complicated plot, make this story of sudden death her most satisfying to date.

ROSEMARY FOR REMEMBRANCE

June Thomson

CONSTABLE CRIME

Constable London

First published in Great Britain 1988
by Constable & Company Ltd
10 Orange Street London WC2H 7EG
Copyright © 1988 by June Thomson
Set in Linotron Palatino 10 pt by
Rowland Phototypesetting Ltd
Bury St Edmunds, Suffolk
Printed in Great Britain by
St Edmundsbury Press Ltd
Bury St Edmunds, Suffolk

British Library CIP data
Thomson, June
Rosemary for remembrance
I. Title
823'.914[F]   PR6070.H679

ISBN 0 09 468260 7

For Garrett and Paul, with my best love.

1

'I think that covers all the points I wished to raise,' Bernard said with a judicious air, glancing at the notes which lay beside him on the top of the desk, each section neatly subdivided under headings. Raising his head, he glanced across at the others. 'Are there any questions?'

Implying, Harriet thought, that if there were they would be entirely superfluous, Bernard having dealt fully with every possible query and contingency which could arise during the creative writing course which was due to begin in less than half an hour at four o'clock with the arrival of the first students.

There was nothing she wanted to ask. The whole meeting in fact struck her as unnecessary, all four of them – Bernard Livesey, herself, Jake Nolan and Ron Arnott – having taken part the previous year in a similar course which had been held at exactly the same location, Morton Grange Girls' School, leased for the summer while its normal occupants of teaching staff and pupils were away on holiday. The same arrangements which had worked well then could surely have been repeated without the need for this hour-long meeting?

But that was simplistic of her, she realised with amusement, and did not take into account Bernard's need to impress on the rest of them that it was he who was the organising genius behind the entire project.

'I preside, therefore I am' summed up not only Bernard's physical presence behind the desk – actually Miss Winthrop's, the headmistress of Morton Grange School, but Bernard's now for the duration – but his whole attitude to his own creative gifts. As a younger man, he had published several volumes of poetry which had won him considerable literary acclaim. Now in his

7

fifties and that small, clear spring of poetic inspiration having dried up, he had been forced to join the critics and commentators on other people's work through articles in academic magazines, on Radio 3 programmes and, more especially, on the teaching circuit in the States, a transatlantic connection which had given him a senatorial air, polished, urbane, his silvery tie matching his silvery hair as his thin, fastidious, high-nosed profile chaired the meeting from behind the gleaming expanse of mahogany.

Harriet Wade, who had been watching him with fascinated attention, glanced across at the other two, passing the buck of Bernard's query to them.

If 'I preside, therefore I am' summed up Bernard, what, she wondered, would epitomise them?

Jake Nolan was easy: 'I screw, therefore I am.'

He was sitting relaxed beside her, one leg crossed high over the other, left hand grasping the right ankle, exposing too much of the crotch of his jeans, looking bored but with the ennui of an actor on stage playing a role, theatrically wearied, dark brown hair becomingly untidy, occupying himself by drawing with his free hand complicated little doodles on the edge of his note-pad, an activity which had annoyed Bernard throughout the meeting as no doubt Jake had intended it should do.

Now that her short-lived affair with him the previous summer was over, Harriet could view him with a new, objective regard. He was a despoiler, an emotional brigand and so damned obvious that she could not understand why she had ever been sufficiently attracted to him in the first place to allow herself to be lured into his bed, except that at the time he had seemed to possess a sexual energy and a ruthlessness of purpose which, lacking both qualities herself to any such positive degree, she had found attractive.

It was all largely a pose, as she had realised too late; part of Jake's image into which almost all of this drive and energy was directed and for which his sexual encounters merely served as fuel, stoking up his fires. But not entirely and for that reason she was prepared to forgive him a great deal for, despite everything, he possessed a genuine talent for writing and directing plays which was why Bernard tolerated his continuing presence as the summer school's drama tutor, just so long as Jake's extra-mural activities remained reasonably within bounds, an unspoken proviso which both men perfectly well understood.

Ron Arnott who, like Harriet, taught that part of the course described in the brochures as 'Aspects of Novel Writing' was less easy to define in any one phrase. Last summer, Harriet might have said of him, 'I confront, therefore I am.' Then he had been a broad, stocky man, already running to seed like a boxer past his prime, but still exuding a strong physical presence and an air of suppressed aggression, despite the beer belly which swelled out over the top of his trousers. But in the intervening twelve months, it seemed that much of that inner strength had collapsed, leaving him grey-faced and slack-bodied, the smouldering anger reduced to a sullen and morose withdrawal.

Jake, who took a malicious pleasure at times in passing on gossip, had told Harriet that Arnott's marriage had broken up, his wife suing for divorce on the grounds of mental cruelty, the details of which some of the popular newspapers had made a point of featuring and, although Harriet had not read the reports, she could imagine their contents. In addition, Arnott had been ill with some kind of breakdown; and that, too, she could believe.

He sat slumped in his chair, apparently totally uninterested in the meeting although as Bernard, gathering up his notebook and pen, was about to declare the conference closed, Arnott roused himself to ask a question.

'I take it we're responsible again this year for setting our students any written assignments?'

He spoke in a flat London accent which Harriet sometimes suspected was deliberately preserved in order to emphasise, along with his hand-rolled cigarettes and his ill-fitting corduroy jacket, his working-class roots.

Bernard raised an eyebrow.

'Of course, Ronald, although if you have any problems you can always consult with me.'

It was said in a tone of surprised but gentle commiseration as if, aware of Arnott's personal problems, Bernard was prepared to be genuinely tolerant of any professional difficulties Arnott might encounter. At the same time, the double-edged insult was perfectly obvious to all of them, including Arnott himself; firstly in Bernard's use of the word 'Ronald', that middle-class extension of his name which Arnott disliked intensely; and secondly in the implication that Arnott would indeed be in need of Bernard's expertise in the matter of student organisation.

Beside her, Harriet heard Jake laugh softly under his breath and, avoiding his eyes, she stared down studiously into her lap.

Bernard, meanwhile, had gathered up his papers and was rising to his feet.

'If that's all,' he remarked. It was a statement rather than a question, signalling the end of the meeting. Harriet, too, got out of her chair in readiness to make a bolt for it before Jake could waylay her.

It had been a mistake to come, she realised. She should have turned down Bernard's invitation to join the course as a tutor for the second time. All her instincts had told her to refuse, not just on account of Jake but because of that quality of male professional bitchiness between Bernard and Ron and, to a lesser extent, between all three men.

But it had been flattering to be asked and, as a writer herself with as yet only one novel to her credit, she was aware that Bernard had considerable influence in the right critical circles. Besides, she was short of money and the salary, though small, was useful. The teaching wasn't hard either and the offer of a six weeks' stay, all meals provided, in the pleasant setting of Morton Grange School, not to mention the well-kept grounds which surrounded it, was not to be lightly turned down, especially when compared to the contemporary ugliness of the London comprehensive school where she taught during term-time or the confines of her tiny flat.

So, she thought wryly, making for the door, one sells one's soul for a mess of pottage.

She wasn't quite quick enough. Jake caught up with her in the corridor.

'Collapse of stout party,' he remarked, glancing back to where Ron Arnott still remained stubbornly seated in his chair, determined to have, if not the final word, the distinction of being the last person to leave the room.

Bernard, with an air of bustling efficiency, had already hurried ahead of them, lists of names, timetables and room allocations grasped in his hand, on his way to pin them up on the notice-board in the main entrance hall, where at least one student would fail to see them during the coming weeks and would wander disconsolately about the corridors.

'Poor old Ron,' Harriet said lightly, only half meaning it.

'Oh, don't waste your pity on him,' Jake replied, giving her a bright sideways look as he fell into step beside her, suggesting that if she had any softer feelings towards anyone they were better spent on him. 'He's a dreadful old pseud really with all that working-class bullshit. It's a wonder he doesn't turn up for his tutorials in a cloth cap with a whippet at his heels.'

He was right, of course; Ron Arnott was something of a poseur. All the same, it was rich coming from him of all people, Harriet thought, and she was about to make some tart comment when Jake forestalled her.

'But who am I to pass judgement?' he continued. 'If it comes to crap, I can dish it out with the best of them with the possible exception of Bernard who is a past master at the art. Ron's trouble is that he takes himself too seriously. He actually believes in his own image. A pity, that.'

'Why?' Harriet asked, intrigued despite herself. One of the reasons why she had been attracted to Jake the previous year had been this ability of his to be totally objective about himself as well as other people, a disconcerting quality because Harriet was not sure how far it was genuine or how much of it was contrived as part of his own image.

'Because he should have traded it in years ago for the latest model. All that working-class spleen – it's outmoded now, like duffle coats or espresso coffee. And if he could summon up the energy to put down his bottle of whisky and heave himself off his backside out of that comfortable Hampstead pad of his and actually walk round the East End, he'd see the changes for himself. The docks? Gone and the dockers with them. The warehouses? Taken over by the property developers. Life's moved on but Ron's still stuck in the fifties. Bernard's going to ditch him,' he added unexpectedly.

'What makes you think that?' Harriet asked.

'Because Bernard is always especially polite and considerate just before he slips the knife in between the ribs. "If you have any problems, Ronald, you can always consult with me."' Jake mimicked exactly Bernard's tone of commiseration. 'So be warned, my dear Harriet, of Bernard's sympathy. It spells death

11

to one's literary career. Not that you need worry yet. You're Bernard's little pet lamb; at least as long as your particular brand of wry, upmarket, feminine protest, ever so perceptive and literate, is the flavour of the month. Bernard likes nothing better than to be in the artistic swim.'

As they had been speaking, they had passed along the corridor leading from Miss Winthrop's study, situated at the rear of the central block, and had entered the main entrance hall.

Like the whole house, it possessed that grace and understated elegance of the early eighteenth century, slightly shabby now and faded, but not even the signs of wear nor of its conversion from a private mansion to a girls' boarding school could detract from the balance and harmony of its architecture. The hall itself was square, floored with black and white marble in a circular pattern, matching the rounded curve of the upper gallery which, supported on columns, swept to left and right of the central staircase.

It had all the simplicity and fascination of a geometrical drawing, Harriet always thought; a circle within a square; a motif which was echoed both above and below in the arched openings which led to corridors and inner staircases, in the semi-circular architraves to the pairs of niches, each surmounted by a plaster shell, which decorated the walls of the lower hall and in the two gilt-framed mirrors which hung between them, the gold-leaf tarnished now and the glass turned watery with age.

There was no sign of Bernard although his notices were pinned up on the square, green-baize board facing one of these mirrors on the opposite wall in which were reflected the white oblongs of paper, exactly aligned and each fastened in all four corners by a brass-headed drawing-pin.

The mirror also reflected Harriet and Jake and, as they passed it, Jake suddenly spun her round towards it, taking up his own position behind her, his hands still resting on her shoulders.

The unexpected action and the appearance of both their images, one behind the other, as if they had jumped up out of the glass at her, both startled and disconcerted her. They looked so dreadfully intimate, Jake's face smiling above hers, eyes crinkled up, lips parted to show white teeth – a *practised* smile, she thought, perfected along with his air of casual charm in many other mirrors – and below it her own face, tucked in under his chin, as if he were wearing it as some damned trophy round his neck. It seemed so oddly unfamiliar in those first few seconds of astonished confrontation that she saw, not herself but a stranger, a young woman in her early twenties with a pale, oval face, dark grey eyes and hair the colour of wheat which hung over one shoulder in a thick, loosely braided plait.

'And what about your image, Harriet?' Jake was asking softly.

She was about to answer angrily that she didn't know what he meant – that, as far as she was concerned, she had no image – when someone behind them cleared his throat and, pulling herself free from Jake's grasp, she turned to see a middle-aged man standing just inside the glass doors which led out on to the porch, suitcase in hand, regarding them wtih an embarrassed yet gratified air, as if pleased to have witnessed such an intimate scene between so young and good-looking a couple.

'Goodyear,' he announced, moving forward towards them. 'Frank Goodyear,' adding with an apologetic smile, 'I'm afraid I've arrived a little early.'

He had; a whole half an hour too early which was exasperating although Frank Goodyear himself seemed not too abashed by this fact. He was a pleasant but undistinguished-looking man, in his fifties, of medium height and a little stooped across the shoulders, with thin brown hair which was turning grey, neat hands and clothes and the subdued, slightly formal manner of a man who has spent most of his life indoors – in a local library, perhaps, or in the office of a minor branch of government – used to small responsibilities but never making any major decisions.

And yet, despite this air of reserve, he had a quiet self-assurance which Harriet liked and which made her instantly warm towards him. The name, Frank Goodyear, was familiar to her as one of the students in her own tutorial group, a list of whom Bernard had given her earlier that afternoon.

Grateful for the excuse to break free from Jake, she smiled as she crossed the hall towards him.

'Welcome to Morton Grange,' she said, holding out her hand. 'I'm Harriet Wade, your tutor. Would you like to go up to your room straight away, Mr Goodyear? Tea will be served in about half an hour when the others arrive.'

He smiled and nodded, glancing about him with a bright-eyed interest as she found his room number on the list pinned up on the board before preceding him up the stairs.

13

'Beautiful place you've got here,' he commented. 'Lovely gardens, too. I noticed those as I drove up. By the way, I've bagged one of the garages round at the back of the house. I hope that's all right. The car's a bit of a nuisance to start if it's not kept under cover. Ignition trouble,' he added in way of further explanation.

'I don't think anyone will mind,' Harriet assured him, noticing that he spoke with a faint Midlands accent, Nottingham, perhaps.

They reached the upper gallery landing and Harriet turned into the corridor leading to the west wing which, like the east wing on the far side of the main building, contained the study-bedrooms of the fifth- and sixth-year pupils and had been set aside for the use of the summer-school students and staff. His was number six and she opened the door, inviting him to enter.

'Nice! Very nice indeed!' he said, putting his suitcase down on the bed and looking about him, clearly delighted with what he saw. Indeed, he seemed almost buoyant with happiness as if the plain, sparsely furnished room with its divan bed, its small fitted wardrobe, the one chair standing in front of the desk which, with the mirror hanging on the wall above it, was intended to serve double-duty as a dressing-table, and the stark white basin in the corner had lifted him up to some high peak of joy. Harriet wondered at his reaction. It seemed too extreme, like a child's at Christmas, raised to too high a pitch of expectation.

No doubt in term-time the room would appear more comfortable and welcoming, strewn with the personal possessions of whoever normally occupied it. Now, stripped of its posters and family photographs, the shelves empty of books, it seemed as vacant and impersonal as any tourist-grade hotel bedroom, offering a clean bed and somewhere to keep one's clothes but nothing more although the view from the window across the lawns at the back of the house towards the high yew hedges which surrounded the school's swimming-pool was probably an improvement on the outlook offered by most such establishments.

Smiling, she said, 'I'll see you downstairs later. Tea will be served at four o'clock when the others arrive,' and, leaving him to unpack, she walked back to the main landing, turning to the right along another corridor to the east wing where her own bedroom was situated.

This separation of the sexes was a deliberate plan on Bernard's

14

part, she assumed, to keep herself and Jake as far apart as possible. The previous summer, the rooms in the two wings had been allocated on an alphabetical basis, regardless of sex. This year, for the first time, men and women had been strictly segregated, the men to the west wing, herself along with all the female students to the east. Not that she and Jake had been at all indiscreet and she doubted if any of the students had been aware that two of their tutors had been conducting a clandestine love affair under the same roof.

But Bernard had guessed. He had an almost spinsterish capacity for scenting out illicit relationships and took a headmistressy delight in frustrating them.

Well, he would be wasting his time this year, Harriet thought. She had no intention of picking up where she had left off with Jake although, as she crossed the room to the mirror to pin up her braid of hair into a more conventional chignon in readiness to meet the students over tea, she felt a small pang of longing for some close contact with another person, if only in friendship. She had friends, of course – colleagues at work and women she had been to school or university with whom she still met from time to time and whose company she enjoyed. But none of them were special and she felt suddenly the irrational need for some close companion, a desire brought on, no doubt, by Morton Grange itself which with its classrooms and playing-fields roused in her memories of the easy companionships of adolescence.

She knew she would never discover that intimacy with someone like Jake. He was entirely predatory, concerned only with satisfying his own desires. As for the students, she doubted either if among those there would be anyone capable of filling that empty hollow inside herself which wasn't so much loneliness as a sense of the absence of something precious but undefinable, like homesickness.

If they were anything like last year's lot, they would be mostly middle-aged and more intent on finding an answer to their own needs than on gratifying anyone else's. As for the younger ones, in her experience they tended to be even more self-absorbed and she remembered one in particular with a small *moue* of distaste – Leon, who had fastened himself like a small, pale, neurotic leech to Jake the previous summer. Even Jake for all his ruthlessness had found it difficult to get rid of him although Harriet suspected that, to begin with at least, Jake had been flattered by Leon's attentions and may even have encouraged them. It was only when Leon had become too shrill and hysterical in his demands that Jake had put an end to the relationship, the confrontation coinciding to everyone's relief with the last day of the course so that Bernard, who had regarded the whole episode with extreme disfavour, had been able to pack the young man off without too much scandal and without any serious damage to the good name of the Morton Grange summer school. But it had been an unpleasant and highly emotional situation and, as she closed the door behind her, Harriet hoped to God that no one like Leon would present himself as a student at this year's classes.

Returning along the corridor, she began to descend the stairs at the same moment that Joyce Yarwood, the school's domestic bursar, kept on for the duration along with other kitchen and outdoor staff while Bernard's students occupied the premises, crossed the hall towards the common room, pushing a trolley containing plates of sandwiches and cakes, already cut into slices. She was followed by Mrs Soames, the assistant caretaker's wife, who worked in the kitchen and who was also pushing a trolley, the top tier of which was loaded with two huge, steaming metal teapots, the bottom with cups and saucers, jingling gently together.

It seemed that tea was about to be served.

Its arrival was nicely time. At the same moment, the grandfather clock which stood just inside the main entrance doors chimed four and almost simultaneously the school's minibus, driven by George Burton, the head groundsman, who had gone to collect those students without cars who had arrived at Chelmsford station on the 3.25 train, drew up on the gravelled forecourt in front of the porch.

Hardly had it come to a halt than Bernard, closely followed by Jake, appeared in the doorway of the staff common room, where presumably they had been waiting for its arrival, Bernard already assuming that professional smile of greeting, designed to make each student feel uniquely welcome, while, behind his back, Jake met Harriet's eyes and twisted up his face into a comic God-help-us-all expression.

Refusing to be drawn into any conspiracy with Jake, Harriet kept her own face neutral and stayed where she was at the foot of

16

the stairs, preferring to remain uninvolved either in the domestic organisation of the tea-trolleys or in Bernard's welcome of the first consignment of students until Bernard himself invited her to come forward to be introduced.

It was therefore as an outsider that she was able to witness the interchange which took place immediately afterwards and which was over so quickly that, had she not remained aloof, she might have missed it.

She was conscious first of Joyce Yarwood's reaction to Jake's appearance at the door of the staff common room. Joyce had halted with her trolley to allow the two men to cross into the hall and, as Jake passed her, Harriet caught sight of the expression on the woman's face.

It was all the more evident, at least to Harriet, because Joyce Yarwood's features were usually so politely and non-committally expressionless. She was in her middle thirties, pleasant enough to talk to, efficient in her work and not unattractive, with soft, brown hair and pale, regular features, redeemed from complete homeliness by the mouth, the upper lip of which slightly protruded over the lower, giving the whole face a look of childlike vulnerability which Harriet found appealing.

During the previous year's summer school, Harriet had tried to draw the woman out, intrigued not only by her mouth but by the whole air of *noli me tangere* which she seemed to exude, as if she had drawn a circle round herself describing a Tom Tiddler's ground into which no one was permitted to enter. But, apart from a few basic facts about her, that she was unmarried, that she had trained in catering in London and that she came originally from Dorset – mere scraps of information which nevertheless Harriet had only been able to extract from her by direct questioning – she had learnt nothing more and Joyce Yarwood remained an enigma.

Thrown back on her own imaginative resources, Harriet had been forced to create a background for her which seemed to fit. She was, she decided, the only daughter of elderly, over-protective parents, with some tragic loss, perhaps a lover who had died or had abandoned her, to account for that expression of sensitivity, very close to tears, which seemed to tremble just below the calm, neutral exterior.

Now, looking across the hall to avoid Jake's glance, Harriet saw

17

that Joyce Yarwood had turned her head in his direction, following his progress as he accompanied Bernard towards the entrance doors. And for a few seconds her face was quite undisguised, the expression totally open. There was no mistaking the look of longing in the eyes nor the eager lifting of that long upper lip.

She was in love with him.

More than that, she was his lover. To Harriet, it was blazoned in Joyce Yarwood's face as clearly as if she had worn a placard round her neck announcing the fact.

The next second, the features closed over again as, turning her head away and holding back the door with one hand, she manoeuvred the loaded trolley into the common room, presenting her back only, in its neat blue overall coat, to Harriet's astonished and aggrieved gaze.

Her anger was directed largely at Jake although also at herself. But before she had the time to collect up her thoughts and to centre them on his perfidy as well as on her own naïvety in assuming that their affair last summer had been exclusive, a new diversion occurred to distract her.

Jake was saying furiously, 'For God's sake, Bernard, how the hell did *he* get on the course again?'

He was flourishing an angry arm at the minibus which was disgorging its occupants on to the gravel in a chattering group which had begun to cluster round the back of the vehicle where George Burton was unloading the luggage.

It was not difficult to pick out the cause of Jake's fury. Leon Murray was only too obvious among the new arrivals. He was standing at the front of the group, pale, golden hair – surely too good to be true? – flopping forward across his forehead in a charmingly casual lick, the petulant, pretty-boy face in profile, lips pouted, chin raised, clamouring to be the first to be handed his suitcase.

'My dear Jake, believe me, I had no idea,' Bernard was protesting. 'If I'd known he'd sent in an application, I would have returned it to him at once.'

He seemed genuinely nonplussed and for once had lost some of his usual bland self-confidence.

Crossing to the notice-board, Jake hard on his heels, he consulted the list of students' names.

'You see,' he began, 'he's not here.'

18

'Yes, he bloody well is,' Jake interrupted, jabbing a finger. 'He's down under B. L. Murray and he's in my tutorial group. Well, I'm not teaching him, Bernard, and that's final. Get rid of him; I don't care how. But if he turns up tomorrow morning for my class, then I shall walk out.'

And with that, he strode away down the passage which led to the kitchens – and, Harriet added to herself, to Joyce Yarwood who, together with Mrs Soames, had already departed in that direction – leaving Bernard to explain in a hurried aside to Harriet, the only person left to listen, 'It's quite a common name, Murray. When my secretary handed over the application forms for my approval, I simply didn't make the connection. And he registered as B. L. Murray, not Leon, so of course . . .'

There was no time to say any more. The students were beginning to file into the hall through the double glass doors, joined by others who had meanwhile arrived by car, setting down their suitcases to look about them at the circular gallery, the arched niches, the elegant sweep of the staircase, obviously delighted at the setting in which they would spend the next six days. And at Bernard who, recovering his poise, hurried forward, one hand extended in a gesture of general greeting, the senatorial smile pinned back into position as firmly as one of his notices – a welcoming committee of one, Harriet thought with amusement.

2

And yet there was a great deal to admire about Bernard. By the time everyone had assembled for tea, he had not only succeeded in rounding up Ron Arnott, still sulking after his earlier humiliation, but had managed to persuade Jake to return to the staff common room and had sufficiently calmed him down for Jake to resume his usual light romantic role of the summer school's charmer which suited his personality better than that of the dramatic heavy. Bernard had also dealt with Leon. During tea, Harriet noticed the pair of them standing by one of the long sash windows which overlooked the front garden, Bernard magisterial, Leon abashed and contrite, like a schoolboy receiving a wigging from the headmaster, but all done so discreetly that no one else appeared to realise that anything untoward was taking place.

In addition, Bernard found time to play host to the new students, circulating genially among them, introducing them to one another and to the course tutors, answering queries, exchanging a pleasantry here, bestowing a smile there so that, scarcely had the first cup of tea been drunk and the first slices of cake eaten, than the long panelled common room, with its informal groupings of chintz-covered armchairs, rang to the sound of voices and laughter.

If the success of a social occasion was to be measured in decibels, Harriet thought, smiling and talking herself until the muscles in her face ached, then Bernard's efforts had been well rewarded. Instead of thirty strangers, they might have been a party of old friends meeting together in joyful reunion.

There were too many in the group for her to assimilate each one immediately although, as in a class at the beginning of a new academic year at Foxwood Comprehensive School, certain individuals stood out for one reason or another whose names, emblazoned on circular identity tags pinned to lapels or the fronts of dresses, she was able to remember without any difficulty.

Frank Goodyear was one, due entirely to their earlier meeting. Otherwise, Harriet might have passed him over for there was nothing really remarkable about him apart from that air of buoyant happiness which had first singled him out but which was less apparent now that he was merely one of the crowd.

More instantly noticeable was an auburn-haired woman in her early thirties, smartly dressed in a well-cut green linen suit, attractive and animated, except that, in rare moments of repose, her face quickly assumed a bored expression. She was Felicity Grayson, whose name was already familiar to her from her tutorial list, Harriet realised, reading the woman's identity tag as she stood nearby talking to a lugubrious middle-aged man, another of her students.

Jake, too, had picked her out. Harriet saw him excuse himself from a plain, elderly woman and push his way across the room towards her, his fires instantly lit.

It was inevitable, Harriet thought, and yet it did not stop her from feeling a sudden surge of exasperated resentment, not at the woman nor even at Jake's immediate desire for her but at the ease with which the pair of them signalled their availability to one another, a form of communication that she herself had never quite mastered but which, like some esoteric language she was not particularly desirous of learning, she could still envy the proficiency of in others.

Turning away, she searched the room for someone with whom she, too, might find an immediate accord and discovered two possibilities, one a woman with dark hair and a thin, mobile face, the other a tall man in his thirties, with blunt features and an air of easy, relaxed good humour, who were standing together talking. Quickly passing the lugubrious man to Ron Arnott, who was conveniently at hand, she went across to introduce herself to them both, reading their identity tags as she did so.

They were Kay Ratcliff, she discovered, and Steve Mayhew, 'Steve' clearly intended as the name by which he intended to be known for the duration of the course and which suited him with its no-nonsense brevity.

Kay and Steve – easy enough to remember. Bernard insisted on this use of Christian names, another example of his transatlantic experience although Harriet sometimes doubted if every one of the students, especially the older women and the stuffier men, approved of this form of instant chumminess. There was a spurious intimacy about it which caused her at times to suspect its worthiness.

Steve was another of her students whose name she remembered seeing on her tutorial list, a fact which pleased her. In the mental columns of plus and minus points already forming about the members of her class, Steve was definitely a plus and would balance out the lugubrious man whose name she had already forgotten and, she suspected, would recollect only with an effort at the end of the six-day course.

She was disappointed that Kay was in Jake's group. She looked interestingly ironic, not the type to suffer fools gladly, and Harriet wondered how Kay and Jake would get on as student and tutor. As they stood in conversation, during which she learned that Kay was a drama teacher and Steve a social worker, she saw Kay glance several times with amusement under deep, sardonic eyelids towards the centre of the room where Jake and the auburn-haired Felicity Grayson were laughing a little too loudly,

21

like an adult observing the behaviour of a couple of adolescents and finding it diverting.

After one of these glances, she looked at Harriet and gave her a brief smile that was nevertheless surprising in its implied intimacy.

I believe, the smile seemed to be saying, that you and I might share the same sense of humour.

It was another invitation to conspiracy and one which, unlike Jake's earlier attempt to draw her into his circle, Harriet found to her liking although, as their eyes met, she quickly veiled her own glance, saying brightly to Steve, 'Tell me, what sort of social work do you do?'

'With deprived families,' he said, 'in Birmingham.'

It was not the answer she had been expecting. It seemed out of keeping with his easy-going good nature. And besides, it invited a more complex response than she was prepared for or for which the occasion gave opportunity. The teacups and the slices of Joyce Yarwood's Victoria sponge cakes suggested the social rejoinder, 'Really? How fascinating!' accompanied by a smile and an interested tilt to the head. But that would be doing them both an injustice.

On the other hand, to embark, as she would have wished for his sake as well as hers, on a genuine discussion of his work was hardly in keeping either with the temporary relationships within the room, groups constantly forming and re-forming, or with the cocktail-party quality of the noise level.

In the event, Harriet was spared having to make any response at all. Seeing that the plates of sandwiches and cakes were depleted and that the teapots were being raided for second cups by those who already felt sufficiently at home in Morton Grange to help themselves uninvited, Bernard decided that the time had come for him to preside once again.

Moving forward towards the fireplace, he took up his position under the portrait of Miss Edith Poulson, MA Oxon., the school's headmistress in the days of its Edwardian expansion, who was posed, one hand on a table piled high with books as if about to distribute end-of-term prizes, presiding herself and smiling down benignly on Bernard through her pince-nez as he tapped on the marble mantelshelf with his teaspoon for silence.

Once he had everyone's attention, he beckoned the tutors

22

forward to join him, acolytes, Harriet thought, to his celebrant priest, signalling them to their places a little to the left and right of him, Jake Nolan still eyeing up the auburn-haired Felicity Grayson, Ron Arnott, who hated these occasions, glowering at the faces of the students now turned in their direction while Harriet, feeling uncharacteristically self-conscious, was too aware of Steve Mayhew and Kay Ratcliff in the front row and turned instead to look at Bernard who now stepped forward.

He began with a short speech of welcome, almost word for word the same as last year's. Great pleasure to have them all here as students at the Morton Grange summer writing school which, as Director of Studies, he counted it a privilege to organise. Hoped they and their tutors, whom he introduced formally by name at this point, would share in the creative endeavours, a voyage of self-exploration in which they were all fellow travellers. In the case of any problems or difficulties, do contact him personally; he was always available.

But not always willing to listen, Harriet thought, remembering Bernard's warning to them at the afternoon's meeting not to encourage students to pester him unnecessarily but to deal with any queries themselves, a proviso directed explicitly at Ron Arnott who, deliberately taking Bernard at his word, had last year directed his own time-wasters straight to the door of Bernard's study.

The speech of welcome was followed by a short homily on the rules that applied during their stay at Morton Grange School although Bernard, in his anxiety to appear one of them, was at pains to point out that the regulations were not of his making but were imposed on him by the board of school governors to whom he was responsible. All buildings such as the laboratories and the lower school houses of residence were out of bounds, together with any rooms in the main block not set aside for their use. So, too, was the assembly hall unless specifically required and then only by the drama students and with his special permission. The grass tennis-courts were also closed to them but – and here Bernard smiled at them as benignly as Miss Poulson on the wall above him, as if bestowing on them a personal gift – the hard courts and the swimming-pool were available for their use. And could he please remind them that, because of reasons of security, all doors had to be locked by 11 p.m. although anyone wishing to return after that hour should sign the late-book by the main entrance after which a member of staff would be available to let them in?

A low murmur of dissent was heard from those who had envisaged convivial evenings spent at the local pub until closing-time. It was also a point of dispute among the tutors who were delegated these late-night portering duties although Bernard disarmed any criticism by laying the blame for this curtailment of freedom firmly at the feet of the school governors. Harriet doubted they were entirely responsible for the regulation, suspecting Bernard may have played a more active part in its formation than he was willing to admit.

'And now,' Bernard concluded, 'I'm sure you've heard quite enough information from me. Classes will begin at nine-thirty tomorrow morning. In the meantime you are free to unpack and to make the most of this glorious afternoon. You will find a list of room allocations on the notice-board in the main hall and signs directing you to the east and west wings at the head of the main staircase. Dinner will be served promptly at seven-thirty in the dining-room which you will find at the end of the central corridor leading from the hall.'

The students began to disperse in chattering groups towards the double doors but, instead of following them, Harriet made her escape through the other door at the far end of the room which opened into a small side vestibule with its own entrance into the grounds behind the west wing, from where she walked round to the front of the house. She longed suddenly for silence and for a respite from the press of other people's personalities.

The garden afforded her both. Here, facing the main building, it was largely lawn, planted with ornamental trees and shrubs to shield from view the new assembly hall at the far end of the west wing although the school chapel, built at the turn of the century when Morton Grange had first been established as a girls' board-ing school, stood proudly alone on its own sweep of grass. Further off still, beyond the chapel, the outdoor swimming-pool was also decently hidden away inside its own box of high, clipped yew hedges.

To her right, at the end of the east wing, more modern extensions, the gym and the laboratories as well as the four solid Edwardian buildings which housed the lower-school pupils, were completely screened from sight behind a dense planting of firs and evergreens.

Viewed from the front lawn where she settled herself down under a tree, her back resting against its trunk, only Morton Grange itself was visible, an eighteenth-century mansion, still retaining its elegantly harmonious façade of rose-red brick and the symmetrical tiers of sash windows each with its white stone pediment. Another huge pediment crowned the central, three-storeyed block which dominated the two lower wings stretching out on either side, the west wing further extended by the addition of a glass and wrought-iron orangery, since turned into a music-room and used by Jake for his drama classes. Calm, serene, Morton Grange rose from its surrounding lawns with a graceful and yet unpretentious beauty, so terribly English that she herself felt composed and in harmony with it. Foxwood Comprehensive seemed a thousand miles away, another experience.

But which, she wondered, was the real England? Morton Grange with its tended lawns and cedar trees, its atmosphere of peace and privilege, or the scrubby, litter-strewn playing-fields of Foxwood, its rows of scarred desks in its modular classrooms, the armies of pupils, 3E and 4C, 1J and 2B, who surged in and out of those desks at regular intervals to the ringing of bells and for some of whom the real world began outside the gates at street corners and amusement arcades and Saturday night discos?

Not all, of course; she would have resigned her post years before had not some classes and individual pupils made it possible for her still to hang on to that ideal of equal opportunities for everyone and the belief that it was only through education that one lifted oneself above the daily grind of getting and spending. All the same, there were occasions when she felt her grasp on those ideals beginning to falter and when she wanted to cry out in a parody of the biblical quotation, 'I offered you bread but you preferred the stone.'

But here at least at Morton Grange for the whole of the summer, she would be able to indulge herself, to make her offering of bread and have it accepted with gratitude by the students. Whether it constituted the greater reality, she herself was uncertain.

Jake was only too real and not part of the pleasure of the occasion either.

No sooner had Harriet settled herself with her back against the tree and her face lifted towards the sun than she saw him come loping down the slope of the lawn towards her with a confident, easy stride, clearly expecting a welcome. She watched him approach through narrowed eyes.

He sat down beside her, stretching out his legs on the grass.

'Go away, Jake,' she told him.

'Bernard sent me to find you,' he replied, not at all put out. 'He's fussing about numbers in the tutorial groups now I've refused to have Leon. I don't suppose you'd agree to teach him?'

Harriet sat up.

'No,' she said. 'I won't. Why should I have to put up with your left-overs?'

To her surprise, Jake nodded in agreement.

'Exactly what I said to Bernard. You can't expect to offload your problems on to Harriet's young but lovely shoulders, I told him. Be a man, Bernard. Face up to your responsibilities. It was you who allowed the little turd back in the first place. Although we can hardly blame poor old Bernard. He's just shown me Leon's registration form. The sly little sod signed under his real name, Brian Murray.'

'So he's not really Leon at all?'

'His second name's Leonard but Brian Leonard isn't nearly as fetching as Leon, is it? It doesn't have quite the same romantic, middle European ring to it.'

'I don't see why Bernard simply doesn't ask him to leave. After all, in a way he's here under false pretences,' Harriet said severely. She felt fussed herself by the potential cross-currents of relationships and tensions which could emerge and which seemed to threaten the pleasant languor of the afternoon, the view of Morton Grange, the garden itself. Not that such considerations seemed to trouble Jake who had lain down beside her, arms comfortably folded behind his head.

'Bernard won't do that. It's much too direct and positive. He prefers the softly-softly diplomatic approach with all its endless comings and goings. As it is, he's already given Leon a lecture on the need to preserve the good name of the school and I gather Leon's promised to be a model student. And besides, if Bernard chucked him out, he'd have to return his fees which would come very hard. So Leon remains on the course.'

'You don't seem too worried at the prospect,' Harried commented. She thought she knew why, too. The presence of Felicity Grayson was more than adequate compensation for any inconvenience caused by Leon's unexpected arrival. She couldn't resist adding, 'I thought you said you'd go if he stayed.'

He grinned across at her, unrepentant.

'A piece of dramatic licence designed to keep Bernard on his toes although I admit I was bloody angry at the time. It pays to throw the occasional tantrum. Remember that, Harriet. It's the best bit of advice I can give you. Bernard will respect you all the more for it. As for Leon, as long as I don't have to teach him, I don't much care and if I have to meet him face to face, I shall be cool and aloof. He hates that.'

It was said in a tone of amused satisfaction which made Harriet suspect that Jake's connection with Leon had not been terminated during the previous summer after all, as he had led everyone to believe.

She said, 'You've been seeing him recently.'

It was almost an accusation.

Jake rolled over on to his stomach so that his face was hidden between his arms. His voice came to her muffled.

'He got hold of the phone number of the theatre in London I'm involved with and rang me a couple of times, suggesting we met for a drink. It seemed rude to keep turning him down. You know how it is, Harriet.'

'No, I don't know,' she retorted. Rudeness had never seemed to bother Jake in the past. When he didn't reply, she added tartly, 'Go on.'

He sat up, looking aggrieved.

'What do you mean – go on? That's all there was to it. I met him for a drink, that's all.'

'And?'

He pulled a face, boyishly rueful. 'Oh, how sharp you are, Harriet! A positive little gimlet, boring away to get at the truth. All right, so I asked him round to the Lion's Head in Camden a couple of times where we run that theatre group I help organise. And why not? He seemed genuinely interested. In fact, he offered to invest some money in a production we were working on. I didn't see anything wrong with it at the time. Leon was trying very hard to be on his best behaviour and, with the Bath

Festival in the offing, it seemed a golden opportunity to take the play out to a wider audience . . .'

He shrugged and left it there.

'But it didn't work?' Harriet persisted. It was, of course, none of her business but all the same she felt irrationally angry with Jake for allowing his opportunism and his need to gratify his own needs to blind him to the risks of continuing a relationship with someone as unstable as Leon. And now all of them would be expected to pay the price.

'You know Leon. Once he'd parted with the cheque, he seemed to think he'd bought the whole bloody production – me, the actors, even the backstage staff. He was constantly turning up and trying to shove his oar in and not just at the Lion's Head but at my flat as well. So in the end, I had a God-almighty row with him, gave him his money back and told him to get lost in no uncertain terms. I haven't seen him since until he turned up here this afternoon. Of course, it meant the play went down the tubes but it seemed a small price to pay. If I hadn't got rid of him, I might have ended up strangling the little creep.'

It had been on the tip of Harriet's tongue to ask if he and Leon had been lovers; lightly, of course, turning it into something of a joke. She did not want to appear jealous of Jake's other relationships, especially now that she had decided that their own affair was over. She was curious all the same. It would account for Leon's persistence in returning to Morton Grange and for Jake's initial anger at his arrival. And she wouldn't have been surprised if Leon had shared Jake's bed. She was quite prepared to believe that Jake's sexuality was all-embracing – an unfortunate and yet appropriate term to use under the circumstances, she thought, with a small, amused grimace.

Besides, as a writer, sexual ambivalence interested her, not in any prurient manner, but because of the added permutations it offered in the range of human relationships.

But it was hardly fitting to question Jake on the subject and anyway he forestalled her by getting to his feet.

'For God's sake, Harriet, let's forget Leon, shall we? Bernard's promised to deal with him if he steps out of line. At least, I got that much out of him. Are you coming back? I've got a bottle of gin in my room. We could have a G and T together before dinner.'

Harriet settled herself back against the tree and lifted her face towards the sun again, half closing her eyes. Cool and aloof, wasn't that what he had said?

'No thank you, Jake.'

She was aware of him standing over her, nonplussed by her indifference.

'All right. Suit yourself,' he replied as, shrugging, he set off across the lawn towards the house.

How absurd he is! Harriet thought, watching him through her eyelashes. For a few seconds, he looked diminished, a small boy sent packing by an adult, but within a few paces he had recovered his jauntiness and, hands in pockets, broke into a jog-trot, making straight, if Harriet guessed correctly, for the fructuous Felicity Grayson.

Good word, that. Fructuous.

Harriet smiled and closed her eyes.

George Burton carefully drew both boots across the scraper outside the kitchen door although they hardly needed this scrupulous attention. He had merely been putting away the school minibus and directing those summer school students who had arrived by car to the garages in the stable block behind the main house.

The boot-scraping activity was entirely to placate Joyce Yarwood whom he could see through the glass panel in the kitchen door, standing at the long preparation table which occupied the centre of the room, slicing up vegetables in readiness for the evening meal.

As he scraped away, he kept his head turned in her direction, watching her profile with its lowered eyes and half-parted lips, a study in concentration, the coil of her hair fitting neatly into the nape of her neck.

His feelings for her astonished him. He was over fifty, widowed for the past two years, and had imagined himself reconciled to a single life although he had not discounted the possibility of remarrying one day to someone of his own age, a widow possibly, who, like him, was looking for companionship rather than any grand passion. He had made no allowances for falling in love and, for him, preparation was everything. He had planned every step in his career from its humble beginnings as assistant employed by a local council to his present position of head gardener and groundsman at Morton Grange School, with his own house and two men working under him, not to mention the part-timers who came in from the village to carry out the more menial tasks of grass-cutting and hedge-trimming.

The possibility of falling in love and with someone like Joyce Yarwood, almost young enough to be his daughter, had not crossed his mind until it had happened. It made him feel ill at ease, both with himself and with her, as if he were to blame for the strength of the passion which overwhelmed him even just watching her from a distance.

She knew he was there. He could tell by the way her shoulders suddenly stiffened that she was aware of his presence on the other side of the door. But she didn't look round. Instead, she put down the knife she was using and moved across to the bank of stoves that lined the far wall of the kitchen where she began moving saucepans about on the hotplates, her back towards him.

He gave a final scrape to his boots and entered.

'Anything you want from the garden?' he asked.

As he spoke, he glanced to left and right, hoping for signs that there might be an offer of a cup of tea. If he were less self-conscious with her, he might have suggested it himself. Any chance of a cuppa? But he could hear the dishwashers pumping away in the pantry and the big teapots from the students' tea had already been washed up and were standing up-ended on the draining board.

'Only some lettuces,' she replied, not even bothering to turn round to look at him.

It was better than nothing. If she had said 'No', he would have had to go away unneeded.

'How many?' he asked.

'Half a dozen.'

He waited but she said nothing more and after a few seconds he was forced to remark, 'Right you are,' before walking back towards the door, conscious of the noise his boots made on the tiled floor.

In the kitchen garden, he went along the rows of lettuces picking out the best for her, parting the outer leaves and choosing those with the densest hearts.

Not that she'd notice, he thought as he twisted off the roots and

30

shook out the loose earth. He was wasting his time. It was that young tutor chap, Nolan, she was keen on, not him. He had seen them the previous summer walking together at the far end of the school grounds and had once come across them one evening in the kitchen, Nolan perched on the end of the table as if he had every right to be there while Joyce had stood at his side, looking flushed and more animated than he'd ever seen her, and the pair of them acting like lovers surprised by his unexpected arrival.

All the same, he arranged the lettuces in the basket as carefully as if they had been bouquets of flowers before carrying them back to the kitchen where Mrs Soames met him on the step.

'Ta,' she said and shut the door in his face.

'Oh, it's you, Ronald,' Bernard said disapprovingly. He had hoped for half an hour of solitude before dinner to enjoy a glass of sherry while admiring the view from Miss Winthrop's study window of lawns and cedars, the school chapel dominating the centre of the vista, deplorably neo-Gothic, of course, although Betjeman had done much to revive its architectural prestige.

It was the time of day which gave Bernard his greatest pleasure. Here, in the study, with its glass-fronted bookcases and swagged curtains, its view of chapel tower and trees, it was possible to imagine himself an Oxford don, quietly and appreciatively sipping a glass of sherry before putting on his gown and joining the others at high table.

And now to spoil it came Arnott, putting his head round the door after the most perfunctory of knocks and, judging by his expression, with some complaint or other which could probably have waited until the morning although Bernard already suspected the reason behind Arnott's unwelcome arrival.

'If you've come about Murray,' he began. It was always better, he had discovered after years of dealing with some television interviewers and the more aggressive questioners after one of his lectures, to anticipate the confrontation. It took the wind out of his opponents' sails and put them immediately on the defensive.

'I'm not teaching the little bugger,' Arnott announced, adding as Bernard raised his eyebrows, 'I use the term technically.'

'My dear Ronald, I had no intention of asking you,' Bernard

31

replied, waving a hand towards one of the armchairs seconds after Arnott had seated himself. 'You'll have a sherry?'

He filled glasses for them both, handing one to Arnott and carrying his own over to the desk. Resuming his seat behind it, he ostentatiously moved some papers to one side at the same time glancing at his watch as if to indicate that, although Arnott had come at a most inconvenient time, he, Bernard, was prepared to give him his full attention. Because Murray was not the crux of the matter. He was merely a peg on which Arnott could hang all his other grievances – his ill health, his falling sales, the break-up of his marriage, the fact that his latest novel had been almost enirely passed over by the critics, certainly those in the quality newspapers while even the popular press had been grudging in its reviews.

Although what he expects I can do about it, Bernard thought, God alone knows.

All the same, he felt almost sorry for the man. He looked so utterly dejected, sitting slumped in his chair, huge, clumsy hands clutching the fragile cut-crystal glass – a navvy's hands, really. It might have been better if Arnott had never written a word but had stayed in his East End tenement among his own kind, working on the docks like his father.

He lacked finesse. He also lacked, in Bernard's opinion, a great many other qualities – the ability to deal with success and now, it seemed, with failure, the sensitivity to see that literary fashions had moved on since the fifties. More importantly, he lacked even the basic good manners of making himself agreeable to the critics at literary functions. There had been too many occasions in the past when Arnott had openly shown his contempt for them. While he had been riding high and his books had topped the best-seller lists, it hadn't mattered so much. But now that his popularity had waned, some of those same critics had sharpened their knives. There had been one or two particularly scathing reviews recently – Bagstock in the *Temple Magazine*, for example, and Halliday in the *Globe*. Unkind, of course, and quite unnecessary. His own experience had taught Bernard to keep aloof from such literary in-fighting and to preserve a dignified silence about those novels he could not decently recommend.

'So you weren't going to ask me to teach Murray?' Arnott was demanding. 'Why not? You asked that Wade woman.'

Bernard sat back in his chair astounded. To be accused of passing Arnott over in the matter of tutoring Murray when Arnott had clearly come with the express intention of complaining about being asked was not only standing logic on its head; it was positively paranoiac.

Arnott would have to go, Bernard decided. It was a decision he had been postponing since the end of the previous year's course, putting off the unpleasant necessity of telling him his services were no longer required as a tutor. While his novels had been best-sellers, his name had been sufficiently well known to attract students to the summer school. Bernard had made certain that it figured prominently in the brochures. It hadn't mattered then that his style of teaching had been abrasive. That could be excused as a writer's eccentricity. But now that fewer and fewer people had heard of him, it could not so easily be passed over. There had been several complaints recently about his rudeness and his lack of sympathy towards the students' own literary efforts. It was the main reason why Bernard had not suggested to Arnott that he took Murray into his tutorial group. That situation was tense enough without having Arnott exacerbating it.

No, Arnott would definitely have to go. It was almost a relief to have come to the decision. It would be done as pleasantly as possible, of course, avoiding any confrontation. A letter would probably be the best method, written several weeks after the summer school had closed, expressing regret and using Arnott's ill health as an excuse. A few likely phrases rose to mind. 'Not wishing to place any further burden . . . sincere gratitude for all you have contributed in the past . . .' It could be done kindly.

In the meantime, there were more immediate concerns – the need to mollify Arnott sufficiently to avoid any unpleasantness during the coming session. Nolan was another thorn in the flesh and not just in relation to Murray but that Grayson woman as well. Bernard could see further problems arising there if the pair of them didn't exercise enough discretion.

He would talk to Jake about her when the opportunity arose. He would keep a strict watch on Murray as well. In addition, he would have to handle Harriet Wade in the future with a little more subtlety although he had been gratified to see that during the afternoon's meeting she had seemed cool towards Nolan, so perhaps that liaison was over. Bernard fervently hoped so. All the same, her refusal to teach Murray had come as a shock. He had not expected her to show so much independence of mind. But he couldn't afford to antagonise her. She was beginning to make quite a name for herself in literary circles.

Bernard pressed two fingers wearily against the bridge of his nose. At times, it all seemed too much and he had the uncomfortable feeling that, unless he employed considerable diplomatic skill, this first session could go disastrously wrong.

'My dear Ronald,' he said, 'I merely suggested that Harriet might tutor Murray in order to save you a quite unnecessary burden of extra work. In the event, Harriet has decided that she would prefer not to have him in her group and so I shall teach him myself. I very much regret you should have interpreted my decision in such a manner. It was intended as a criticism neither of your teaching ability nor of your capacity to handle the situation. I know only too well from our past experiences together over the years at Morton Grange that I can rely on you absolutely. Now, more sherry, my dear fellow?'

Carrying the glasses over to the decanter – and a damned good sherry, too, entirely wasted on Arnott – Bernard glanced again at his watch but covertly this time.

In another two or three minutes, the gong should be sounding for dinner. Thank God, Bernard added to himself.

3

The following morning at half-past nine, Harriet arranged her notes on the table in front of her before glancing up to face her students.

She had been assigned one of the upper-school classrooms, the former morning-room when Morton Grange had been in private hands. Small, sunny, its panelled walls painted apple-green with the beading picked out in tarnished gold beneath a ceiling swagged with plaster fruit and flowers, it formed a charming and intimate setting. Harriet hoped that she could live up to it by being as charming and intimate herself.

Her students clearly had high hopes of her. Arranged round a horseshoe of tables, their faces, full of bright expectation, were turned in her direction. No rows of desks here; no muffled giggling in the back row; no cries of protest about mislaid text-books and forgotten pens. Each table was a paradigm of neatness, new notebooks laid out as if for kit inspection alongside a choice of biros in case one should run out in the middle of note-taking. Cynthia Eversham had even come equipped with a box of paper handkerchiefs and a tin of throat lozenges as if expecting to be struck down by a sudden virus in the middle of the tutorial.

And yet their eagerness and preparedness was intimidating and, as she rose to her feet, it occurred to Harriet that what she had to offer was unworthy and that she was there under false pretences. Would it not be more honest to say to them, 'Look, I can't teach you to write. Go away and try it for yourselves. If you have any quality of the writer in you, you'll learn far more that way than from anything I tell you.'?

But, of course, she couldn't say it. It would be betraying a trust; not only that which existed between herself and this particular group of students but between all teachers and their pupils, the belief that the one had some special knowledge worth acquiring by the others which would make them better educated or happier or more highly developed as individuals. It was a fundamental doubt about the whole efficacy of education which she had been most keenly aware of when teaching poetry to 3E in the last two periods of a Friday afternoon.

She felt a twinge of it now as she smiled round at the half-circle of faces, summing them up quickly, at the same time counting heads to reassure herself that all were present and that no one had got lost in the corridors between the dining-room where breakfast had been served and the tutorial room.

There were eight of them, three only being instantly recognisable – Felicity Grayson, of course, in blue silk this morning with a plunge neckline which revealed the top of her bra every time she leaned forward and wearing not quite the same expectant expression as the others as if she were already resenting her presence in Harriet Wade's tutorial group; the nice man, Frank Goodyear; and Steve Mayhew, looking relaxed and cheerful.

The lugubrious man was there, too, and, as her glance passed over him, Harriet reminded herself that she really must make the effort to remember his name.

Next to him sat Cynthia Eversham, a retired Civil Servant, small, grey and quiet, who had already chummed up with Miss Grace Mott, also retired and a former primary school head-mistress, a large-bosomed woman with a keen gaze who was extending towards Miss Eversham that condescending and slightly bullying attitude which she must have shown towards her staff and which Miss Eversham, contrary to Harriet's initial doubts over the friendship, seemed to welcome.

The remaining two students were William Harvey, an elderly former solicitor, one of those who clearly resented the use of Christian names between students and staff and who looked the type to ask awkward questions, and a formidable-looking young woman in horn-rimmed spectacles and a severe black fringe, Elaine Sherman, who had quizzed Harriet over tea the previous afternoon about her opinion of D. H. Lawrence's anti-feminism.

In other words, it was very much the same mixture as before.

Gathering up her papers, Harriet launched into her first lecture on the subject of characters – their importance in the novel; their role in plotting; action springing from, example Jane Austen's *Emma* – watching as, heads bent, her students scribbled away taking notes of her notes, an absurdity which had struck her before.

At the end of the session as the gong sounded for the mid-morning break, she handed round the visuals with which she had come prepared, photographs of portraits or busts on which her students were to base their first written assignments – descriptions and a character assessment of the individuals portrayed. Stopping at Felicity Grayson's table, Harriet, in a sudden small impulse of malice, handed her a photo of a portrait bust of a Roman senator, thin-lipped, cold-eyed, passionless except for greed and cruelty.

As a gesture, it was wasted. Felicity Grayson merely shoved it into her notebook without even glancing at it before following Harriet to the door, smiling appealingly.

'I do hope you're not going to take this the wrong way,' she began, 'but would you think me frightfully rude if I swapped tutorial groups? You see, I don't think the novel is quite my subject after all.'

'And what is?' Harriet asked, pausing in the doorway. She could guess the answer but she was damned if she was going to help the woman out.

'Well, actually, drama.'

'I'll have to speak to Bernard,' Harriet said coolly. 'I'm not sure he'll agree to the change. Or Jake either.'

'Oh, Jake won't mind,' Felicity Grayson assured her. 'I spoke to him about it yesterday and he said it'd be quite all right by him.'

I bet it would, Harriet thought. She doubted if Jake had already bedded her. Even he wasn't quite as crude as that, preferring some pretence at seduction, however minimal. But it wouldn't be long delayed. He only had until Saturday, after all, when the present batch of students was due to leave.

She walked slowly along the corridor which led to the staff common room where coffee was to be served, allowing Felicity Grayson to hurry on ahead of her, high heels clicking so purposefully on the polished parquet that Harriet was sure her intention was to find Bernard at the earliest opportunity and persuade him to allow her to change to Jake's class. Whether or not Bernard would agree was a moot point and one which would exercise all his skills of diplomacy. On the one hand, he would be anxious to satisfy a request coming from a student, knowing that the success of the summer school depended largely on word-of-mouth recommendation. On the other, Bernard was no fool and must already be aware, after yesterday's tea-party, that Jake was likely to attempt a liaison with Felicity Grayson, a situation which Bernard would disapprove of even more strongly than Jake's affair with Harriet the previous summer. A sexual relationship discreetly conducted between two members of staff was one thing; one involving a tutor and a student was quite another. Bernard held very firm opinions about unprofessional conduct.

It would be interesting, Harriet thought, to see which side of Bernard emerged the victor – the businessman or the moralist. It would probably be a very close-run contest.

She turned from the corridor into the main entrance hall where groups of students were already gathering after the first teaching sessions of the morning before moving into the common room for coffee. Among them was Cynthia Eversham, anxiously consulting the notice-board, Grace Mott at her elbow, while it appeared that Felicity Grayson had successfully waylaid Bernard for the two of them were just passing into the common room, Felicity Grayson talking animatedly, Bernard listening judiciously, head tilted but his shoulders held a little stiffly as if not entirely in agreement with what she was saying. It was evident to Harriet that Bernard was postponing the moment of decision.

They were followed by Steve Mayhew in company with Frank Goodyear which pleased Harriet. Shy and yet so eager to be friendly, Frank Goodyear was the type to be ignored, especially by the younger students, and she was just about to catch up with them when a sudden outburst of raised voices coming from the gallery which ran above the hall caused her and everyone else present to look up to see what was happening.

It was like watching a performance in an Elizabethan theatre, the two players, Jake and Leon, acting out some passionate balcony scene while the rest of them, the groundlings, stood below, mouths agape, craning their necks upwards although the lines being spoken were hardly high Shakespearian.

Jake was shouting angrily, 'I wish to Christ you'd piss off, Leon! I've just about had enough of you.'

Leon's appeal, 'For God's sake, can't we even talk?' was cut short as Jake was seen striding away from him towards the head of the staircase in a furious exit, spoiled by his sudden realisation of the audience below. For a few seconds his face, still angry but its expression changing to one of consternation, looked down at them over the banisters before disappearing from sight. Shortly afterwards, a door was heard slamming shut in an upper corridor.

It was Harriet who reacted first. Bernard, who was standing a few feet inside the common room, seemed transfixed, his face turned towards the hall, aware of some disturbance but unsure of its exact nature.

Hurrying forward, Harriet collected up the scattered groups, observing brightly, 'Coffee is ready. Do come through. We only have twenty minutes' break before the next tutorial,' as she ushered them towards the double doors of the common room. She was gratified to see that Steve Mayhew had also turned back and was jollying along the more reluctant students who were still hanging about the hall in the hope, no doubt, of a continuation of the quarrel. Harriet gave him a quick smile of thanks before glancing up at the gallery to assure herself that this was unlikely. There was no sign of Jake. Nor, thank God, of Leon.

But the incident wasn't passed over without comment. As the students moved into the common room, one of them asked her,

'What was all that about?' to which she responded with a smile and a shrug while Grace Mott remarked to Cynthia Eversham in a loud voice clearly intended to be overheard, 'Quite disgraceful language! And from one of the tutors, too!'

It was inevitable that Bernard should waylay her as soon as he could do so discreetly. She had hardly helped herself from one of the coffee urns and moved away from the trolley than Bernard was beside her, holding her by one elbow and steering her towards an unoccupied corner of the room, remarking for the benefit of those around them, 'I wanted to consult you about the timetable, Harriet.'

Once they were established in their corner, he lowered his voice.

'I gather there was a quarrel between Jake and Leon. What was it about?'

'I have no idea,' Harriet told him. 'You'd better ask Jake.'

'But several students overheard it?'

There was no point in lying to him.

'Yes, I'm afraid they did.'

'Blast!' Bernard said.

Although it was mild enough expletive, it sounded shocking coming from Bernard who rarely swore. He was standing with his back to the room so that no one else apart from Harriet could see his expression. He was, she realised, very angry, his nose quite beaky with suppressed rage, the lips a mere line.

'I shall be calling a meeting in my study at half-past six this evening,' he informed her. 'Please make sure you are there.'

He then walked away to find Ron Arnott to whom he passed on the same instruction. Harriet saw them in conversation on the far side of the room, Arnott's face heavy with disapprobation but whether at the convening of this unexpected meeting or at the news of Jake's and Leon's behaviour Harriet could not tell.

Probably both, she decided.

She felt angry herself at the situation. All through the school year at Foxwood, she was expected to attend meetings with year tutors and class teachers to discuss individual pupils' problems and breaches of discipline. She had not expected to find the same demands made of her at Morton Grange which had seemed a haven from such extra responsibilities.

Damn Leon! she thought. And damn Jake, too!

And damn Felicity Grayson, she added a quarter of an hour later when, the coffee break over, she faced her students again in her tutorial room and saw the woman sitting in front of her, looking as sulky and uncooperative as any third-form pupil at Foxwood, Bernard having decided, in view of the problems already facing him over Jake and Leon, not to compound his difficulties by allowing her to change to Jake's group, at least for the time being.

It was fortunate for Bernard that only Steve Mayhew witnessed the second confrontation which took place later that day.

There were no teaching sessions in the afternoons, the time being allocated, at least in theory, to private study and the preparation of any written assignments and, as soon as lunch was over, Steve Mayhew took himself off to the gardens of Morton Grange with the visual that Harriet Wade had given him that morning and a pad of writing-paper, his intention being to find a quiet corner, well away from everyone else, where he could enjoy the sun and perhaps even make a start on his essay.

He found the ideal place leading off the stable-yard, where the garages were situated, behind the main building. A wooden door at the far end of the yard led into a small herb garden, totally enclosed, the back of the stables forming one side, high brick walls the others, through one of which an opening, closed off by a tall wrought-iron gate, gave a glimpse of the kitchen garden beyond, with a long greenhouse, its panes glittering wickedly in the sun, and vegetable plots neatly laid out between grass paths.

A bench seat had been placed in a sunny position at the far side of the herb garden, facing the stable block and the wooden door which led into it and which Steve Mayhew carefully closed behind him as he entered to discourage any other intruders. Crossing to the bench, he sat down, spreading his notebook and Harriet Wade's visual aid on the slatted seat beside him although he made no attempt to pick up either. Instead, he looked about him with a relaxed and indolent pleasure.

The garden was laid out in formal beds, each separate plot, edged with low hedges of box, containing clumps of herbs – mint, sage and rosemary, tarragon and thyme, and more whose names were unknown to him, each releasing its aromatic scent into the warm, still air. Their perfume seemed almost visible, part of the heat haze which quivered over the beds and the paved paths which ran between them, softening all angles and hard edges so that even the surrounding walls seemed diffused in the bright, trembling light.

It was like finding himself alone in a sanctuary, not just in the sensation of physical withdrawal from other people but as a spiritual escape into an idealised garden of childhood or into one of those illuminations, all gold and blue, of a medieval manuscript in which a similar enclosed plot of fruit and herbs and flowers offered a refuge from the real world of toil, squalor and danger which lay behind the walls.

In his own experience, the toil and squalor were real enough – a caseload of twenty inadequate and deprived families whose problems ranged from poor housing, unemployment and debt to alcoholism and drug abuse. And child abuse. He had on his books at least one case of suspected incest between a father and his seven-year-old daughter although he had yet to produce the necessary evidence, both the wife and child being too terrified to talk.

The danger was real, too, and not only among the families he visited. He himself had been attacked on several occasions, once in his own office by an alcoholic mother whose children were being taken into care. He had carried the scratches on his face from that particular encounter for several days.

But here, in this garden, it was possible, if not to forget, at least to banish that world temporarily behind the walls and the closed door and with a sense of increasing pleasure he took out a pen, opened the pad of writing-paper and settled back to study the picture which Harriet Wade had given him that morning.

It was a reproduction of a Holbein drawing of some young, anonymous Tudor gentlewoman, a sweet face with a tender mouth and eyes beneath the smooth hair and the curve of the coifed cap she was wearing; at first glance too winsome and demurely pretty to inspire him to write anything about it apart from a few descriptive banalities. But Harriet Wade did not invite the banal; neither, come to that, did Holbein. And studying it again with greater care, Steve Mayhew saw the firm, almost stubborn line to the chin and, behind the gentle expression in the

41

eyes, a glint of that same intelligence and humour which had no doubt persuaded Harriet to hand it to him in the first place, as a test, perhaps, of his own powers of perception.

Smiling, he began to write.

He was disturbed a little later by the sound of footsteps moving along a gravel path on the far side of the wall which backed on to the kitchen gardens. Glancing up from his work, he saw Joyce Yarwood, the school's domestic bursar whom he had already encountered in the dining-room supervising the serving of meals, pass in front of the wrought-iron gate. She did not notice him. She seemed more intent on whatever errand had brought her out to the garden – collecting vegetables, he assumed, judging by the basket she was carrying in one hand.

She crossed his line of vision, moving towards one of the beds which contained long rows of runner beans, supported on tent-shaped poles, where she put the basket down on the ground. He had only an oblique view of her through the tracery of the gate, a figure in the middle distance, dressed in a pale blue overall coat, alternately lifting one arm and then lowering it as the beans were picked and dropped into the basket at her feet, a silent activity which struck him as oddly emblematic, part of the setting, as if she, too, had strayed out of a medieval illustration and had become part of his landscape, he with his pen and paper, seated within the garden, symbolising intellectual endeavour, she, outside it, depicting human toil, but still idealised, showing none of the hard, back-breaking labour which would have been the lot of a real peasant-woman.

He watched her for several moments, intrigued by the concept and aware that it was unlikely she could see him. The bench on which he was sitting was placed at too acute an angle to the gate to allow her to look in at him, giving him the uninterrupted pleasure of observing unobserved.

A few minutes later, she was joined by another figure – George Burton, the school's head gardener, who approached her from the other end of the long row of bean-poles, walking with a heavy, purposeful tread.

They spoke to one another, their voices, carrying clearly through the still afternoon air, coming as a small shock to Mayhew who had assumed that their encounter would have been as silent as the woman's solitary occupation.

He heard Burton say to her, 'You should have asked me. I could have picked those for you and saved you the trouble.'

Without so much as pausing in her task, Joyce Yarwood replied, 'It's no trouble. I'm enjoying it.'

Her indifference was apparent to Mayhew even at that distance. Burton did not reply but remained beside her, shoulders hunched, looking awkward but standing his ground.

After a short silence, he spoke again.

'If you're free later this evening, I could run you down to the White Hart for a drink.'

'No thank you,' she said. Picking up the basket, she moved away, walking back along the row, her face turned in Mayhew's direction so that he could see the closed expression on it before she passed in front of the iron gate and out of his line of vision.

Burton took a few steps forward and then gave up the attempt to follow her. Standing legs apart, he called after her, 'I suppose if *he*'d've asked you, you'd've gone with him like a shot.'

He seemed to regret the remark as soon as he made it. For a few seconds, he remained where he was and then, kicking out at a clod of earth which lay between the rows of beans, scattering it into granules, he too walked away across the garden in the opposite direction to be lost to sight behind the greenhouse.

It had been a small, intriguing episode but one which Mayhew soon dismissed from his mind, apart from wondering briefly who the 'he' was to whom Burton had referred, as he turned his attention back to the essay he was writing.

A second but much shorter interruption occurred about half an hour later when the door into the stable-yard was opened and Frank Goodyear appeared in the opening. He hesitated but, seeing Steve was already there and absorbed in his work, he quickly retreated, closing the door so quietly behind him that Steve, raising his head momentarily from his task, hardly registered either his arrival or departure.

At about the same time, Bernard, too, was interrupted from his work but in his case his visitor was expected.

Rising from his desk, he indicated one of the armchairs.

'Ah, Leon,' he said. 'Do sit down.'

And resuming his own seat, he made a steeple of his fingers before settling himself back to listen.

Bernard seemed to have recovered his urbanity when, a little after half-past six that evening, Harriet knocked and entered the study. A decanter and four glasses had been set out in readiness on the desk and, as soon as she came into the room, Bernard poured them each a sherry, carrying hers over to the armchair where he had installed her.

So Bernard intended the occasion to be a civilised affair, Harriet thought. There would be no confrontations and no recriminations. The unfortunate episode between Jake and Leon was to be tactfully papered over, allowing no cracks to appear in the smooth surface of Morton Grange summer school. A cosmetic job, in other words.

She wondered how the others would take it, Jake in particular.

They had, it appeared, no option. Bernard had already made up his mind what line he proposed to take, a fact which he made quite clear to them when, Jake and Ron Arnott having arrived, Jake ten minutes late – on purpose, Harriet suspected – Bernard took his place behind the desk, clasping his hands together as he addressed the neutral space between them.

'Thank you for coming,' he began. 'I shan't keep you long. I merely wanted to inform you that I spoke to Leon Murray this afternoon and, in view of everything, I have decided it would be best if he withdraws from the course . . .'

'Wait a minute,' Jake broke in. 'Just what the hell do you mean by "in view of everything"? Exactly what did Leon say to you and why wasn't I asked to the interview? He's quite capable, you realise, of twisting anything to suit himself . . .'

'I'm well aware of that,' Bernard interrupted in his turn, 'and the purpose of the interview was not to ask for his version of this morning's events, I can assure you, but to inform him of my decision which is also why I convened this meeting. Murray has agreed to leave tomorrow morning immediately after breakfast while the rest of the students are engaged in tutorial classes. In the meantime, he will keep to his room and make himself as unobtrusive as possible. I have arranged with Miss Yarwood that one of the domestic staff will take his meals upstairs to him. In return, his fees will be refunded to him in full.'

For a moment, he looked pained, an expression which Arnott must also have seen for Harriet heard him give a small snort of derisive amusement.

Ignoring it, Bernard continued, 'I suggest that we make no reference to Murray's departure and refrain from discussing the incident with any of the students unless directly asked in which case we should simply say that Murray is unwell and has withdrawn from the course for that reason. Otherwise, I think it more prudent that we consider the whole incident closed. Is everyone agreed?'

For the first time he met their eyes directly. Harriet nodded briefly in response. It seemed the best way out of the situation. At least, with Leon gone, there would be less likelihood of any more confrontations taking place. Arnott, too, agreed but with a shrug as if he considered Bernard's decision was none of his business.

Jake said, 'I don't care what happens to him as long as I don't have to meet the little sod face to face again.'

He began to unfold his long legs and get up out of his chair but Bernard hadn't quite finished.

'Just one further point before you go,' he continued. 'Felicity Grayson has asked permission to transfer from Harriet's tutorial group to Jake's and I have reluctantly given permission although I prefer not to encourage students to change courses once they are here. However, I have made an exception in her case. And lastly, may I impress on you the necessity of behaving with the greatest discretion although I'm sure none of you will need reminding of that?'

The warning was quite clear although it was said with a small, chilly smile, and was intended for all of them; for herself, Harriet assumed, because of her affair with Jake the previous year; for Arnott whose treatment in the past of some of his less able students was known to be undiplomatic; and for Jake, of course, not just over his relationship with Leon but as a prior notice to him that Bernard would not tolerate any obvious liaison with Felicity Grayson.

'Thank you for coming,' Bernard was saying, rising from behind the desk. 'I don't propose keeping you any longer.' He waited until they had reached the door before adding as if struck by a sudden afterthought, 'Oh, Jake, if you wouldn't mind, there's one small additional point I'd like to discuss with you.'

Outside in the corridor, Arnott remarked to Harriet, 'Bernard's going to give Nolan a bollocking; deserved, too, in my opinion.'

It was said with obvious satisfaction. For once, Arnott's morose, jowled face looked almost animated. It was one of the few occasions when he had ever spoken to her directly and it seemed to her typical of the man that he should choose it to make a derogatory comment about a colleague.

To her relief, she was spared the need to reply. The gong sounded in the hall for dinner and, taking it as an excuse, she hurried ahead of him down the passage, leaving him to follow more slowly behind her.

Jake said, 'So what was this small additional point, Bernard?'

After the door had closed on Harriet and Arnott, he had come lounging back into the room to resume his seat, deliberately lighting a cigarette although he knew Bernard disapproved of anyone smoking in his presence. Bernard opened the sash window at the bottom and moved a small glass ashtray to the edge of the desk.

'About Murray,' he began.

'But Leon's leaving tomorrow. As you said, isn't it best to consider the whole incident closed?'

The dinner gong was heard faintly, muffled by the closed door, and Bernard waited until the sound had died away before continuing. 'I was disturbed by what Leon had to tell me about your relationship with him.'

Jake, who had been sitting sprawled negligently in his chair, sat up, suddenly alert and angry.

'You bloody well did question him this afternoon!' he said, his voice rising. 'It's none of your damned business.'

'The good name of the summer school *is* my business,' Bernard reminded him gently.

'Then where the hell were you this morning? I thought you were supposed to be Leon's minder while he's here. If you'd been doing your job properly, he wouldn't have had the chance to follow me upstairs and the row wouldn't have happened.'

'Ah, yes.' Bernard seemed prepared to concede this point. 'Unfortunately the Grayson woman detained me in the hall and my attention was distracted. And that's another point I wanted to take up with you. I should like to make it quite clear that I shall tolerate no nonsense between a member of staff and one of the students.'

'If by "nonsense" you mean you object to my screwing her, then why don't you come straight out and say it?'

Bernard drew in a small, sharp breath.

'I must protest . . .' he began. But Jake hadn't finished.

'God, you're a sanctimonious old hypocrite, Bernard! But you're hardly whiter than white yourself, are you? Remember Mike?'

'Mike?'

Bernard was genuinely nonplussed.

'Michael Bryant who died so tragically after you'd panned his collection of poems in the *New London Review*.' Jake seemed to take pleasure in reminding him. 'Surely you haven't forgotten him?'

'But he killed himself with a drug overdose,' Bernard protested. 'The inquest returned a verdict of accidental death. It had nothing whatever to do with anything I wrote about him.'

'No? But inquests can be reopened, you know, Bernard, especially if fresh evidence turns up.'

'What evidence?' Bernard asked sharply.

'A letter, perhaps. Who can tell? You see, I knew Mike quite well. I was going to stage a reading of some of his poetry at the Lion's Head with strobe lighting and electronic sound. It could have been very effective. Then he died. Sad, wasn't it? Tragic even. But supposing he wrote to me shortly before he killed himself telling me how desperate he felt over your review and how life no longer seemed worth living . . .'

'I don't believe you,' Bernard told him.

'No?' Jake got up and strolled casually over to the door where he paused to add, 'Then remind me to show you his letter some time, my dear Bernard. It makes such poignant reading that I carry it about with me everywhere, just to remind me how cruel life can be. I'm sure a coroner would be interested in it, not to mention the popular press whom you so rightly despise.'

'You're lying,' Bernard said. 'There isn't any letter.'

But Jake had already gone, slamming the study door shut behind him.

4

The dining-room was at the rear of the main building, constructed at the time of the school's Edwardian expansion from a series of smaller rooms, and panelled in mahogany which gave the impression that one was sitting inside a large, dark, beautifully polished box hung with black-painted wooden shields on which were emblazoned in gold letters the academic and sporting achievements of the Morton Grange pupils since its foundation. The view from the windows hardly alleviated this feeling of worthy gloom for they overlooked an enclosed service area, neatly paved but denuded of any greenery except for the heavy swags of ivy on the wall of the adjoining stable-yard, above which the little white-painted clock tower with its blue dial and gilt Roman numerals seemed almost a frivolity.

By the time Harriet arrived, the queue at the long serving-hatch had shortened and, as soon as Mrs Soames had served her with cheese and onion quiche, baked potatoes and salad, Harriet moved away with her tray to look for a place where she might sit down.

At Bernard's suggestion, the normal term-time arrangement of tables joined end to end to form long refectory seating had been dispensed with and the furniture had been moved apart into more intimate six-person placings, most of which were already taken. She saw an empty place at one table at which Steve Mayhew was sitting and then decided against joining him. She liked him but to seek out his company might be misconstrued, not only by him but by others including Bernard whose recent strictures about the need for discretion had made her over-scrupulous in showing even the most innocent demonstration of personal preference.

There was an empty chair at a nearby table at which Kay Ratcliff was sitting together with four other students from Jake's drama

48

group and, deciding that by choosing that spare place not even Bernard could accuse her of favouritism, Harriet carried her tray across to it.

'May I join you?' she asked of all five of them.

'Help yourself,' one of them replied. 'There's plenty of room. We were just about to go anyway.'

And with that, the four of them took their used plates back to the hatch, leaving Harriet alone with Kay Ratcliff which was not at all what she had intended.

For some inexplicable reason, she felt ill at ease, not because of any particular reaction on the part of Kay Ratcliff who seemed genuinely pleased to see her. Or perhaps that was the cause of Harriet's disquiet. Perversely, she might have felt more comfortable had Kay shown greater indifference towards her.

Anxious to establish some space between them, she said brightly, 'And how are you enjoying the course?'

Kay looked across the table towards her and Harriet was aware of the woman's eyes, dark, heavy-lidded, almost languorous but with a glint of ironic amusement in them like small, sharp pin-points lighting up the pupils.

She waited before replying, letting Harriet's trite little social remark hang in the air between them almost like a reproach.

Then she said, 'It's fine. A damn sight better than teaching anyway. But perhaps I shouldn't say that to you as you're on the staff.'

'I don't mind. In fact, I'm inclined to agree with you,' Harriet replied. She had lowered her own gaze and was concentrating on cutting up her quiche. But the humour of the situation suddenly struck her. Leaning forward, she said in a theatrical whisper, 'But don't tell Bernard. He'd mind dreadfully.'

Kay laughed, putting her elbows amicably on the table.

'You teach too, don't you? I mean not just here but in a London comprehensive as well.'

'How do you know that?' Harriet asked, surprised.

'I read it on the jacket of your novel. As a matter of fact, when I applied to come here, I was torn between your course and drama.' Unexpectedly, she added, 'Why do you teach?'

Disconcerted, Harriet retorted, 'Why do you?'

The little points of amusement were very bright, Harriet noticed, as Kay replied, 'God knows. Because I can't do anything else? Because I'm a masochist at heart? Perhaps. When it's going badly it's hell, but on a good day it's exhilarating, like . . .' She laughed again as she searched for a comparison. 'Free-fall parachuting or driving a fast car.'

'Yes, exactly,' Harriet said in quick agreement. She knew that sensation, the almost heady sense of excitement when a lesson was successful, the heightening of response as she and her pupils shared in the experience of learning, ideas crackling between them, but she herself in control, conducting them, she felt on these occasions, as if they were an orchestra and she were drawing music out of them.

'Or like making love,' Kay Ratcliff added.

This time it was her remark which hung between them as Harriet laid her knife and fork down on her empty plate.

Before she could think of a reply, Jake, looking more than usually jaunty and well-pleased with himself, placed his tray on the table, drew back a chair and seated himself with the easy confidence of someone sure of a welcome.

'Hi, there, folks!' he said in a quite unjustified parody of Bernard's transatlantic familiarity which made Harriet suspect that, whatever had passed in private between Jake and Bernard after that evening's meeting, it was Jake who had emerged the winner. As if to emphasise the point, Bernard himself entered the dining-room at this moment, looking subdued and oddly diminished as he waited his turn at the hatch to be served by Mrs Soames.

Jake noticed him, too.

'What a bit of luck!' he exclaimed. 'Just the person I wanted to see,' and as Bernard passed their table in search of a place elsewhere, he raised his voice. 'I say, Bernard, could I have the keys to the assembly hall? I forgot to ask you earlier when we were having our little chat.'

Bernard halted, his tray held defensively in front of him like a shield.

'Why?' he demanded, his lips pressed so tightly together that they were almost invisible.

Jake looked from Harriet to Kay as if inviting them to join in his amusement at Bernard's obtuseness.

'Because I need them to unlock the doors. Or if you want a more lengthy explanation, I'd like to use the hall tomorrow to teach voice projection and stage movement. That stupid little dais in the music-room's no good. It's almost entirely taken up by that bloody great grand piano.'

The use of the swear word was meant to be provocative. Heads at neighbouring tables turned in Jake's direction and, aware of this, Bernard approached nearer, his tray still held in front of him.

Kay took the opportunity to leave, rising from the table with an apologetically wry glance at Harriet whose own escape route was blocked by Bernard who was standing almost immediately behind her.

'But why do you need to open the hall up this evening?' he persisted. 'Surely that could wait until tomorrow morning?'

'Because last year the stage was full of chairs which some fool had stacked on it. So, unless you want me to spend part of tomorrow morning's tutorial moving furniture . . .' Jake shrugged as if the rest of the sentence should be obvious even to Bernard.

'Very well,' Bernard said stiffly. 'I shall have to fetch the keys from my study and give them to you later. I don't carry them about with me.'

He moved away, walking the length of the dining-room to a far table.

As he left, Jake looked across the table at Harriet, remarking as she pushed back her chair in readiness to leave, too, 'She fancies you, you realise?'

The apparent inconsequentiality of the remark caught her off-guard.

'Who does?' she asked.

'Kay Ratcliff.' He waved his fork at her. 'So be warned, dear Harriet, by your uncle Jake who has only your best interests at heart. Kay's a very determined woman who eats young lady novelists like you for breakfast.'

Harriet thrust her chair back into place and walked away, head high but aware that the blood had run up into her face.

It was absurd! All of it! Jake's interpretation of Kay's behaviour towards her, absurd; her own reaction to it equally ridiculous. As if it mattered a damn to her what Jake chose to say out of malice.

But she stopped there.

He could possibly be right. No – correction; he most probably was right. She had noticed before this talent of Jake's in uncovering the hidden flaws and weaknesses in other people with a cruel but objective perception. And if she were equally objective, hadn't she herself been aware at tea yesterday afternoon of some dangerous and yet fascinating quality about Kay Ratcliff which had both repelled and attracted her?

As she considered these questions, she turned from the corridor into the entrance hall where she hesitated, wondering whether to enter the common room where coffee was being served and where no doubt Kay Ratcliff would be found or to go straight upstairs to her room. But to do so would be to admit her inability to cope.

No, she decided. She wouldn't run away. Instead, she would behave normally, have coffee, nod pleasantly to Kay Ratcliff if she had to and then seek out someone else to talk to.

She chose the lugubrious man who was standing by himself at one of the long sash windows, looking out across the garden.

'Going to be a storm,' he told her.

The clouds were already beginning to gather behind the trees and the chapel tower, quenching the sunset. As he spoke, there was a brief, pale flash of summer lightning very far away, followed seconds later by the low rumble of distant thunder.

'Listen to that!' he remarked. He seemed pleased to be proved right.

'And how are you enjoying the course?' Harriet asked him, knowing it was safe to repeat the question she had asked of Kay Ratcliff. It was unlikely he would respond in the same ironic manner. As he wasn't wearing his identity tag, she still didn't know his name.

It seemed he was enjoying it quite well – better anyway than another course he had been on the previous summer about Elizabethan literature. Couldn't say he was all that keen on Shakespeare himself – overrated in his opinion, and the food had been disgraceful.

As she listened, Harriet looked about the room which was now crowded. Jake was there, talking to Felicity Grayson, of course. She noticed Steve Mayhew as well on the far side of the room who, catching her glance, smiled and made a small beckoning gesture with his head, invited her to join him. But she pretended not to notice and let her eyes move on. Ron Arnott had installed himself in the next window embrasure with two middle-aged women, presumably his students, who, judging by Arnott's unusually cheerful expression and the pile of books on the low coffee table between their chairs, had asked him to autograph copies of his novels. As her glance passed over him, he was in the act of feeling in his inside pocket for a pen.

And there was Kay Ratcliff, standing alone by the fireplace, a coffee cup in her hand, also looking about the room as if searching for someone.

Hurriedly, Harriet turned back to the lugubrious man.

Ten minutes more, she told herself, and I can decently leave.

The ten minutes up, she excused herself and moved across to the trolley with her empty cup, passing behind Jake and Felicity Grayson, who had meanwhile been joined by two of the drama students, just as Bernard approached the group from the other direction.

She heard him say, 'Here are the keys for the hall, Jake. May I rely on you to turn the lights off and lock up when you've finished? And may I also remind you that the front door is supposed to be secured at eleven o'clock?'

He spoke in a clipped, efficient voice, very much in charge, very much the Director of Studies.

'Yes, thanks, Bernard,' Jake said casually.

By the time Harriet had deposited her cup and had turned back, Bernard had gone while Jake was still talking to the group of students, the bunch of keys dangling in his hand.

Looking neither to left nor right, and certainly not in the direction of the fireplace, Harriet let herself out by the double doors, unaware that someone was behind her until she was half-way to the stairs and heard her name called.

'Harriet!'

But it was only Steve.

'Care for a walk?' he asked as he joined her.

'Sorry,' she replied. 'I've got some work I ought to do.'

Which was true although none of it was urgent. All the same, to discourage Kay by encouraging Steve was, she felt, not the solution and might lead to further complications.

He didn't seem all that disappointed.

'Some other time perhaps?' he suggested cheerfully. 'I'll watch the athletics on television instead then with some of the others.

Would you like to join us?' he added, addressing Frank Goodyear who had at that moment emerged from the common room where he, too, had presumably been drinking coffee although Harriet had not noticed him among the crowd.

'Thanks for the offer, Steve,' he replied. He seemed pleased to be asked. 'I might join you later.'

Harriet said good-night to them both and went on up the stairs, glancing down as she reached the upper landing. Steve was no longer in sight, having gone, she assumed, into the television room, the former writing-room which opened off the hall. But Frank Goodyear was still there, standing with hands clasped behind his back, apparently absorbed in studying the notices pinned to the board.

It was the last time that Harriet was to see him.

At approximately twenty to nine, George Burton took his dirty supper dishes through to the kitchen where he left them in the sink, after running a little water perfunctorily over them. He should have washed them up. In fact, the kitchen and the whole house needed a damned good clean. It had originally been the gatehouse, modernised and updated, and, when his wife had been alive, had been spotless, every stick of furniture polished to a high gloss. It would break her heart to see it now.

But first her death and then his unaccountable passion for Joyce Yarwood had left him feeling restless, incapable of settling down to anything as humdrum as housework. The gardens and grounds of Morton Grange were a different matter. That was man's work, out of doors and where he was in charge.

Turning away from the sink, he took his jacket from the hook on the back door and let himself out.

Just a short stroll round the grounds, he told himself. Get a breath of fresh air before bedtime.

But even before he set off up the drive, he knew exactly where his walk would take him – past the chapel and round by the back of the west wing to the service yard where, unseen in the shadows, he would watch Joyce Yarwood through the un-curtained kitchen window clearing up after the students' supper. It was the same route he took every night and at exactly the same time, once the car, driven by Soames, the assistant caretaker, passed the gatehouse, taking Mrs Soames and the other women who worked in the kitchen back to the village.

It was darker than usual that evening. Although the sun had barely set, the twilight was already thickening under the heavy cloud-cover which was piling up behind the trees, lit from time to time by a flicker of lightning. But the storm was still a long way off and wouldn't break yet. He'd be back home before the rain came.

In his bedroom in the west wing, Leon Murray took his tray on which his supper had been brought to him earlier by one of the kitchen staff and dumped it down in the corridor outside his room where someone else could bloody well come and fetch it. He didn't see why he should carry it downstairs himself. Anyway, hadn't Bernard ordered him to keep to his room?

Standing in the doorway, he waited for a few moments, head cocked towards the head of the stairs, listening to the sound of voices coming from the common room before, slamming the door loudly behind him, he went back inside the room.

It was a bloody nerve on Bernard's part to banish him in this manner, like a child sent up to bed early by the grown-ups, and Leon had protested bitterly when Bernard had first imposed it at the interview that afternoon.

He had paid his fees, he had pointed out, and the quarrel which had taken place on the landing that morning had been as much Jake's fault as his. All he had wanted to do was to talk things over with Jake. After all, they'd been friends – well, more than friends really, Leon had hinted – and then Jake had turned on him for no real reason. It was all so unfair, especially as only last October Jake had been only too eager to take Leon's two thousand pounds – money he'd had to borrow from his mother – for that stupid play he'd wanted to put on. And then, instead of being grateful, Jake had lost his temper and had accused him, Leon, of interfering and had refused to have anything more to do with him.

So was it surprising, he had appealed to Bernard, that he had wanted to come back to Morton Grange and try to find out what had gone wrong? Jake wouldn't speak to him on the phone or answer his letters and whenever he had tried to get in touch with Jake at the theatre that stupid bitch, Mo Cunningham, who helped run the place, wouldn't let him inside the door.

Surely Bernard could understand?

The infuriating thing was that Bernard had at first seemed sympathetic, encouraging him to talk. It was only at the end of the interview that Bernard had come out with all that crap about how he, as Director of Studies, was responsible for the good name of the Morton Grange summer school and that, on mature reflection, he had decided that Leon would have to leave.

Leon had tried every gambit he knew – protestations of out-raged innocence, promises of future good behaviour, even at the end of a tearful plea to Bernard's better nature. But none of it had worked. Bernard had remained unmoved and the interview had ended with Leon flouncing out of the study with the threat that he wouldn't leave without making a final protest.

The trouble was he didn't quite know how to carry it out. Bernard had made it quite clear that a taxi would be sent for to take him to the station at half-past nine the following morning when everybody else would be in class so a scene in the hall would be wasted with no audience to witness it. As for any other scheme he might have devised to get his own back, such as leaving his mark on the room in some way, Bernard had thought of that one, too, and had pointed out that, before the taxi was allowed to leave, he would personally make an inspection of the room and its contents and any missing or damaged item would have to be paid for or its value deducted before the fees were reimbursed.

Moving restlessly, Leon went over to the chest of drawers which stood under the window overlooking the front of the main building, and, jerking open the top drawer, began to throw its contents on to the bed in readiness for packing when his attention was caught by a figure crossing the lawn and he paused in his task to watch.

It was getting dusk but there was still enough light left for him to see that it was George Burton, the school's head gardener, and that there was something furtive in the man's behaviour. He was keeping to the grass, avoiding the drive and the lights streaming out from the common room windows as he struck off along the front of the west wing in the general direction of the assembly hall and school chapel.

Very quietly, Leon leaned across the top of the chest of drawers and pushed the sash window open at the bottom. By craning his head out, he was able to follow Burton's progress as he turned right at the far end of the west wing where a sudden flash of lightning seemed to spotlight his stocky, hunched figure with a dramatic intensity for a few seconds before it disappeared from sight behind the domed glass and iron structure of the music-room.

Intrigued by this curious little incident and by the view of the garden settling down into dusk, Leon remained where he was at the window, waiting for the next flash of lightning. There wasn't much else to do anyway except his packing and he was bored with that already.

A few minutes later, he heard the front door of the main building below him close and footsteps cross the gravelled drive under his window. Someone else beside Burton was out and about, it seemed.

It was Jake. Craning his head out again, Leon had no difficulty in recognising Jake's tall figure nor the easy, loping stride as, hands in pockets, Jake walked briskly away towards the assembly hall where, shortly afterwards, lights sprang up in the interior behind the long rectangles of glass which formed its façade.

From his vantage point in the angle formed by the back of the stable wall and the brick pillar which supported the gateway into the service yard, George Burton was able to observe the kitchen window without being seen.

The light poured out through the uncurtained glass, giving him a clear view of what was going on inside. He could see Joyce standing at the sink, drying off the large saucepans which had been washed up earlier and left up-ended on the racks to drain before carrying them one by one across the kitchen to the wall hooks beside the stoves.

Every moment was neat and quiet and contained. As she lifted her arms, the hem of her blue nylon overall coat lifted too, revealing the backs of her knees, the skin stretched taut above the curve of her calves.

She looked too slight for such heavy work which he would gladly have done for her and, as he watched, he was aware of a protective tenderness towards her which he had not felt before even for his wife except in the last few months before her death and which rose up in him again, transferring itself to this small, slender figure moving backwards and forwards under the bright strip lighting against the background of white tiles and polished stainless steel.

But she would not welcome his attentions. If he went up to the back door, he knew exactly what would happen. She would turn towards him that formal, unsmiling face, the mouth, even that long upper lip, pressed shut.

It wasn't worth it. At least, standing there in the dark, he could go on watching her without arousing her displeasure.

But as the thought crossed his mind, lights sprang up somewhere over to the right behind the trees, too far away to illuminate the yard although their sudden appearance made him realise that someone else beside himself must be about in the grounds.

He retreated quietly by the route by which he had come, keeping to the grass so that his footsteps were inaudible and aware, as he crossed in front of the school chapel and struck off across the lawn towards the far end of the drive, that the assembly hall was now brilliantly lit up and that a figure, whose he couldn't quite make out, was moving about inside.

Jake carried the last few chairs, stacked up in fours, which had been left on the stage, into the wings where he dumped them against the back wall. Only the lectern was left now and he was in the act of moving it when the door at the far end opened and someone crossed the parquet floor.

Turning, Jake half expected to find it was Felicity Grayson coming towards him. She had offered to help earlier over coffee in the common room but Jake had turned her down, not because of Bernard's warning against staff and student fraternisation – Jake was damned if he was going to take any notice of anything bloody old Bernard might say – but because she was a little too obvious, unlike Harriet who was being cool and aloof towards him that summer and was therefore much more of a challenge. Besides, Jake had other plans for the rest of the evening, once he had finished in the hall, and Felicity Grayson was not part of them.

But it was not Felicity who was walking up the length of the hall towards him; it was someone much more unexpected.

Surprised and a little impatient, Jake demanded, 'What do you want?'

5

For the third time, Bernard broke off from his task of drawing up lists of room allocations and tutorial groups for the following week's batch of students and, rising from his desk, drew aside one of the curtains and looked out across the darkened side lawn towards the school chapel and the assembly hall, checking his watch as he did so.

It was now a quarter to eleven and quite dark except for the intermittent flashes of sheet lightning which had drawn closer and which lit up the whole sky for a few seconds in sudden bursts of white brilliance, so bright that it was possible to pick out the chapel tower and the trees which surrounded it. But even after it had faded, the oblong shape of the school assembly hall still remained clearly visible, every window ablaze with light.

It was damned irresponsible of Nolan, Bernard thought angrily, letting the curtain drop back into place. When he had handed Nolan the keys, he had made it perfectly clear to him that the place had to be locked up and the lights switched off by eleven o'clock although he could guess what had happened. Nolan had been entertaining that Grayson woman in there; indeed, it was probably the motive behind his asking for the keys in the first place. Moving furniture from the stage had been merely an excuse. And they were either still in there or, alternatively, had returned to the main building leaving the place unlocked and every light blazing.

His suspicions regarding Nolan and Mrs Grayson were the reason why Bernard had been keeping watch on the hall on and off all evening; not that he had seen even Nolan go in there and the place was too far away for him to distinguish who might still be inside it now.

He would have to make some sort of inquiry, he supposed, if

only to check up exactly where Nolan was and what he had done with the keys. With a frown of impatience, Bernard put the cap back on his pen and, letting himself out of his study, walked briskly along the corridor to the common room.

But Nolan was not there, the room being almost empty apart from a few students who were sitting about talking and Arnott who, together with two middle-aged women from his tutorial group, still occupied one of the window embrasures where they had drawn their armchairs together in a comfortable tête-à-tête half-circle.

Bernard beckoned Arnott to join him by the fireplace, keeping his voice low so that the others could not overhear their conversation.

'Have you seen Nolan?' he asked.

'No, not since he left here about ten to nine,' Arnott replied. 'Why?'

'Because every light in the hall has been left on and I'm concerned about the place not being properly secured for the night. Did Mrs Grayson go with him?'

Arnott gave a small, pleased smile, amused not only by Bernard's anxiety and Nolan's irresponsibility, which would probably earn him another bollocking, but at Bernard's assumption that Jake and the Grayson woman had been having it off in the hall.

'I don't think he's with her,' he said. 'At least, when he went he was on his own and she was still here until about half-past nine.' As Bernard turned to walk away, Arnott added, deliberately raising his voice, 'Have you tried Harriet Wade's room? He could be there.'

But Harriet was alone. When Bernard knocked and entered, she was seated at the table writing, still fully dressed and with no sign that Bernard could see as he cast a surreptitious glance towards the bed that anyone had occupied it.

She hadn't seen Nolan either and had no idea where he might be found.

'He's probably still in the hall,' she concluded. It seemed the most obvious explanation.

'At this time of night?' Bernard asked disbelievingly. 'Arnott said he left the common room at about ten to nine. It couldn't have taken him more than half an hour to move a few chairs off the stage.' He turned towards the door, adding in an aggrieved voice, 'I suppose I'd better go and look for him but it's a confounded nuisance. I still have a great deal of organisation to do for next week's students as well as going over my notes for my lecture tomorrow on Eliot.'

'I'll go,' Harriet said, coming to a sudden decision.

'Are you sure?' Bernard asked, torn between the inconvenience of having to look for Nolan himself and the undesirability, in view of Harriet's previous relationship with Jake, of allowing her to undertake the task. But she seemed to have made up her mind.

'Quite sure,' she told him. 'A walk will do me good.'

She was already out of the door, giving Bernard no option but to follow. As they went down the stairs, he continued, 'You won't be too long, will you? You know part of the agreement with the school governors stipulates that all doors must be securely fastened by eleven o'clock.'

She seemed to guess what was in his mind because she looked back at him with amusement over her shoulder.

'Ten minutes?' she suggested, smiling.

'I'll be in my study,' Bernard said stiffly. 'Please make sure Nolan returns the keys to me personally. I am, after all, responsible for their safe-keeping.'

And with that he marched off along the corridor which led to his study, leaving Harriet alone.

But not for long. She was half-way across the hall when the door to the television room opened and a group of students emerged, among them Steve who, breaking away from the others, hurried forward to join her just as she reached the double glass doors leading into the porch.

'Changed your mind about a walk?' he asked. 'Mind if I join you?'

'All right,' Harriet agreed, trying not to show her reluctance.

Pleasant though he was, he was becoming a little too persistent and she had had quite enough that evening of other people's interest in her. Besides, there were few opportunities to talk to Jake alone during the day because of the presence of others and she had hoped that, by meeting him in the hall but merely as Bernard's messenger, she could make it quite clear to him by her continuing indifference that their relationship was finished. And if he wasn't prepared to take the hint, she would tell him so outright. None of this could, of course, be explained to Steve and it seemed easier to accept his company although, as they set off along the drive, she gave him a brief account of the reason behind her apparent change of mind regarding the walk.

The drive ran along the front of the west wing before turning off to the right by the music-room where it continued on towards the service yard and the stable block at the rear of the main building. At the point where it swung behind the west wing, several broad asphalt paths radiated from it, one leading to the hall, one to the school chapel, while a third, a little further off, branched off in the direction of the outdoor swimming-pool, screened from the other buildings by a high yew hedge so that, even in daylight, not even the little peaked roofs of the changing-rooms could be seen, only the top of the diving-board being visible.

But it was dark now although the lights first from the main building and then from the assembly hall were sufficiently bright to illuminate the drive. Flashes of summer lightning, lasting only a few seconds, also lit up the scene, quenching momentarily the brilliance of the artificial lighting and making it seem pallid.

The hall was modern, built in the sixties, and reminded Harriet of Foxwood in the stark utility of its design – oblong, flat-roofed, with huge plate-glass windows, softened a little by the shrubbery which surrounded it but still, in comparison with the Gothic intricacies of the chapel which stood a little distance from it, too boxy and functional. With all its lights blazing, it looked like part of an air-terminal complex.

The door on the near side was unlocked. Harriet pushed it open and went in, followed by Steve. The place appeared to be empty. The floor had been cleared of chairs which were stacked up along each side while, at the far end, the curtains had been drawn back, revealing the stage, also empty apart from a reading lectern in the centre and a large white screen which hung down on the back wall.

'He doesn't seem to be here,' Steve remarked.

'But he must be,' Harriet replied. Suddenly she could appreciate Bernard's exasperation. It was typical of Jake to switch on every light in the building and then apparently wander off. She added, 'He's probably backstage.'

Two short flights of steps led up at either end of the stage and she chose the nearest, crossing the platform to the prompt side where more steps led down to the green-room at the back.

Jake was not there either. Nor was he in any of the small dressing-rooms nor the lavatories which opened off it while the props store was locked. It stood at the end of a short corridor from which another door led out into the grounds. Harriet discovered when she tried it that it was not only unlocked but had been left ajar. It seemed likely therefore that Jake had left by this side exit. But where could he have gone? The door led away from the main building towards the school chapel. And the swimming-pool.

It was absurd that she felt so certain that it was here that he would be found. Afterwards, she tried to rationalise that moment of absolute certainty with the explanation that, as she stood by the door looking out through the glass panel, a sudden flash of lightning, much nearer now as the storm rumbled towards them, seemed to pick out the yew hedge and the top of the diving-board so that, in those few seconds of blue-white, drenching light, she was able to see quite clearly the metallic sheen on the frame, the sharp-cut edges of the opening in the tall hedge and, beyond it, the sheet of water, mirroring momentarily the brilliance of the sky.

'We'll try the pool,' she said to Steve.

'But why?' he asked. He seemed surprised by her decision which appeared so irrational even to her that she felt obliged to add as she pushed open the door and set off along the path which ran past the chapel, 'He might have decided to go for a swim.'

It was unlikely. Jake was too hedonistic to take any pleasure in a late-night dip in an unheated, outdoor pool which was more-over unlighted and, apart from the occasional burst of sheet lightning, very dark indeed.

Harriet was aware of the darkness as soon as she walked through the opening cut in the surrounding hedges. The dense foliage of the yews seemed to extrude even the smallest glimmer of light although a very faint gleam was given back from the water by the turquoise-blue tiles which lined the pool as a dim, almost phosphorescent glow, barely discernible and yet appearing so close despite the broad expanse of paving stones which enclosed it that she stopped short, afraid of stepping over the brink.

It was Steve who first saw Jake's body. Harriet had taken it to be a shadow cast by the hedges, a deeper mass of darkness, that was all.

She heard Steve give a muffled exclamation as he began pulling his T-shirt off over his head but before she could register what he had said, he had kicked off his shoes and jeans and had plunged into the pool, the splash sending water spraying over her.

'What's happened?' she cried out, crouching down at the edge and peering forward into the blackness.

Steve seemed to be struggling with something in the water, trying to lift it up over the coping and, as she stretched down her hands into the darkness, they came into contact with arms covered with sodden fabric and then with wet hair.

It was the texture of the hair, rough and springy, which told her it was Jake and in that shock of recognition she found the strength to lift him. Running her hands down over the face and shoulders, she fumbled for the armpits and, with Steve somewhere in the darkness below her lifting the rest of the body, she was able to drag it towards her until its weight was resting on the edge.

Steve hauled himself out of the pool beside it, turning the huddled form roughly over on to its back. And then the outline of his body seemed to mount Jake's while his head rose and fell, rose and fell with a regularity of motion which she could not understand until she heard the gasp and blow of his breath as he tried to force air into the lungs.

A flash of lightning illuminated them briefly, Jake sprawled out as she had seen him in bed, relaxed and sleepy, with Steve straddling his body, his mouth pressed on Jake's in a parody of love-making as she crouched beside them, voyeur to this bizarre passion in which for once Jake was the passive and unparticipating partner.

It seemed to last for a long time before Steve finally knelt upright.

'It's no good,' he said.

Harriet tried to push him away.

'Let me try!' she protested.

He seized her wrists.

'It's no good, Harriet,' he repeated. 'He's dead.'

She cried out, 'He can't be!'

It was absurd. Jake couldn't be dead. He was so much on the

side of living – the smile, the jaunty tilt to his head, the physical energy which he seemed to carry about him like an electric charge, attracting anyone who came close to its field. Death was a negation and Jake could never be accused of that.

She put out a hand in the darkness and touched his chest, feeling the arch of his ribs and the slight hollow which ran between them. The skin was cold and there was no movement under the rib cage but she kept her hand on the place where she thought the heart would be, with the ridiculous hope that the warmth from her own flesh might coax it back into life.

Beside her, Steve was struggling back into his clothes. Then she heard a faint metallic click and the yellow flame of a cigarette lighter spurted up suddenly and was carried down to Jake's body.

It flickered over the face, turned away from her so that she could see only the profile and a patch of rough, wet hair where the flame paused, went out and was relighted. This time it was carried closer to the area above the ear where it seemed to hover like a small, incandescent moth, lighting up with its fluttering wings the side of the head near the temple. In its light, she saw the broken flesh where the wound gaped beside the hair-line like another black, open mouth.

And something else. As the flame wavered and flared, she noticed the right hand lay close beside the head on the paving stones, drawn up as a fist on the same level as the wound, the fingers tightly clutching a small sprig of leaves which, in those few seconds of illumination, she recognised.

The next moment, the flame had gone out and Steve was helping her to her feet, saying urgently to her in the darkness which now seemed thicker and more intense than before, 'Go back to the house, Harriet. Call an ambulance and the police. I don't think he died accidentally.'

'Yes, of course,' she agreed quite calmly. It made sense, standing there in the muffled darkness with Steve's hands on her arms. He was right. Jake was dead but it was not an accident. Absurdly, Ophelia's words came into her mind and, before she could stop herself, she had spoken them out loud for no better reason than they seemed a fitting epitaph.

'"There's rosemary; that's for remembrance."'

Then, breaking away from Steve's grasp, she began running

back across the grass towards the lights of Morton Grange, ignoring the question he called out after her.

'Rosemary? Why rosemary, Harriet?'

6

Detective Inspector Jack Finch of Chelmsford CID made a similar remark about an hour later as he bent over the body of the young man which lay on the flagstones surrounding the swimming-pool at Morton Grange. The halogen lamps which shone down on the area gave it a theatrical brilliance as if the scene were part of an open-air production, the tall yew hedges, very black and dense, forming the backdrop while, in the foreground, the water in the pool was constantly shifting and dissolving into loops and whirls of turquoise and silver as the lights reflected back from the tiles which lined it.

The dead man had the same dramatic unreality. Left arm extended, right hand close to the head which was turned away to show the profile, he might have been waiting for the applause to break out before springing to his feet and coming forward to make his bow, the wound which disfigured the temple only grease-paint after all.

But why the sprig of leaves clutched in his hand? It seemed incongruous unless it was a symbol, the significance of which Finch had not yet grasped although he recognised the stiff, grey-green foliage. Leaning forward, he pinched the top of it between finger and thumb before lifting them to his nose.

Rosemary.

'But why rosemary?' he asked of no one in particular.

The scent was redolent of his childhood. There had been a bush of it by the front gate of his home. Every morning as he left for school, he had brushed against it, releasing the same aromatic fragrance.

Detective Sergeant Tom Boyce, who had been hanging about with the rest of the men, waiting for instructions, took the question to be directed at him and stepped forward. This keenness to be in the forefront of any investigation was typical of the

66

Sergeant and was prompted by his dislike of those moments of inactivity before a case got properly under way. Boyce preferred to see the men set about their business, a search started, the fingerprint experts on the job, not all this standing about doing nothing.

But recently a new element had crept into his eagerness to claim his place as Finch's right-hand man. Ever since Finch's widowed sister Dorothy, who in the past had kept house for him, had remarried, leaving the Chief Inspector on his own, the Sergeant had assumed an extra responsibility for him – almost like a nanny, Finch thought at times with exasperated amusement, although the comparison hardly suited the tall, burly Sergeant. Nevertheless, there had developed a gruff, awkward concern in his relationship with the Chief Inspector which extended into off-duty times as well so that Finch was constantly being bombarded by invitations to supper or Sunday lunch at the Boyces' house which he was forced from time to time to accept even though these occasions reminded him too acutely of his own bachelor status.

He could only thank God that Boyce knew nothing about his relationship with Marion Greave, the young woman pathologist who had taken over temporarily when Pardoe, the regular pathologist, had been on leave. Finch had fallen in love with her; as absurd to think of now as it had been then. He, a middle-aged bachelor, losing his heart like any romantic, moonstruck adolescent! But when he found the courage to propose to her, she had turned him down, preferring his friendship. Since then she had moved to Leeds to take up a hospital appointment. They still corresponded so the relationship, if you could call it that, continued, leaving him with the faint hope that perhaps one day . . .

But he had learnt not to look too far ahead. All the same, to sit at other people's tables, the Boyces', his sister's and Goodall's, still caused that painful hollow of loss and regret to open up somewhere deep inside him.

Boyce was saying, bringing him back to the present reality, 'If you mean the stuff he's holding in his hand, there's more of it in the pool. Do you want me to send Kyle in to fish it out?'

The offer was well meant but did not prevent Finch from feeling a momentary stir of impatience. Although he and Boyce had worked together for many years and made, he liked to think, a good professional team, the Sergeant had never quite grasped the importance to the Chief Inspector of those few moments of contemplation, especially in a case of sudden death, when, alone and as yet unaffected by the pressures which would build up as the investigation developed, he could make his own silent assessment. A kind of communion with the dead, he supposed. Not that he could explain it in those words to the Sergeant.

He straightened up. The moment had passed. All the same, he had absorbed enough of the corpse and its setting for him to acquire some feeling for this particular case. Each had its own individual aroma, like the scent released from the sprig of rosemary grasped in the dead man's hand. And this one smelt to him of murder, not accidental death.

Pardoe, the police pathologist, would no doubt confirm that the wound on the temple could not have been caused by a fall. It was too deep and extensive, spreading from just above the right eyebrow to the tip of the ear, crushing in the skull like an eggshell whacked with a damn great spoon. And you didn't get that kind of injury simply by falling and banging the side of your head. It looked to him like a classic case of the blunt instrument wielded with considerable force and deadly intention. Murder in other words. But he'd have to wait for Pardoe's report to discover whether or not the man had been killed by the blow or by drowning in the pool.

The fact that the body had been discovered in the water intrigued him. It suggested the murder had taken place here, at the pool-side. But why in this particular place? Because it was secluded? It seemed a possibility. The pool was some distance from the main house and the high hedges which surrounded it gave it an air of secrecy. It would make a perfect meeting place for lovers.

But it was too early in the case to come to any such conclusions although, as he stepped back a few paces to allow McCullum, the photographer, to take some close-up shots of the head, he went on contemplating the body in a ruminative fashion, hands stuffed deep in his pockets, a stocky figure standing four-square on the damp paving stones like a farmer at a stock-sale, waiting for the right moment before putting in his bid.

The victim had been young and good-looking. Even the shattered side of his head could not detract from the clear lines of the profile, the eyes open and very bright under the arc-lights and McCullum's flash-bulbs, the lips parted as if in a gasp of surprise at the awfulness of death. And physically strong, too. The chest, lifted by the upstretched arms, was almost naked where the shirt had been ripped open by whoever had tried to resuscitate him, showing firm flesh and arched muscles. He wasn't the type who would have stood meekly by while his killer struck him down, which suggested the blow had come unexpectedly from someone he knew and trusted. It was possible. Certainly there was no sign that he had fought for his life. The face, apart from the wound on the temple, was unmarked. So were the hands.

Finch contemplated them. The left hand was loose and flaccid, the right clenched round the sprig of rosemary as if to a lifeline, indicating a cadaveric spasm in which the muscles had violently contracted in the last few seconds before he died.

So the chances were that he had still been alive when he had gone into the water. But whether he had been pushed or had fallen made in fact little difference. Death had resulted.

But why the hell rosemary? It made no sense at all.

Skirting round McCullum, Finch moved to the edge of the pool, squatting down carefully to peer at the water where more sprigs of the stuff were floating gently about, rocked to and fro on the surface and forming little clusters as if attracted like to like.

He let the word rock in the same idle manner on the surface of his thoughts. Rosemary. Herb. Bush. Scent. Small, pale blue flowers in summer. Used in cooking. His sister had always put a spring of it in with a roast chicken. But that particular memory roused too many other painful and complex recollections – guilt that he had not appreciated her enough in the past mingled with a vague sense of resentment that, while he wished her well, it was after all she who had found the happiness which he had so ardently hoped for.

He began again.

Rosemary. A girl's name, of course. He was surprised that he had not made the connection sooner although how relevant that association might be to the investigation had yet to be established.

Rising to his feet, he took a last look about him before the business of getting the investigation under way overwhelmed him.

Yes, it would make a good trysting place for lovers, he decided. The bulk of Morton Grange loomed behind the yew hedge but some distance away, only the roof and the upper lighted windows being visible, while over to the left, the rectangular shape of a more contemporary building, every light switched on, stood out against the dark trees and shrubbery which surrounded it. From time to time a brief burst of summer lightning gave its own momentary brilliance to the scene, as fleeting yet as revealing as McCullum's flash-bulbs, scalding everything in a few seconds of blue-white radiance in which chimneys, branches, leaves, even the underside of the clouds, jumped forward into sudden focus.

Thunder sounded like a roll of drums still some distance away but circling closer as if the storm were prowling round the perimeter of the scene.

It was time to get started before it finally broke.

As McCullum finished and began packing up his equipment in his usual laconic, unhurried manner, Pardoe, the small, irascible, sandy-haired pathologist, with a God-help-us-all look up at the sky, bustled forward impatiently with his own bag of instruments to lay claim to the corpse, pulling the jeans down over the hips before turning the body briskly over on its side to take the rectal temperature.

Finch also stepped forward, Boyce at his side alert for orders.

Minutes later, the scene had lost any of the special atmosphere it had possessed during those first few moments. Men were given instructions and moved off, the uniformed men under Inspector Stapleton to make a search of the area, the scene of crime officers to complete their meticulous inch by inch inspection of the immediate vicinity, the plain-clothes experts to look for any likely surfaces for blood and hairs although they would be largely wasting their time. Finch had already given Stapleton's men orders to look for anything that might have struck that blow to the temple even before Pardoe, straightening up and turning to address him, confirmed the Chief Inspector's suspicions.

'Dead a couple of hours at a rough guess,' he said snappily as if Finch were about to query his expertise. 'And, if I were a betting man, I'd put my money on murder.'

'Murder!' Bernard repeated for the fourth time.

They were seated in his study, Bernard behind the desk, the bottle of sherry in front of him. It should have been brandy, of course, and its lack fretted him but he had not thought to bring any to Morton Grange. The sudden death of a member of staff was not a contingency for which one could come prepared.

After all, *murder!*

Behind him, the curtains over the window had been drawn back, revealing, like a huge oil painting hung on the wall, the darkened garden, the tower of the school chapel, dramatically highlighted from time to time by the flashes of sheet lightning, occupying most of the centre of the canvas while, over to the far right, a smaller patch of steady brilliance marked where the police were carrying out their activities under the arc-lamps, behind the black, cubist oblongs of the yew hedges.

The others sat facing him, Ron Arnott, elbows on knees, leaning forward and looking into the depths of his sherry glass, contributing nothing except for a powerful silence which Bernard was beginning to find increasingly exasperating. The man might find something to say if only a few words of reassurance that Nolan's death might have been accidental.

'You're sure?' he demanded of Steve Mayhew yet again.

As a mere student, not a tutor, he shouldn't have been present at the meeting, called hurriedly by Bernard as soon as the news of Nolan's death had reached him, but as Mayhew, together with Harriet Wade, had found the body, it seemed to Bernard expedient that he should be present as a *pro-tempore* staff member although, as the bringer of bad tidings, Bernard considered him with considerable disfavour across his desk.

It was Harriet who answered. She had been sitting in silence, legs drawn up under her, arms about her knees, as if finding solace in this close physical contact with herself, the hem of her skirt still damp where it had brushed against Jake's body.

Now, pushing back her hair, she sat up, suddenly impatient at Bernard's continuing obtuseness.

'No, we're not sure,' she retorted tartly, 'and we won't be until the police choose to tell us the truth although, like Steve, I don't believe Jake died accidentally. You didn't see the injury to his head, Bernard. We did. And there was something else about the

71

body which makes me feel quite certain that Jake was killed deliberately.' She looked across at Steve Mayhew as if seeking his approbation of what she was about to add. 'There were sprigs of rosemary scattered in the swimming-pool. In fact, Jake had one of them clutched in his hand. They didn't get there accidentally. I believe someone must have thrown them into the water for a particular purpose.'

On returning to the pool having telephoned the police and the ambulance service from Bernard's study, Harriet had taken a torch with her by the light of which she and Steve had examined the wound in the side of Jake's head as well as the spray of rosemary in his right hand. It was then that they had discovered the other sprigs of the same herb scattered on the water, confirming Harriet's feelings about their significance, an interpretation which Steve had listened to with some scepticism, considering it too far-fetched. For this reason, she had said nothing until that moment about it to Bernard who appeared bewildered by this additional information.

'Rosemary?' he demanded. 'But I don't see why anyone would want to murder Nolan and then scatter rosemary about the place.'

To Harriet's surprise, it was Arnott who supplied the explanation. She had not thought him capable of such imaginative perspicacity.

Rousing himself, he looked across at Bernard, his expression derisive.

'*Hamlet*,' he said abruptly, as if the answer were obvious. 'In the mad scene, just before Ophelia commits suicide, she hands out herbs and flowers. How does the line go? "Rosemary; that's for remembrance." Something like that anyway. She was drowned, too.'

The last remark fell like a heavy weight into the silence which followed it.

Then Steve spoke; the voice of reason, Harriet thought with an amused impatience, more concerned with the practicalities of the situation than with its dramatic interpretation.

'Whether it's murder or not, the police are going to ask questions and I think we ought to be ready for them.'

'Ask questions?' Bernard's voice was full of outraged incredulity. 'Of us?'

'Of everyone. They'll want to know what each of us was doing this evening, staff and students alike.'

'But most of the students have already gone to bed,' Bernard protested. 'Are you suggesting that we rouse them?'

Steve Mayhew shrugged as if the decision was entirely Bernard's affair.

Rising abruptly from his chair, Bernard went to stand by the window. The scene in the darkened panes of glass reflected two worlds; the study interior with the light falling on bookcases and paintings, the desk top piled with files and papers and the neatly stacked copies of Eliot's *The Waste Land* which he had intended discussing with his tutorial class the following morning; a safe, lamplit, academic domain of which he alone was king. Beyond the glass stretched the shadowy garden, still dominated by the chapel tower. But the change of position had brought into Bernard's viewpoint another building to the left of the frame – the assembly hall, lights still blazing, forming a balance with the other lighted area round the swimming-pool to his far right.

It occurred to Bernard that Nolan must have walked from the hall in front of the chapel to the pool where he had met his death. For a few seconds, he seemed to see Nolan's figure, so damned jaunty and cock-sure, traversing the darkness which now seemed full of menace and danger.

If Nolan had been murdered, he was thinking, then there would certainly be questions asked, uncomfortable and disturbing questions. Who was the last person to see Nolan alive? Who knew Nolan had gone to the hall? Who had the opportunity and the motive for killing him?

As he stared out bleakly through the glass, Bernard realised he himself would fit all too neatly into those categories of suspicion. It was he who had handed the keys of the hall to Nolan in the common room shortly before he must have met his death. As for opportunity, he, Bernard, had been alone for the rest of the evening. It would have been easy for him to slip out unseen from the study through this very window and cross the side lawn under cover of the darkness to seek Nolan out.

Wouldn't that be the line of reasoning the police would take?

As for motive, there was the letter from Bryant which the police might find in Nolan's room when they came to search it; that is, if the letter existed at all and if Nolan had brought it with him as he had hinted although God alone knew if Nolan had been lying or not. He was so damned plausible that it was difficult to tell.

But if it was in his room and if the police found it, it could contain details of Bryant's suicide which the police might very well interpret as a motive for his murdering Nolan in order to secure his silence.

If. If. If.

The uncertainty was as terrible as the fact of Nolan's death.

He must get hold of the letter at all costs, Bernard decided. But first he must make arrangements for the police to interview the staff and students. Once everyone was safely downstairs and the upper floor was vacated, he would then have the opportunity to search Nolan's room before the police arrived to make their own examination.

Closing the curtains with a sudden clatter of brass rings on the pole, he turned to face the others, his decison made.

'I shall make the staff common room available to the police,' he announced. 'Harriet, may I ask you to be responsible for making sure all the women students are assembled there? Perhaps you would also inform Joyce Yarwood of what has happened and ask her to be kind enough to supply everyone with tea and biscuits. I myself will be in charge of the male students.'

'But what am I to say to them?' Harriet asked.

'As little as possible at this stage. Merely tell them that there's been an accident – you needn't even say who is involved – and that the police, who have been sent for, may want to make inquiries. I assume,' Bernard added, turning to address Steve Mayhew as if he were the expert in these matters, 'that the police will be interested in *alibis*?'

He spoke the word with considerable distaste.

'I would imagine so,' Steve replied. 'Anything I can do?'

'Yes; once the students are assembled, you can help Harriet and myself check the names so that we're sure no one is missing.'

Opening a folder on the desk, he took out four copies of the students' lists, handing one each to Harriet and Steve Mayhew and setting the other two aside.

Arnott chose the moment to offer his own contribution. Getting up awkwardly from the low armchair, he held out his hand for one of the remaining copies.

74

'I suppose you'll want me to check my own students?' he asked grudgingly.

'No thank you, Ronald, I really don't think it will be necessary to put you to all that trouble,' Bernard replied briskly. Now that the worst of the shock was over and decisions had been made, he seemed to recover some of his usual authority. 'Harriet and I can cope perfectly adequately with Mayhew's help. Besides, I have only two copies of the list left, one for myself and the other which no doubt the police will need to carry out their inquiries. I'd be grateful if you simply made yourself generally *available*.' He gave the last word a gentle but dismissive emphasis before addressing the other two. 'Please make sure you behave as diplomatically and as discreetly as possible. I don't want the students unnecessarily alarmed nor do I wish unfounded rumours and speculation to start circulating before we ourselves know all the facts. Remember we have the good name of Morton Grange to uphold.'

He sounded, Harriet thought, like the headmaster at Foxwood, addressing the fifth-year pupils about their behaviour at a coming Saturday night school disco, hoping for the best but expecting the worst, although Bernard was human enough to add unexpectedly, his face looking suddenly very drawn and tired, 'I only hope to God none of this gets into the newspapers. It could be the finish of the summer school if it does.'

The creative writing course evidently meant a great deal more to him than Harriet had realised. But he had, after all, been running it for fifteen years and had seen it build up from small beginnings to its present position. Its reputation was excellent and the courses were generally oversubscribed, points which Bernard had been at particular pains to emphasise when he had invited her to join the staff.

It was also evident that Bernard intended dispensing with Ron Arnott's services as course tutor. Jake had been right about that. Bernard's decision not to involve Arnott in the arrangements had been a deliberate snub, disguised under a cloak of concern for Arnott's well-being but nevertheless significant in its dismissiveness. Arnott himself seemed aware of it for, as she accompanied Steve Mayhew to the door, she caught a glimpse of his face, the heavy jowls drawn down into an expression of ponderous and settled gloom.

She ought, she supposed, to feel sorry for him but there was no time. Hardly had she and Steve turned out of the passage leading into the main entrance hall than the first students came down the stairs to meet them, some in dressing-gowns, aware from the comings and goings of the staff as well as the arrival of the official police cars that something unusual had happened and clamouring for information.

So much for Bernard's diplomacy and discretion, Harriet thought wryly. They were almost as bad as a third-year form at Foxwood. Raising herself on tiptoe and pitching her voice above theirs, she waved Bernard's list at them, her badge of authority.

'If you'd all please come into the common room,' she announced, 'I'll explain what's going on.'

It was a measure of her experience at Foxwood that they fell in meekly enough behind her, Steve bringing up the rear to round up those who might prefer to linger in private discussion.

As the double doors closed behind her, Harriet caught a glimpse of Arnott mounting the stairs, clutching the banister rail with one hand and hauling himself up painfully step by step as if suddenly very old and very tired.

7

Three of the students were missing, Harriet discovered when, having collected the others together in the common room and made her announcement, she and Steve did a quick head count.

The news of the sudden death and the arrival of the police shocked most of them into silence although one or two voices were heard demanding 'Who's died?'

Harriet ignored them, stepping forward with her list to call out names and putting a cross beside those for which there was no answer. She had almost finished the task when Bernard joined them.

'Who's missing?' he asked, drawing her to one side.

'One woman, two men,' Harriet informed him. 'Felicity Grayson, Frank Goodyear and Leon Murray.'

She saw Bernard give a quick little frown of impatience at

Leon's name and felt like reacting in the same manner over Felicity Grayson's. It was typical of the damned woman not to conform with everybody else and to have to be sent for specially. The absence of Frank Goodyear surprised rather than annoyed her. He was the type to follow the group and she had expected to find him among those already assembled. But perhaps he was asleep and had not been disturbed by the sound of voices and footsteps as the other students came downstairs.

'Then I suppose we'll have to find them and inform them what's happened,' Bernard said. 'But apart from those three, everyone else is accounted for?'

'Ron Arnott isn't here.' Harriet felt she was sneaking on Arnott by passing this information on to Bernard but she supposed he ought to know. 'I saw him going up to his room before we started the check.'

'As far as I'm concerned, he can stay there,' Bernard said snappily. 'I'm sure we'll cope a great deal more efficiently without him. Before we start looking for the ones who are missing, I'd better say a few words to the rest of the students.'

It was remarkable, Harriet thought, as Bernard stepped forward to his usual place in front of the fireplace under the portrait of Miss Poulson, how quickly he could assume the correct expression, almost as if he carried about with him a bag of facial disguises which he could don in a moment to suit the occasion. In this particular instance, it was the noble, grieving look of the elder statesman, announcing tragic tidings to a stricken nation. Even his voice changed, taking on a deeper, more sonorous timbre.

'I believe Harriet has already informed you that there has been a fatal accident. The police have been sent for and arrived a short time ago. No doubt, they will want to interview everyone in due course. In the meantime, may I ask all of you to remain here? Arrangements will shortly be made for refreshments to be served.'

It was only as Bernard made this last statement that Harriet realised Joyce Yarwood was not among those assembled in the common room and would also have to be sought out and informed. She was the only member of the domestic staff who had her own room in Morton Grange, the rest, who lived locally, arriving by car or minibus for work on a daily basis.

As Bernard turned away, someone, bolder than the others,

77

repeated the question which so far Harriet had managed to ignore.

'Who was involved in the accident?'

But Bernard had already gone, striding straight-backed although with head decently lowered towards the door, managing to express even in this back view of himself his dual role as Director of Studies, very much in charge of the situation, as well as the sorrowing individual suffering some deep and personal loss.

He had heard the question, however. As she followed him into the hall, Harriet was quite convinced of that. Which left her, she thought angrily, with the task of informing the students not only exactly who was the victim but also of the unpleasant fact that the fatal accident, as Bernard euphemistically described it, was most probably murder. As a piece of buck-passing, it was very neatly contrived.

On the upper landing, she left Bernard to make a search of Leon's and Frank Goodyear's rooms in the west wing and turned into the east wing towards Felicity Grayson's which she found empty, the lights on but the bed unslept in. It was only as she closed the door and stood hesitating in the corridor outside, wondering where else to look, that it occurred to her that, of the four of them not yet accounted for, three – Joyce Yarwood, Felicity Grayson and Leon Murray – might have had a motive for murder. All had been involved with Jake in some special relationship, Leon and Joyce Yarwood in particular. Felicity Grayson's contact with him was of a shorter duration and therefore presumably less intimate although that was not necessarily a proof of innocence. Jake might already have got her into bed. He might even have arranged to meet her that evening in the assembly hall. Certainly she had been talking to Jake when Bernard had handed over the keys so she must have been aware that Jake intended going to the hall that evening.

And there was herself, too, of course. After the first shock of finding the body had passed, she had managed to push to the back of her mind the memory of her own affair with him in the flurry of the subsequent events which had overtaken her – informing Bernard, telephoning the police, taking part in the meeting to discuss arrangements; a deliberate suppression on her part, she realised, because to compare the dead flesh with the living had been beyond contemplation. He was no longer Jake, her former lover, but a victim, an object of general horrified compassion in which all other emotion had been burnt away.

But not entirely forgotten. She assumed that if Jake had indeed been murdered, the police would ask much more searching questions than if his death had been an accident. They would want to know not only who had the opportunity to kill him but also who had a reason for wanting him dead.

In their eyes, she would have both. She had been alone in her room all evening. She and Jake had been lovers. Moreover, she had been one of those who knew he had gone to the hall that evening and later had helped find his body. Remembering that flash of intuitive recognition which had persuaded her to lead the way to the swimming-pool, she was suddenly afraid. Might that also be regarded as suspicious?

She could keep silent, of course, about her affair with Jake although hiding the truth could be more dangerous than admitting it. Bernard knew about the relationship and might have confided his knowledge in Ron Arnott, however unlikely such a possibility seemed.

No, she decided, it was probably better to answer any questions the police might put to her frankly and openly, hoping to God that the investigation uncovered the true facts behind Jake's death as quickly as possible.

Meanwhile, there were more practical problems on her mind – to find Felicity Grayson and Joyce Yarwood as quickly as possible, especially Joyce who would have to be informed of the need to prepare refreshments. Felicity Grayson could wait until last.

Although she had never been inside it nor even explored that part of the upper floor of Morton Grange, she understood that Joyce Yarwood had a small flat over the kitchen quarters at the rear of the main building. Returning to the gallery landing above the central staircase, she therefore set off down the unfamiliar passage which led in that direction and which, after taking her through a pair of swing doors, down some steps and round an L-shaped corner, brought her eventually to a smaller back landing from which a flight of narrow stairs, presumably the servants' staircase when the Grange had been in private hands, descended to the ground floor.

Seeing the layout of this part of the house for the first time, Harriet was struck that, from the point of view of conducting a secret liaison, it was perfect. It would have been easy for Jake to come upstairs by this back way in order to carry on his affair with Joyce Yarwood, without running the risk of being seen using the more public main staircase and corridors.

There was a door on her right with Joyce Yarwood's name on a small card attached to it and, having knocked and received no answer, Harriet tried the handle, overcome with a sudden curiosity to see inside. Finding the door unlocked, she opened it and put her head round the jamb.

The bed-sitter beyond was large, chintzy and comfortable, probably converted out of several smaller rooms, with two more doors on the far side which had been left ajar and which gave her a glimpse of an adjoining bathroom and what seemed to be a small kitchen. A pair of windows faced the back of the building across the service yard towards the swimming-pool while a large double sash in the left-hand wall looked out towards the school chapel and assembly hall to the west of the main block. None of the curtains had been closed, giving a perfect view to anyone inside the room not only of Jake as he crossed from the drive to the hall and from there to the swimming-pool where he had met his death but of anyone else who might have accompanied or followed him.

But the room was empty, the single divan bed, disguised as a sofa under its flounced cover, unslept in, the cushions neat and plump; an unlikely setting for fornication, it seemed to Harriet. It was too tidy and spinsterish, too tucked in. There were girlish touches about the place as well which hardly conformed with a grand and illicit passion – a collection of photographs on the mantelpiece, Mummy and Daddy and the family dog, a black and white rough-haired terrier; a little basket of china flowers; a small, furry koala bear wearing a blue and white spotted bow tie. It was as difficult to imagine Jake, naked and randy, against such a virginal background as for Harriet to grasp the fact that he was now lying dead at the side of the pool.

Abruptly, she closed the door and returned along the passage to the east wing. Joyce Yarwood must still be in the kitchen. Felicity Grayson also had to be found.

Harriet discovered her in one of the bathrooms at the far end of the east wing, the last place she had decided to try before going downstairs in search of Joyce Yarwood.

The sound of running water and a transistor tuned to Radio 2 could be heard coming from behind a closed door. Banging on it, Harriet heard both music and water turned off and Felicity Grayson's voice call out, 'Who is it?'

'It's Harriet Wade,' she called back.

The door opened part-way and the top half of Felicity Grayson appeared, plump white shoulders, still beaded with water, revealed above a towel wrapped like a sarong under her armpits, the auburn hair covered with a shower-cap. Without her make-up, she looked older but the damp flesh had an exotic, pearly lushness to it which Harriet was in no mood to admire.

'There's been an accident,' she announced briskly in her best I-shall-stand-for-no-nonsense classroom voice. 'The police are here. Would you please get dressed immediately and come downstairs to the common room?' And with that she marched away, not giving Felicity Grayson time to ask any questions.

Let her damn well find out about Jake from someone else, she decided.

Leon had evidently been found. As she reached the top of the main staircase, Harriet could see him descending it ahead of her, dressed in a white towelling robe which suggested he had just got up although the blond hair, glistening like gold patent leather under the lights, had been carefully combed into its boyish, sideways flick.

The police, too, had arrived; at least two figures, both in plain clothes, were standing in the hall just inside the main doors in company with Steve who appeared to have let them in only a few seconds before; one a short, stocky man who stood, hands in pockets, head tilted upwards to observe Leon's and her own descent, a bland expression on his face but nevertheless giving out an impression of a watchful and intelligent alertness. The man accompanying him was taller, broad-shouldered, altogether heavier.

Seeing her, Steve called out, 'Is Bernard up there?'

He had intended the question for Harriet but it was Leon who answered.

'Yes. He's still looking for someone called Frank.'

Harriet, her foot on the top step, said, 'I'll go and find him.'

81

She turned back, recrossing the landing, and was about to enter the corridor leading to the west wing when she realised the shorter of the two men was following her, having come up the stairs with surprising alacrity.

'Miss . . . ?' he prompted as she waited for him to catch up with her.

'Wade,' she told him. 'Harriet Wade. I'm one of the tutors.'

She was aware that he was appraising not only her but their surroundings, taking in the details of the long corridor of facing doors, even the dark brown matting on the floor, with quick little sideways glances which missed nothing.

'I'm Detective Chief Inspector Finch,' he announced, adding unexpectedly before she had time to reply, 'Who's Frank?'

'Frank Goodyear, one of the students.'

'And he's missing?' he asked.

'He's probably in bed asleep,' she said dismissively so as not to over-dramatise Frank Goodyear's non-appearance. Walking on ahead of him to escape his scrutiny, she thought that she would be a fool to try and hide anything from him. He might give the impression of a countryman, genial and fresh-faced, more like a farmer than a Chief Inspector, but that was, she felt, only a disguise. Underneath that affable exterior was a sharp-eyed professional policeman who had already summed her up in those first few seconds.

'This is his room,' she continued, knocking at Frank Goodyear's door and waiting for a few moments before opening it to reveal it empty, not only of Frank Goodyear but of Bernard as well.

God knows what prompted her to try Jake's room. Later, she tried to analyse her motives. It was facing Frank Goodyear's. It seemed natural to take the few steps towards it if only to avoid the proximity of the Chief Inspector and to divert his attention from both Frank and Bernard's absence. But mostly it was to convince herself that Jake wasn't there after all and that she had indeed left him lying at the side of the pool, the water running from his clothes and hair as he stared up at her with those blank, fixed eyes.

She flung the door open without knocking, intending to remark for the Chief Inspector's benefit, 'And this is Jake Nolan's room.' But the words were never spoken.

On the far side of the room, Bernard had whirled about to face them, his expression full of appalled guilt, his hands still in the act of searching the top drawer of the chest which stood under the window.

For a few seconds, they looked at one another in silence which was broken by Finch who, stepping forward, said with a twinkling air of good humour, as if secretly amused by the situation, 'Mr Livesey, I presume? I wonder if I could have a few words with you downstairs?'

8

Bernard led the way downstairs to his study where he took his usual seat behind the desk although it no longer seemed to afford him quite the same sense of authority that it had on previous occasions. Detective Chief Inspector Finch, accompanied by Detective Sergeant Boyce whom he had collected up on their way through the hall, sat opposite him, both very much at ease as if they had as much right to be there as Bernard; more so, in fact, for, as they assumed their places, the Detective Sergeant took a notebook and pen from his pocket with an unhurried air, glancing sideways at Finch as he did so to signal that he was ready for the Chief Inspector to begin.

Bernard also waited. In the time it had taken them to reach the study, he had been searching his mind for a plausible excuse to explain his presence in Nolan's room but had thought of nothing. Words which had never failed him before either in the giving of his lectures or the writing of his reviews and which had slipped so easily from tongue or pen refused to materialise.

In the event, the Chief Inspector seemed in no hurry himself to reach that particular point and the interview began with a few innocuous questions about Morton Grange summer school, its students and staff and the exact role that Jake had played in its organisation.

Bernard took his time giving his answers, padding them out with any details he could think of which might have even a peripheral relevance, postponing the moment when Finch would reach the crucial part of his examination. To all of this the Chief Inspector listened with apparent interest although, when Bernard had finished, he summed up the information in a few brief and, to Bernard, cruelly concise sentences.

'So, Mr Livesey, there are thirty students staying at Morton Grange at the moment on a week's course, all of whom arrived yesterday; four tutors including yourself and Mr Nolan who taught drama, and one member of the domestic staff who lives in. Is that right?'

'No, not quite,' Bernard corrected himself. 'I should also have included the gardener, George Burton, who, although he doesn't live in the main building, does have a house in the school grounds.'

He realised he had forgotten to mention Burton to Harriet Wade when making arrangements for the students and staff to be assembled in the common room but he assumed that the police would send for him themselves if they considered it necessary.

Handing a copy of the list of names to Finch, he continued, 'You'll find all the students listed there in tutorial groups. I might add that I've asked everyone to gather in the common room in case you might wish to question them. I thought it expedient under the circumstances.'

The remark was offered as a small sop to the Chief Inspector. By appearing co-operative, Bernard hoped to allay any suspicions Finch might be holding against him.

The choice of phrase proved unfortunate. Finch pounced on it at once.

'Circumstances? Exactly what circumstances had you in mind, Mr Livesey?'

Bernard hastened to retrieve the situation.

'In case Nolan's death wasn't accidental.'

'Have you any reason to believe it might not have been?'

'No, no; that wasn't what I meant at all. I was merely making an assumption on what I was told by Harriet Wade and Steve Mayhew who found the body. Both of them seemed to think that, judging by the nature of the injury, it was unlikely Nolan had struck his head in a fall. Of course, I had only their assessment to rely on. Nevertheless, I thought it wiser to assume . . .'

He waved a hand to indicate that the rest of the sentence was better left unsaid. Finch promptly picked it up.

'That Mr Nolan had been murdered?' he suggested.

'That the circumstances surrounding his death were suspicious,' Bernard corrected him coldly. It was time, he felt, that he began to re-assert his own authority. After all, Finch was hardly as impressive figure. Dressed in a shabby jacket and trousers which had seen better days and wearing shoes which were a positive disgrace, he looked and sounded, Bernard thought, his ear detecting the faint sing-song intonation of the local Essex accent, more like a farmer than a professional policeman.

To his relief, the Chief Inspector seemed to lose interest in this aspect of the investigation and turned his attention to the list of students.

'No one called Rosemary down here, I notice,' he remarked.

'Rosemary?' Bernard asked sharply. 'I have a Miss Rose Deacon in my tutorial group, a rather elderly lady . . .'

For a moment, he had forgotten Harriet Wade's comment about the sprig of rosemary in Nolan's hand and the bizarre interpretation which both she and Arnott had put on it but, as he recalled it, Finch appeared to lose interest in that subject as well. List in hand, he was asking, 'Were any of these students known to Mr Nolan before they joined the summer school?'

It was a theory he and Boyce had discussed as they walked from the swimming-pool to the main house. Although the forensic and pathologist's reports had yet to confirm the fact, Finch's money, like Pardoe's, was on murder and moreover a murder which had been planned. He was willing to bet a month's salary that Nolan had been lured under some pretext or other to the swimming-pool, no doubt because the high yew hedges offered concealment, by someone he knew who had good reason to want him dead.

Bernard hesitated before replying, weighing up the likelihood that Leon Murray's name could be kept out of the inquiry before deciding that there was small chance that it could. Too many people had witnessed the quarrel which had taken place that morning between Jake and Murray. For his own sake, he decided, it was far better that he admitted what he knew before someone else blurted out the truth, giving Finch further grounds for suspicion against him for withholding evidence.

All the same, he spoke circumspectly.

'There is one young man, Leon Murray, who, I believe, knew

85

Nolan outside Morton Grange.' When Finch made no reply apart from cocking his head to show interest, Bernard was forced to continue, 'In fact, they met here last year on a similar course when Murray was a student in Nolan's drama class. Unfortunately, Murray caused difficulties . . .'

'Difficulties?' Finch prompted. 'What sort of difficulties?'

'He was rather demanding; expecting far too much attention and special treatment. But as it was nearly the end of the week's course and he would shortly be leaving, I saw no reason to intervene. However, he re-enrolled this year under a different name – B. L. Murray, not Leon Murray. Had I realised this, I would have refused his application. Nolan was very angry when he found out about it. I gather that he and Murray had been in contact with one another since last year's summer school. In fact, Murray had supplied financial backing for a production Nolan was involved in at some London fringe theatre but there'd been some dispute between them and Leon had withdrawn from the agreement. I ought to add that I have only heard Leon Murray's side of the dispute, not Nolan's, at least not in full. I had reason to speak to them both earlier today following an unfortunate quarrel which took place in front of other students, in the light of which I decided Murray would have to leave. Consequently, I arranged for him to be kept incommunicado in his room until his departure tomorrow morning.'

'He accepted your decision?' Finch asked.

'With bad grace,' Bernard admitted. 'But he was given no option.'

He would have preferred not to expand on this aspect of his interview with Leon who had tried every trick in his not inconsiderable repertoire of emotional manipulation, including cajolery, defiance, threats to make trouble and even tears, before finally accepting the inevitability of Bernard's decision. It had been a painful and embarrassing experience.

But Finch persisted.

'He was angry?'

Bernard weighed his answer judiciously before replying.

'He was displeased.'

'So as far as you know he was alone in his room all evening?'

'I believe so but you would have to ask him yourself, Chief Inspector. I made arrangements with the school's domestic bursar, Joyce Yarwood, that supper should be taken to his room on a tray but, apart from that, I have no personal knowledge of his movements this evening.'

'About your own,' Finch began.

They had reached, Bernard realised, the crux of the interview and, now that it had arrived, it was almost a relief.

'I dined as usual with the students and the other members of staff at half-past seven and joined them for coffee afterwards in the staff common room. The time would then have been about half-past eight. Over coffee, I handed Nolan the keys to the assembly hall which he had asked for earlier. Normally it's kept locked and out of bounds to the students except those on the drama course and only then under special circumstances. However, Nolan wanted to use the hall tomorrow morning to teach voice projection and stage movement to his class. I agreed and, having fetched the keys here from my study, gave them to Nolan in the common room. I understand he left about twenty minutes later at ten to nine.'

'To go to the hall?'

'I assume so. I didn't myself see him leave. He wanted to check that the stage was cleared of any furniture that might have been stored on it before his tutorial class tomorrow morning.'

'Who else, apart from yourself, knew he was going to be in the hall this evening?'

'Any number of people. Several were sitting nearby when he asked for the keys and most of the students and staff were present in the common room having coffee when I handed them over to him. He was in a group on both occasions.'

'Their names, sir?' Boyce asked, lifting his head from his notebook.

'Oh, really!' Bernard protested. 'I can't be expected to remember every single individual. But if you insist, Harriet Wade, one of the tutors, was sitting at the same table in the dining-room with Jake when he asked for the keys. So was Kay Ratcliff, a drama student. As for the others in the common room, I believe Felicity Grayson and Mark Anderson were present. I can't recall the others. Nolan had quite a little audience round him at the time.'

It was said with a bitterness which was not lost on Finch, nor on Bernard himself for, aware of the effect his remark might have had on the Chief Inspector and his Sergeant, he added hurriedly,

'Jake was an actor as well as a writer and producer. He could be very amusing and entertaining when he wished. But apart from the people I mentioned, others could have overheard our conversation. Neither of us made any secret of the fact that he was going to prepare the hall this evening for his drama class.'

'And what about your own movements this evening, Mr Livesey?' Finch asked, resuming the questioning.

'As soon as I'd handed over the keys, I came back here to the study to prepare some work for my own tutorial class.'

'You were alone?'

'Yes, I was.' Bernard looked across the desk at the Chief Inspector, his expression almost defiant. 'I had a great deal to do, including drawing up class lists and room allocations for next week's students who are due to arrive on Sunday. At quarter to eleven, I realised Nolan hadn't returned the keys. As part of our agreement with the school governors stipulates that all doors should be secured by eleven o'clock, I decided to go and look for him. I thought it was unlikely he was still in the hall. It couldn't have taken him all evening to clear the stage and I assumed he'd forgotten to turn the lights off and hand back the keys. I checked the common room but, as he wasn't there, I went upstairs to Miss Wade's room.'

He was about to continue when Finch interrupted him.

'A couple of points, Mr Livesey,' he put in with a casual air. 'First of all, how did you know the lights were still on in the hall?'

'I saw them,' Bernard explained.

'But from where? You said you were here in the study all evening from about half-past eight to quarter to eleven. So how could you be sure Mr Nolan hadn't turned off the lights?'

Damn! Bernard thought. He had not even seen that particular trap although he had been aware as he had mentioned Harriet Wade of the potential danger of introducing her name in connection with Jake's.

'I saw them through the window,' he explained, getting up from the desk and lifting aside the curtains, conscious as he did so that there was only one possible inference that could be drawn from his actions – that he had been surreptitiously checking up on Jake's movements.

The scene was revealed through the panes of glass which

were now spattered with the heavy drops of rain which were beginning to fall.

Finch also rose from his chair and came to stand beside him, hands in pockets, contemplating the oblong of lighted windows which was the assembly hall as well as the dazzle of brightness which marked the swimming-pool where the arc-lamps, their brilliance refracted by the raindrops on the glass, shone out with a more sinister radiance.

'A good view,' he remarked cheerfully. 'Did you see Nolan?'

'I saw nobody, Chief Inspector,' Bernard said stiffly, letting the curtains fall back into place.

'And you didn't go across to the hall to look for him?' Finch continued. 'Instead you went to Miss Wade's room.' He rattled the curtains back on their rings so that the panes were completely uncovered. 'Why?'

Bernard resumed his seat, turning his back on the uncurtained window.

'I've already explained, I thought it unlikely that Nolan was still in the hall.'

'But why Miss Wade's room?' Finch repeated. He had sat down again opposite Bernard who, noticing the expression of smiling affability on the Chief Inspector's face, felt both exasperated and afraid. The man might give the impression of a genial country-man but there was an acute and perceptive intelligence behind those deceptively bland and genial features. 'Why not the other tutor's room – what's his name? – Mr Arnott?'

It was a double jeopardy but Bernard no longer cared. An instinct for self-preservation overcame any scruples he might have regarding the others, certainly Arnott.

'Arnott and Nolan weren't exactly friendly,' he replied although he was quick to add, 'There was no quarrel that I know of. They simply weren't on good terms with one another.'

'But Mr Nolan and Miss Wade were?'

Caution persuaded Bernard to answer more prudently. After all, although he felt under no obligation to protect Arnott, in the case of Jake and Harriet, he had the good name of the summer school to consider.

'They were friends,' he replied.

'Nothing more? Not lovers?' Finch persisted and, when Bernard didn't answer, he continued, 'Oh, come on, Mr Livesey!

You went looking for Jake Nolan in Miss Wade's room at a quarter to eleven at night. Now that suggests to me that there was something more than mere friendship between them and that you suspected it. Wasn't that the case?'

'There may have been an intimacy between them last year,' Bernard admitted, hesitating over the word 'intimacy' which had all the prurient overtones of a divorce court report in the more sensational daily press but he could think of no other term to use. 'I have no direct knowledge of their exact relationship. You would have to ask Miss Wade about that.'

Finch nodded as if he intended doing just that before adding, 'Go on.'

'Miss Wade said she hadn't seen Nolan but, as I was busy, offered to go over to the hall to look for him in case he was still there. I agreed and we went downstairs together where I returned to my study. I understand one of the students in Miss Wade's class, Steve Mayhew, went with her. About quarter of an hour later, Miss Wade returned to report that she and Mayhew had found Nolan dead in the swimming-pool. She used the telephone in here to ring for an ambulance and the police. But were she and Mayhew right, Chief Inspector? Did someone kill Nolan or was it an accident?'

If he had hoped for a direct answer, Finch didn't oblige him, merely replying in a non-committal voice, 'We're not sure ourselves yet, Mr Livesey, but no doubt the experts will come up with the facts in good time. I take it you didn't see the body?'

'Certainly not!' Bernard said with a shudder.

'And now,' Finch went on, settling himself back in his chair as if in readiness to give Bernard his undivided attention, 'would you mind explaining exactly what you were doing in Mr Nolan's room when Miss Wade and I found you?'

'I was looking for some papers,' Bernard replied.

He saw the Sergeant raise his head from his notebook as if scenting out the equivocation.

'What papers?' he demanded.

'Just what I was going to ask Mr Livesey myself,' Finch said with a maddeningly cheerful air. 'What papers?'

It was useless, Bernard realised, to try to fudge the issue. The two of them, the Chief Inspector and his Sergeant, would go on passing the question backwards and forward between them until they learnt the truth. He was suddenly overcome by an unutter-able weariness. Better perhaps to confess the truth and have done with it.

'As I've already told you, I spoke to Nolan earlier today about the quarrel which took place between him and Murray this morning for which I felt Nolan was partly to blame because of his previous relationship with Murray. Nolan resented what he termed my interference in his private affairs. In the course of the interview, during which he became quite offensive, he men-tioned a letter which he said he had in his possession and which could have caused me considerable professional embarrassment had it been published. It had been written, he said, although I had no means of knowing that Nolan was speaking the truth and the letter even existed, by a young poet who, according to Nolan, committed suicide about two years ago following a review I wrote about his work in one of the quality papers. The young man certainly died although the coroner recorded a verdict of accidental death due to an inadvertent overdose of heroin. If such a letter exists and if it had been sent to the coroner, I understood there could have been further inquiries or so Nolan said. I don't know about these matters. But had the inquest been reopened and my name mentioned, it could have led to a great deal of adverse publicity. It was that letter I was looking for when you and Miss Wade found me, Chief Inspector.'

'And what had you intended doing with it?' Finch asked.

'I should have destroyed it, of course,' Bernard said promptly, as if that much were obvious. Rising abruptly again from his chair, he went to stand behind the desk, looking out through the window although he was less aware of the distant view of the school hall and the swimming-pool, obscured by the falling rain, than the nearer reflection of the interior of the study, brightly lit, in which the seated figures of the two policemen seemed to fill up the darkened glass, their faces turned in his direction.

With his back still towards them, he continued, 'If Nolan was murdered, I would seem to have both a motive and the oppor-tunity for killing him. Isn't that what you're thinking, Chief Inspector?'

But the tableau in the glass was already breaking up. Finch was getting to his feet. The Sergeant, too, was preparing to leave, closing up his notebook and restoring it to an inner pocket.

'I'd like to interview the rest of the students and staff, Mr Livesey,' Finch was saying.

Bernard turned back.

'Of course,' he replied, drawing himself upright as he stood behind the desk. 'You'll find them in the staff common room. I don't know if they're all assembled yet. When Miss Wade checked the list a little earlier, Miss Grayson and Miss Yarwood, the school bursar, were still unaccounted for. So were Murray and another of the male students, Frank Goodyear. However, I've since found Murray in his room and he should now have joined the others. I couldn't locate Goodyear but he may have since made his own way downstairs. Is that all?'

'If you'd remain here for the time being, I'll send along a Detective Constable to take down details of Mr Nolan's home address.'

'I have it on file,' Bernard assured him, escorting Finch and the Sergeant out of the study and watching as they walked away down the corridor. It was only when he had closed the door behind him that he allowed his anxiety to find expression.

Oh, God! he thought. Where was it all going to end? Even though he had confessed about the letter, the worst was not yet over. Indeed, he suspected that it had only just begun.

9

As soon as they were out of earshot of the study, Boyce said, 'He's right, you know. If Nolan was murdered, Livesey would have both the motive and the opportunity for killing him.'

Finch merely grunted in reply. They had walked down the corridor and had reached a small inner vestibule, floored with worn black and white marble tiles, where the passage formed a T, one branch turning off to the left towards the main hall, the other leading to the right to run the length of the west wing.

Several doors opened off this vestibule, including one with a glass panel which gave direct access into the garden. It seemed to catch his attention for he opened it and peered out into the night and the rain. Across an expanse of darkened lawn and shrubbery behind the west wing, the lights round the swimming-pool where the men were continuing the search were clearly visible although only a corner of the school assembly hall could be seen.

Closing it, he remarked, 'It's a warren of a place, Tom. Remind me to check how many separate exits there are apart from the front door. This one seems to lead directly on to the side of the main building.'

As he spoke, he was opening more doors, one revealing a large cloakroom, equipped with lockers and wash-basins, the other, on the opposite side of the vestibule, a lighted classroom, converted, it appeared, from a sitting-room, with faded wallpaper and an ornate marble mantelpiece still in place, contrasting oddly with the utilitarian chairs and tables drawn up in a half-circle facing the uncurtained window which overlooked the same view of the side lawn that Finch had seen through the glass-panelled door.

A large desk of plain wood stood in front of this window at which was seated a man who looked up from a folder in which he was writing and demanded angrily as the Chief Inspector's head appeared round the door, 'Who the hell are you?'

'Detective Chief Inspector Finch,' Finch replied blandly. 'And my Detective Sergeant, Boyce.'

The answer seemed to mollify the man a little for he said with better grace, although the impatience was still apparent in his voice, 'Well, come in, come in. I'm Ron Arnott, one of the tutors. I suppose you're here to question everybody about Nolan's death. What do you want to know?'

He gestured abruptly towards the chairs drawn up in front of him and, with a smile and a nod at Boyce, Finch took his place at one of the tables as if amused at the situation, the Sergeant seating himself with a more disapproving air before getting out his notebook.

Together, like pupils at school, they faced Arnott; a large, slack man, Finch noted, who sat, head thrust forward at them across the desk so that, even before the interview began, it had already taken on the quality of a confrontation.

It was because of this that Finch began casually, dropping into the gentle rhythms of the local Essex intonation, a throwback to his own village upbringing, which he could still produce whenever he wanted to create the impression of a country copper and which, in this instance, contrasted, to his apparent disadvantage, with Arnott's harsher and more aggressive London accent.

'At the moment, Mr Arnott, we're merely checking on everyone's movements at about the time we think Mr Nolan may have met his death. So, if you don't mind, sir, we'd like you to tell us what you were doing after supper from about half-past eight onwards.'

'I joined the others for coffee in the common room,' Arnott said.

It was evident from his reply that he was going to be one of those difficult witnesses who merely answered the question that was put to him, offering no additional information. Finch had met his type before. Naturally parsimonious in conversation, they made any interview hard going, turning it into a mere question and answer session with none of the easy, gossipy approach which, given the opportunity, Finch preferred.

It was a pity but it couldn't be helped. Hitching his chair nearer, Finch propped his elbows on the table and settled himself down to the task.

'I understand Mr Nolan was there?'

'That's right.'

'Can you remember who he was talking to?'

'No, I can't. I didn't take that much notice. I think the Grayson woman was one of them.'

It was said dismissively as if neither Nolan nor the woman counted for much in Arnott's estimation, although it was interesting that both Livesey and now Arnott had specifically mentioned her in connection with Nolan.

'And then Mr Livesey came into the common room?'

'I believe so.'

Again there was that offhand tone in his voice as if Arnott didn't think much of Livesey either.

'Did you happen to overhear the conversation between Nolan and Mr Livesey?'

'No, I didn't. I was on the other side of the room, talking to two of my students.' Arnott paused deliberately before adding, 'If it's the keys to the hall you're on about, I saw Livesey hand them to Nolan.'

'So you knew Mr Nolan intended going to the hall that evening?'

Arnott looked pleased at having succeeded in confusing the Chief Inspector over this issue.

'I heard Nolan ask for the keys during supper. I was sitting at a nearby table. Livesey didn't seem all that keen on him having them.'

'I see. What happened after Mr Livesey handed them over?'

'Livesey left the common room.'

'And Mr Nolan? What time did he go to the hall?'

'About twenty minutes later, at roughly ten to nine.'

'What about the other tutor, Miss Wade? Did you happen to notice when she left?'

'Can't say. I told you, I was talking to a couple of my students. I wasn't bothered about who was coming and going.'

'Interesting conversation, was it, Mr Arnott?' Finch asked, switching tactics. He was beginning to grow a little weary of Arnott's manner which gave the impression that, as far as Arnott was concerned, the Chief Inspector's questions were a waste of time. On several occasions, he had glanced down at the folder on the desk in front of him as if its contents were far more worthy of his attention.

'We were discussing books,' Arnott said. For the first time since the interview had begun, he showed some animation, rousing himself to sit more upright in his chair. 'My books, as a matter of fact. The two women happen to be students of mine, both here on the course and outside.' He waved a large hand, indicating the wider world of readers beyond the walls of Morton Grange. 'They were anxious to discuss the social background to my novels, especially in *Dark Tenements* and *The Pool*. Have you read any of them?'

'Yes, indeed I have,' Finch replied, lying agreeably. He had, in fact, read only one of Arnott's novels years before, *The Pool*, the first which had been a huge, popular success. Although he could remember it only vaguely, it seemed safe to add, 'I enjoyed all of them very much.' Bringing the conversation back to the business in hand, he added, 'How long did you stay in the common room, Mr Arnott?'

'Until Livesey called me out into the hall to tell me that Nolan had been found dead in the swimming-pool. That must have been about a quarter past eleven although I knew Nolan was missing roughly half an hour earlier than that. Livesey came

95

looking for him at about ten to eleven, all steamed up because the lights were still on in the hall. He seemed to think Nolan might have been in there with the Grayson woman but it didn't seem very likely to me. She'd still been in the common room until nearly half-past nine. I suggested he tried Harriet Wade's room.'

It was an unexpectedly long speech from Arnott and raised several issues which could have important bearings on the investigation. Firstly, that Arnott not only knew about Jake Nolan's relationships with Harriet Wade and Felicity Grayson which Livesey had already referred to but that, secondly, Arnott had been at particular pains to introduce the information into the conversation, out of malice, Finch suspected, which in itself raised all manner of other interesting and potentially significant implications about Arnott's own relations with both Harriet Wade and Livesey.

But he was disinclined to question Arnott on these matters at this stage of the inquiry, preferring instead to concentrate on that part of the statement which directly involved Arnott himself.

'So you were in the common room talking to two of your students from about ten to nine when Mr Nolan left to go to the hall until approximately quarter past eleven when his body was discovered?' he asked. He wanted this point clarified. If this were indeed the case, it would seem Arnott had an alibi to cover the time of Nolan's death and could therefore be ruled out of the investigation as a suspect.

The brief moment of loquacity had passed. With undisguised impatience, Arnott retorted, 'I thought I'd made that clear. If you want witnesses, I can give you the names of the two students – Barbara Fulton and Margaret Nokes. You ask them. They'll tell you exactly the same.'

It was said with an air of satisfaction as if Arnott took a personal pleasure in thwarting any suspicions Finch might be holding against him which prompted Finch to ask with a touch of malice of his own, 'What did you think of Mr Nolan?'

'Didn't like him,' Arnott said without any hesitation. 'He was a damned sight too big for his boots, especially where women were concerned. And I'll tell you this for nothing, Livesey was keeping a very close eye on his activities, especially after last year.'

'Because of Miss Wade?' Finch suggested.

Arnott smiled, if the slight pursing of the padded flesh round his mouth could be so described.

'It didn't take you long to pick up the gossip, did it, Chief Inspector? Who told you? Livesey? Even though Nolan and the Wade woman were discreet, Livesey'd sniff out anything that might cause a scandal to his precious summer school. But he's got a hell of a lot more on his mind now. Fornication's one thing. Murder's quite another.'

'Murder?' Finch pounced on the word at once. 'Who suggested it was murder?'

'That student who discovered the body with Harriet Wade. Matthews, is it? Mayhew? I don't know. He's not in my tutorial group. But I gather he had his suspicions from the head injuries that Nolan didn't die accidentally. Was he right?'

'We haven't yet had the pathologist's report,' Finch said in his official, formal voice, at the same time making a mental note to interview Mayhew personally and not leave it to one of his subordinates. Which reminded him that he still had one other tutor to question, Harriet Wade herself, as well as any domestic staff such as the bursar whom Livesey had mentioned. And that took no account either of the students. It was time he began organising that part of the investigation.

Before he closed the interview, he put one last question, not because it had any bearing on the inquiry but out of mere curiosity. Livesey had said that he had asked all the members of staff and the students to assemble in the common room. What therefore was Arnott doing by himself in one of the classrooms?

'Weren't you asked by Mr Livesey to join the others?'

'Yes, I was. After Nolan's body was found, Livesey called a meeting to discuss what to do at which he asked the Wade woman and that student, Mayhew or whatever his name is, to collect everybody together. As there seemed no need for my presence, I went upstairs to my bedroom. A little later, I realised I'd left some notes on my latest book in my desk so I came downstairs to get on with them. I'd no intention of sitting about with the others in the common room, speculating on Nolan's death. I've got better things to do with my time.'

'Yes, I see, sir,' Finch said in a non-committal voice although he saw a great deal more than the simple phrase suggested. The bitterness in Arnott's voice when he had spoken of Livesey's decision to ask Mayhew, one of the students rather than Arnott himself, a member of staff, to help with the organisation implied a deep resentment at being passed over in this manner and Finch suspected that Arnott had deliberately absented himself for this reason rather than from any overwhelming urge to complete the notes on his novel. It was an example of sheer bloodymindedness of which Arnott was quite capable, if only to chuck a spanner in the works where Livesey was concerned. He wondered how Livesey reacted to this form of psychological Luddism. Probably badly.

But it was a side issue, with no bearing, as far as Finch could see, on Nolan's death.

Thanking Arnott, he walked across to the door, with Boyce in tow, conscious of Arnott's heavy presence behind him, watching their departure with an amused and lugubrious triumph as if well-pleased with the outcome of the interview.

It was inevitable that, once outside the door, Boyce should state the obvious. He had at times the unfortunate knack of rubbing salt into the Chief Inspector's wounds.

'So Arnott's got an alibi,' he remarked.

'It would seem so,' Finch said sourly. On a purely personal level, he would have liked some suspicion to attach itself to Arnott, if only to give him the opportunity to question the man again and watch him squirm just a little. It was very rarely that he reacted in this manner. Mostly, he managed to remain un-affected. Emotions tended to cloud the judgement and, as a professional policeman, he could not afford to indulge himself in too subjective a response apart from a sense of exasperated compassion, even towards the guilty, for the pity of it all – the waste of life and human endeavour which might have been spent on better causes, the sheer volume of negative energy which went into so much crime.

He felt Arnott possessed a measure of that destructiveness, a strange conclusion to reach considering Arnott was a writer and therefore ought to be a creator rather than a destroyer; on the side of life, not against it. But the encounter with him had left Finch with an unpleasantly sour flavour in his mouth, like the small crab apples he remembered eating as a child, withering to the taste-buds – Arnott's bitterness not his own.

All the same, he walked quickly down the corridor, distancing himself from the experience and concentrating his attention on the next interview, that with Harriet Wade who was young, attractive and, Finch felt, unlike Arnott, one of life's enhancers.

10

After her encounter with Finch and Bernard, Harriet returned to the common room in no mood to parry questions from the assembled students who clustered about her as soon as she entered and whose curiosity had been whetted rather than dispelled by Bernard's earlier statement.

What was happening? Who was involved in the accident? Why had the police been called in?

She had enough questions of her own on her mind, concerning not merely Jake's death but Bernard's presence in Jake's bedroom where he had so obviously been searching the chest of drawers.

What in God's name had he been looking for? And where were Frank Goodyear and Joyce Yarwood?

In the absence of Bernard or even Ron Arnott to take charge of the situation, she pushed her way over to the fireplace and took up her position, or rather Bernard's, under the portrait of Miss Poulson, glancing quickly round at the faces as the others formed a half-circle, looking for Frank's but not finding his among them, before, pitching her voice above the general hubbub as she had done many times at Foxwood, she called for silence.

It was time, she thought, that the truth was announced and the charade finished with. Bernard would probably disapprove of her decision but she was past caring. Bernard himself was no longer above reproach although she still blamed herself, however obscurely, for her part in his uncovering.

'If you'd all please listen,' she began, aware that, as she spoke, the doors leading into the hall had opened and a uniformed policeman had slipped quietly inside the room, taking up his position, hands clasped behind his back, at the entrance as if guarding it from any attempted escape.

Well, she didn't care about that either. He, too, was welcome to listen to what she had to say.

'As Bernard explained earlier, there's been an accident. I'm very sorry to have to tell you that Jake has been found dead.'

She had prepared herself for the sudden shocked outcries of disbelief and the horrified expressions on their faces and, while she waited for the outbursts to die down, she searched among them for two faces in particular, curious, despite her own reluctance to play the part of the bringer of bad tidings, to watch their reactions.

Felicity Grayson, wearing a flowered housecoat, her hair loosely combed and her face hastily made up, looked merely stupid, the mouth, with its quick dash of bright lipstick, hanging open.

She would look like that in twenty years' time, Harriet caught herself thinking. Raddled, slack-jawed, a little foolish.

Letting her glance pass quickly on, Harriet sought out Leon. He was, as usual, with his exhibitionist's need to be noticed, in the front of the group. For a few seconds, his eyes met Harriet's, his features quite rigid, a white mask under the gold hair. Then, with a curious ducking motion of his head, he turned sideways and was absorbed backwards into the crowd, almost as if he had melted away in front of her. But not before she caught a glimpse of his profile, eyes lowered but the corners of his mouth lifted in a smile which disconcerted her in its malicious and secretive satisfaction.

But the others were pressing forward, demanding more information and she was forced to turn her attention back to them.

'Please! Please!' she protested. 'I can't answer you all at once. Anyway, there's not a lot more I can tell you. Jake was found dead this evening in the swimming-pool. It was probably an accident but the police have been informed and will no doubt want to take statements which is why we've asked you to meet in here. Now, if you'd please sit down, I'll make arrangements for tea to be served.' As they began to disperse about the room, she added, 'By the way, has anybody seen Frank Goodyear?'

By the blank looks and shrugs which greeted her question, it appeared no one had. And, moreover, no one seemed to care either except Steve Mayhew who followed her towards the door as the others scattered to claim armchairs, turning them round to form small, intimate circles, the initial shock of Jake's death already transformed into a subject of excited and animated speculation to which the presence of the uniformed policeman at the door seemed to set the seal of official significance, causing voices to be lowered and the atmosphere of conspiratorial excitement to be heightened.

There was nothing like tragedy, Harriet thought wryly, to bring out the worst in people.

'Frank Goodyear's still missing?' Steve asked as he caught up with her. He, too, she noticed, had lowered his voice and for some irrational reason it exasperated her. Surely he wasn't going to join in the charade with the others? She had thought him more forthright and outspoken than that.

In a loud, clear voice, she replied, 'Yes, he is. We couldn't find him in his room. I've no idea where he is.'

As she made the last remark, she realised she was expressing an anxiety which, until that moment, she had hardly considered but which nevertheless had remained at the back of her mind as a small, nagging doubt.

Where in God's name *was* he?

The absence of the others did not trouble her to the same degree. Bernard was presumably being questioned by Finch following his discovery in Jake's bedroom while Ron Arnott was no doubt sulking somewhere, his refusal to join them serving as some kind of pig-headed protest against Bernard's authority although his presence would have been welcome in the common room if only to give her support from another member of staff.

As for Joyce Yarwood, she was probably in the kitchen quarters if she hadn't meanwhile returned to her bedroom by the service stairs. Isolated at the back of the main house, it was perfectly feasible that she was unaware of the comings and goings which had alerted the others that some unusual event had taken place.

But Frank Goodyear couldn't have remained in ignorance. If he had been in his bedroom or even one of the bathrooms, he would have heard the sound of voices and footsteps. Besides, his room had been empty. The same factor applied to the rooms downstairs such as the dining-room and the television lounge, both of which were within earshot of the hall. She would search them, of course, but there was no doubt in her mind that she would find them empty.

The other possibility that he had gone for a walk in the grounds was equally feasible but still didn't account for his continuing absence. The rain, the lateness of the hour, for it was now nearly a quarter to one, would have surely driven him back to the house long ago?

Some of her anxiety must have appeared in her face for Steve said quickly, 'Do you want me to help look for him?'

'Yes, if you would,' she replied. 'Try the other rooms downstairs, including my tutorial room. It's possible he's there.' They had reached the double doors leading into the hall and as much for the Constable's benefit as Steve's she added, 'I'm going to the kitchen to find Joyce Yarwood. She hasn't turned up either. Besides, I promised I'd organise tea for everyone.'

She half expected the policeman to bar her exit but, after a momentary hesitation, he stood aside to allow her and Steve to pass into the hall where his apparent willingness to let them leave was explained. The hall was guarded by another policeman, a Sergeant this time, who had taken his place in the stand-easy position at the foot of the stairs but who moved forward as soon as Harriet and Steve emerged from the common room.

'I'm sorry, miss,' he told her. 'I'm afraid I'll have to ask you to go back inside. It's the Chief Inspector's orders, not mine.'

'But it's absurd!' Harriet protested. She had begun to explain the reason for her need to leave in order to search for Joyce Yarwood and Frank Goodyear when Finch himself, accompanied by his Sergeant, entered the hall from the side corridor which led to Bernard's study and she turned instead to him in appeal.

'And I'm concerned about them,' she concluded, 'especially Frank.'

'I see,' Finch commented. He had listened to her account in silence, his head cocked to one side. 'When did you last see them?'

'I last saw Joyce Yarwood in the dining-room at about eight o'clock where she was supervising supper. Later, after Bernard asked me to make sure all the women were assembled in the common room, I checked her room but she wasn't there. She could either be in the kitchen or could meanwhile have gone upstairs. As for Frank Goodyear, I haven't seen him since I went up to my own room at about half-past eight, I suppose.' She turned to Steve Mayhew. 'Do you remember? He came into the hall and you asked him to join you and some of the others watching athletics on television. He said he might later on.'

'And did he?' Finch asked of Mayhew.

Steve shook his head. 'No, he didn't. I haven't seen him since then.'

'And he wasn't in his room,' Harriet pointed out. 'Bernard checked it and so did I when you followed me upstairs.'

She left it there, feeling there was no need to remind either herself or the Chief Inspector of the embarrassing encounter with Bernard which had followed.

'Anywhere else he might be?' Finch asked with a casual cheerfulness which Harriet felt he had assumed in order to allay her anxieties.

'My tutorial room?' she suggested. 'Although that's not very likely.'

'We'll try there,' he replied. 'But I suggest we look for Miss Yarwood first. Where are the kitchens?'

'This way,' she said, starting to walk ahead of them but turning back when she realised that Finch had remained behind to speak to Steve Mayhew.

'I think Miss Wade and I can manage,' she heard the Chief Inspector say to him. 'If you'd like to wait with the others.'

She watched as, dismissed, he re-entered the common room, looking a little crestfallen, before Finch, accompanied by his Detective Sergeant, hurried to catch up with her. Which left her alone with the two detectives, a deliberate ploy on Finch's part, she felt, to begin the questioning of her under the guise of helping her search for her two missing colleagues.

It was also designed to seek her help in establishing the layout of the house, confusing to anyone unfamiliar with its corridors and passageways.

The corridor leading to the kitchen passed the dining-room, empty now and in darkness, the tables cleared and the shutters covering the serving-hatch closed down. A little way beyond it, the passage opened out into a small, square, paved hall from which the service stairs led upwards and a heavy outer door gave access to the service yard beyond, details which seemed to catch Finch's interest for he paused to look up the staircase and to open the door and peer outside, breaking off, to Harriet's relief, his casual-seeming questioning of her about her role at Morton Grange and her relationship with Jake.

'Knew him well?' he had just asked. But she was spared having to reply by this sudden diversion of his interest away from her.

'And this is the kitchen,' Harriet announced, drawing his attention to the other door which opened off the vestibule. Opening it, she revealed the interior of the kitchen, brightly lit by fluorescent strip lighting after the low-watt bulb in the little hall, the brilliance, striking back from surfaces of tile and porcelain and stainless steel, giving it the clean starkness of a laboratory or dissecting room.

At first, Finch did not notice the woman. His eyes were distracted by the polished reflections and by the lines of neatly organised cooking paraphernalia, the batteries of saucepans lining the walls, the racks of knives, the range of cooking stoves drawn up opposite the double steel sinks.

She was sitting facing them at the far end of a long preparation table which occupied the centre of the room, so quiet and self-effacing that, until he heard Harriet Wade exclaim, 'Oh, here you are, Joyce!' his glance had passed over her.

She was, he saw, in her middle thirties, pale-skinned, with brown hair drawn back from her face, giving her the anonymous, almost sexless appearance which some nurses or clinical assistants acquire; unremarkable except for the traces of tears which had puffed up the eyelids and given the skin across the cheekbones a tight, shiny glaze. But apart from these signs of recent grief, the features were taut and expressionless.

Harriet Wade, too, was aware of these signs for, leaving Finch and Boyce standing just inside the door, she hurried forward to place an arm about the woman's shoulders, a contact which Joyce Yarwood rejected, flinching away and addressing Finch in a voice as expressionless as her face.

'He's dead, isn't he?'

With a gesture of his head at Boyce to take Harriet Wade outside, Finch walked forward and, drawing up a chair, seated himself at the table.

If her question had surprised him, there was no sign of it in his expression which remained bland and open.

'If you mean Mr Nolan, then I'm afraid he is,' he replied,

adding after a moment's pause, 'How did you know it was him, Miss Yarwood?'

As far as he could make out, she had at no point joined the others in the common room and could not therefore have been informed of the facts.

In reply, she got up from the table as much to distance herself from him, Finch suspected, as to demonstrate her actions.

'I went out into the yard,' she explained, indicating a glazed door beside the long, uncurtained window above the sinks, 'and I saw the lights round the swimming-pool. So I guessed something had happened.' Moving aside, she allowed Finch to step round her, waiting to continue her explanation as he opened the door and went briefly outside.

It led into a large, paved yard, partly in shadow although the lights from the kitchen window illuminated the area nearest to him. As far as he could make out, opposite him was a high, blank, brick wall, surmounted by what appeared to be a white-painted cupola or clock tower while, over to his left, an opening wide enough to take a cart, which was probably its original function, gave access to the grounds at the side of the main building behind the west wing.

It was still raining but not so heavily as earlier in the evening and puddles glistened on the stones. The storm was passing over, rumbling off towards the east and leaving behind only a few ragged clumps of cloud through which a pale moon, surrounded by a watery nimbus, was endeavouring to shine, casting a pallid glow on his surroundings so that, as he walked forward towards the opening, he was able to pick out across the lawn and shrubbery, the tower of the school chapel. The assembly hall and the swimming-pool needed no such illumination to make them visible. Both were brilliantly lit up, the arc-lamps round the pool, out of sight behind the yew hedges on his right, nevertheless casting a white, almost incandescent brightness which shone upwards on to the branches of the trees. Even at that distance it was possible to pick out the line of parked cars, including an ambulance, drawn up along the edge of the drive where it swung past the end of the west wing and the figures of the men moving backwards and forwards in front of the yew hedges as the search spread out beyond the immediate area of the pool.

So Joyce Yarwood, and anyone else come to that, Finch was

thinking, could have stood where he was standing and had a ring-side seat. It explained her awareness that some accident must have taken place at the swimming-pool. But it did not entirely satisfy him. How had she known that it had involved Jake Nolan?

She answered the question when, shortly afterwards, on re-entering the kitchen, he put it to her.

'He gave me this,' she said simply. Putting her hand into the pocket of the plain blue dress she was wearing, she took out a folded slip of paper and handed it to Finch.

Opening it, he read: *Shall be busy until about ten. See you after that, usual place. Love J.*

'The usual place?' Finch asked. 'Where was that?'

'Here,' she replied.

'And when did he give you the note?'

'At supper this evening. He slipped it into my hand when I was passing him his plate.'

'I'll have to keep it,' Finch told her, putting it away in his own pocket.

'Yes, of course,' she agreed quietly with that same air of patient resignation with which she had waited for him to return from his brief inspection of the yard. She seemed also to be expecting him to question her further but he hesitated to do so, not with Harriet Wade, herself not interviewed yet, still waiting outside. A longer examination would have to be postponed to a more convenient time. All the same, he wanted to establish a few facts.

'Can you give me a brief account of what you were doing from say about eight o'clock onwards after everyone had finished supper?'

'I cleared up with the help of the three other women who do evening duty. They left about twenty to nine, I suppose, once the tables had been cleaned and the washing-up machines loaded. I stayed on to finish the clearing up and then went upstairs to get showered and changed. I came down again at twenty to ten.'

She looked across at the clock which hung on the opposite wall, indicating how she had known the time so precisely. It also explained why Harriet Wade had not found Joyce Yarwood in her room when she had gone looking for her later after the discovery of Jake Nolan's body. By that time, Joyce Yarwood had returned to the kitchen, presumably by the back stairs which he had

106

passed on his way through the small vestibule, to wait for the arrival at ten o'clock of Nolan – her lover, Finch assumed, although that fact would have to be established when he interviewed her a second time.

And there, it seemed, she had remained alone and therefore without an alibi until the arrival of the police cars and the ambulance had alerted her to the fact that something had happened.

There was a great deal more he would have to check with her – for example, had she known Nolan had gone to the hall? Had she seen anyone in the vicinity of the swimming-pool? – but those questions also would have to wait until another occasion.

Time was passing. There were others to interview, as well as the whereabouts of the missing Frank Goodyear to be discovered.

He said, 'I'll talk to you again later, Miss Yarwood. In the meantime, if you're feeling up to it, I believe everyone would appreciate tea. The others are waiting in the common room.'

'Of course,' she agreed.

'There's a couple of WPCs on the team who can give you a hand,' Finch continued. Turning to Boyce, who had re-entered the kitchen after having escorted Harriet Wade outside, he added, 'Get that organised, will you? I'll be with Miss Wade for the next half an hour.'

11

In the event, the search for Frank Goodyear was completed in a much shorter time. Walking briskly ahead of him, to discourage him from questioning her, Finch suspected, Harriet led him upstairs and along corridors, examining a succession of rooms, her tutorial room, the bathrooms and, for the second time, Frank Goodyear's bedroom in the west wing as well as a small television lounge off the main hall, all of which were empty. After looking briefly inside the last, she closed the door with an air of finality.

'And that's the lot,' she announced. 'The rest are either locked up because we don't use them or Frank would have no reason for going into them, such as the other tutorial rooms or Bernard's study.'

Which Bernard himself had been occupying for most of the evening, Finch silently commented to himself, so Goodyear could hardly have gone there nor into Arnott's classroom which had also been occupied. As for Nolan's tutorial room, it seemed a long shot to search it although he suggested doing so all the same, as much out of curiosity to see it as out of any genuine hope that Goodyear might be found there.

'Very well,' Harriet Wade agreed in a tone of voice which suggested that she, too, considered it a waste of time.

It was situated at the end of the long corridor which ran from the small vestibule near Arnott's tutorial room along the length of the ground floor of the west wing and had been, Finch guessed, as they entered it and Harriet Wade turned on the lights, a conservatory added on to the original building in the Victorian period when ornamental cast iron was in its heyday. It was large; its elaborate metal structure of pillars, surmounted by palm leaves which supported girders intricately arched and fretted, reached up to a domed glass roof; and it was glazed with Gothic windows through which the hall, school chapel and swimming-pool were as clearly visible as they had been from Livesey's study or the service yard outside the kitchen area.

It was also fitted with a pair of double glass doors which led, by means of a series of stone steps, down to the lawns and the drive on the far side of this wing and which formed yet another exit into the grounds, making five which Finch had so far discovered, and adding to the ease by which anyone could have slipped unseen out of the main house. But these, at least, were locked and bolted as he discovered when he crossed the conservatory to try them.

The question of security was a point he raised with Harriet Wade once he had glanced about him and confirmed that this room, too, was empty, apart from a dais at the far end on which stood a grand piano covered with a dust sheet, a collection of music-stands in one corner, and ten plastic and metal chairs, drawn up informally in groups of twos and threes as if the last class which Nolan had conducted had been in the nature of a group discussion.

'Who's responsible for locking the place up at night?' he asked

108

when Harriet Wade had turned off the lights and they had re-emerged into the corridor.

'Joyce Yarwood makes sure the back door and any other doors and windows in the kitchen quarters are fastened,' she replied. 'We're responsible for our own tutorial rooms. Bernard takes care of the rest. According to his agreement with the school governors, all outside doors have to be locked by eleven o'clock so he makes the rounds himself, checking that everything's secure. That's why he was so annoyed when the hall lights weren't turned off and the keys returned to him this evening. He holds the keys, you see, for the whole building, in case of fire.'

'So there's no caretaker on duty?'

'Only the assistant at the moment,' Harriet explained as she led the way back to the entrance hall. 'Normally there's a resident caretaker and his wife who have a flat over the stable block but they're away on holiday for the first two weeks we're here. Soames, his assistant, doesn't live in but, as there are so few of us compared with term-time, we manage until the head caretaker comes back. Soames is here for most of the day to look after the boilers and so on. I believe he goes off duty about half-past eight.' She broke off her explanation to add a little impatiently, anxious to bring the Chief Inspector back to the subject which concerned her most, 'You saw for yourself that Frank wasn't in Jake's room. I didn't think he would be. I've no idea where else to look apart from the grounds.'

'My men will find him,' Finch assured her with more confidence than he really felt. After all, it was very strange that Goodyear had not been seen for over three hours. 'Young, is he?' he added casually, wondering if there were some emotional relationship between Harriet Wade and Goodyear which might account for her obvious concern about him although, if he had read the signs correctly, it seemed more likely that it was Nolan who had been her lover. At least, that appeared to be both Livesey's and Arnott's interpretation of the situation.

And Nolan had, he suspected, also had some involvement with Joyce Yarwood, another aspect of the case which needed further investigation.

'No, he isn't young,' Harriet Wade corrected him sharply as if she knew what had been in the Chief Inspector's mind. 'He's middle-aged; a quiet, pleasant, unassuming man.'

'Not the type to go missing?' Finch suggested cheerfully.

As they had been speaking, they had re-entered the main hall where he added, 'Leave it with me, Miss Wade. I'll get my men on to it straight away,' before, opening the doors into the common room with a flourish and not giving her time to protest, he ushered her inside to join the others, closing the doors firmly behind her.

Boyce, who had been waiting for him in the hall whiling away the time in quiet conversation with the uniformed Sergeant on duty – about football, Finch suspected, catching the words 'Manchester United' as he had emerged from the corridor – walked across to join him, announcing, 'I've got one of the WPCs and young Grant organised to help with the tea. What else wants doing?'

'A hell of a lot,' Finch admitted. 'We've hardly made a start yet on the interviews. Tell the SOCOs I'll want Nolan's room searched as soon as they've finished at the pool. And then get Kyle and Barney in here along with a couple of uniformed men. They can make a start on questioning everyone on this list apart from those I've underlined. We'll deal with them ourselves.' As he spoke, he produced from his pocket the list of students which Livesey had given him and went rapidly down the names, underscoring some of them before handing the list to Boyce. 'It leaves about twenty-eight which Barney can divide up into groups as he sees fit. He'll be in charge. Basically, all I want to know at this stage is what each of them was doing between half-past eight and quarter past eleven this evening when Nolan's body was discovered in order to establish alibis. Those who haven't got one, we'll interview again ourselves later. And hang on a minute, Tom,' he added, raising his voice as Boyce began to move away towards the door, 'at the same time, ask Stapleton to spare me a few men. I want a search made of the grounds and any outbuildings in the immediate vicinity of the main house. One of the students, a chap called Frank Goodyear, is still missing and I want him found.'

Boyce made no comment apart from raising his eyebrows significantly at this last piece of information before leaving by the front door to carry out Finch's orders.

He returned within ten minutes with Barney and Kyle in tow,

together with two uniformed men, whom Finch directed towards the television room and Harriet Wade's tutorial room, the next nearest vacant room, both of which he had decided could be used for interviewing the majority of those still waiting in the common room.

As Barney went into the common room to start organising this part of the inquiry, Boyce remarked to the Chief Inspector, 'Stapleton could spare only three men although he's put a Sergeant in charge of them. I've told them to make a start. Okay by you?'

Finch merely nodded in reply before adding out loud, 'We'll get cracking on our own interviews, Tom. There's four we haven't yet had a chance to question properly – Mayhew and Harriet Wade, who found the body, Joyce Yarwood, who I've so far only talked to briefly, and Leon Murray who, according to Livesey, had some relationship or other going with Nolan last year.'

'So who do you want to see first? Miss Wade?'

It was evidently a temptation because Finch hesitated and then seemed to change his mind.

'No, we'll make it Murray,' he replied.

So far, he had seen nothing of this particular individual apart from a brief glimpse of him coming down the stairs when he and Boyce had first arrived at Morton Grange. As Boyce walked over to the door of the common room to fetch him, Finch added, 'I'll be in Livesey's study which I think we'll commandeer for the time being.'

If necessary, turning Livesey out, he added silently to himself.

He was damned if the man should go on enjoying exclusive occupation of the room, forcing him, Finch, to seek out some hole and corner for his own use, however much Livesey might object to such a requisition.

And Bernard did object.

'But I have a summer school to run, Chief Inspector!' he protested.

'And I have to conduct an official investigation into a suspicious death, Mr Livesey,' Finch countered at which Livesey capitulated but not without bad grace, picking up his folders in an ostentatious manner and stalking over to the door, leaving Finch in sole possession not only of the study but of the desk as well, behind which he installed himself in time for the arrival of Boyce who ushered in Leon Murray.

There was an ingratiating quality about Murray to which Finch took an instant dislike. Smiling, head tilted at a becoming angle, he set himself out to be charming as a precocious child might try to disarm an adult with his winning little ways; unattractive enough in a child but for a young man in his twenties there was an artificiality about his mannerisms which roused the Chief Inspector's disfavour although he tried not to show it as Murray sat down on the upright chair facing the desk, running a hand over his gleaming hair and crossing one leg gracefully over the other so that the pale blue pyjama trousers were visible under the white towelling robe.

Boyce, who had taken the other chair, made no effort to conceal his reactions, getting out his notebook and pen with an air heavy with disapprobation.

Finch began courteously, apologising for having kept Murray waiting, a formality which Murray accepted with a small, gracious wave of one hand, rather like the Queen Mother, Finch thought with amusement, acknowledging the crowd.

'And I understand you knew Mr Nolan well,' he continued more briskly. It was time to get down to brass tacks.

The smile on Murray's face was replaced by a small pout of mock annoyance.

'Someone's been gossiping,' he replied, 'and I can guess who. Bloody Bernard. He's a frightful old woman where tittle-tattle's concerned. Yes, I knew Jake. As a matter of fact, I put some money into that squalid little theatre company he runs in London.'

'The address, sir?' Boyce put in.

'They hang out at the Lion's Head in Huntley Street, Camden, Sergeant,' Murray said. 'Do you want me to spell that for you? H, U, N . . .'

'Go on,' Finch interrupted sharply. 'You were saying you put up some money?'

'Only a couple of thou,' Murray went on carelessly with a shrug and another gracious wave of the hand as if bestowing the largesse there and then. 'But Jake wouldn't play fair with me. Instead of treating me as a partner, he wanted everything all his own way so I had to withdraw my backing. That's what the quarrel was about yesterday. I suppose Bernard told you about that as well? It was entirely Jake's fault. All I'd wanted to do was to make friends again. He'd been so terribly cold and distant ever since I'd arrived and I do hate that sort of thing. I much prefer to kiss and make up. Don't you, Chief Inspector?'

He looked appealingly at Finch, his eyes very bright, but Finch merely nodded to him to continue.

Murray seemed disappointed at this lack of response.

'Well, perhaps you don't,' he remarked lightly. 'Anyway, Jake was extremely rude and told me to piss off.' He turned to Boyce. 'Do get that down correctly, Sergeant. He actually said "Piss off." Of course, it caused a stir, especially among the old biddies, so Bernard decided to punish me, not Jake, for being a naughty boy and banished me to my bedroom but not before he'd pumped me about Jake and found out all the juicy details. But that's Bernard all over – an undercover voyeur disguised as a prude. It wouldn't surprise me in the least if he isn't a secret subscriber to the *News of the World*.'

'So you were alone in your room this evening?' Finch asked, bringing him back to the main issue.

Murray twitched his shoulders as if he found this approach a bore but was forced to comply.

'Yes, I was.'

'Did you know Mr Nolan had gone to the assembly hall this evening?'

'How could I when I was kept incommunicado?'

Which was a valid point although Finch countered it with one of his own.

'I believe your bedroom's in the west wing, Mr Murray. Does it overlook the front of the building?' As Murray hesitated, he added, 'I can check on that.'

'All right, it does,' Murray conceded with a sulky air.

'So you could have seen Mr Nolan leave the main building and walk towards the hall?'

'I suppose I could have done, but I didn't,' Murray said so quickly that Finch guessed he was lying. 'And if you're trying to suggest that I followed Jake and bashed him over the head after luring him to the swimming-pool, then you really know very little about human nature, Chief Inspector. I mean, that kind of rough stuff's hardly my line, is it? Far too macho. If I'd wanted to murder Jake I'd've gone about it with much more finesse.'

'"Bashed over the head"?' Finch repeated. 'How did you happen to know that?'

'Gossip again,' Murray countered. 'The common room's awash with it. It'll be the ruin of Bernard, poor sweetie. Is that all, Chief Inspector?'

As Finch indicated that the interview was over at least for the time being, Murray rose from his chair, smiling and patting his hair before strolling over to the door, escorted by Boyce, where he paused to remark, 'But I did happen to notice someone lurking in the shrubbery this evening as a matter of fact – the gardener chappie. Don't ask me his name. I have no idea. I've only seen him about the place doing unmentionable things to the rose-bushes. And, as I said, lurking about this evening.'

'When was this?' Finch asked sharply, waving Murray back inside the room where he stood, eyes wide with mock surprised innocence at the effect this parting revelation was having on the Chief Inspector.

'Time? I have no idea but it must have been about quarter to nine, I suppose. I just happened to glance out of the window, not looking for Jake, as you so unkindly suggested, but merely watching the lightning – marvellously theatrical, don't you agree? – when I saw this figure come skulking across the lawn and make off in the direction of the hall, looking for all the world like William Corder intent on murder in the Red Barn.'

'Were the lights on in the hall?' Finch asked.

Murray thought for a moment, head on one side.

'No, I don't think they were. I wasn't particularly looking, of course, not knowing that Jake intended to go there, but I'm sure I would have noticed if the place had been lit up. One can hardly miss it, can one? It's so dreadfully *contemporary*.'

'Did you see the man come back?'

It was Boyce who asked the question.

'No, I didn't, Sergeant. I got bored with the lightning. After all, one flash is much like another, as the actress said to the bishop. I drew the curtains.'

'Thank you, Mr Murray. You can wait outside,' Finch said, his face expressionless. 'My Sergeant will escort you back to the common room.'

114

'Golly, how super!' Murray remarked, eyeing Boyce up and down with an ogling air before, with a wriggle of his shoulders, he left the room.

'And before you say anything,' Finch put in quickly as the door closed behind him, 'keep your voice down. He's probably listening at the keyhole.'

'The little . . .'

For once, Boyce seemed at a loss for words.

'Yes, I agree, but a lot of it's pose,' Finch replied, 'although I'm surprised he didn't finish up in the swimming-pool instead of Nolan. You can understand Livesey's decision to get shot of him. But that's not the point, Tom. If he's speaking the truth about seeing the gardener in the grounds this evening, then we must add him to the list of people we ought to interview.'

'You want me to get him?' Boyce asked, his hand already on the door knob.

'No, not yet. He can wait. I'll talk to Harriet Wade first. Apart from wanting to find out from her exactly what her relationship with Nolan was, I'd like to ask her about this gardener, whoever he is, and whether or not he had any grudge against Nolan. So when you take Murray back to the common room, fetch her here, will you? You can also tell any of the students whose statements have been taken by Barney and his team to go to bed. There's no point in keeping everybody up.'

'What about Murray?'

'Tell him to wait. It won't hurt him to kick his heels for a bit longer.'

It was a decision which Boyce evidently approved of for Finch saw him smile as he left the room.

12

Harriet Wade had been expecting the summons and had been dreading it. There would no chance of evading the Chief Inspector's questions as she had done earlier when she had escorted him about the building in search first of Joyce Yarwood and then of Frank Goodyear whose continuing absence still concerned her.

Joyce Yarwood had at last put in an appearance in the common room, along with a uniformed woman police officer and a young PC who had evidently been delegated to helping her with the tea – and also, Harriet suspected, of acting as her escort for they entered the room together with the trolleys of cups, teapots and plates of biscuits, their arrival welcomed with exclamations of relief and pleasure by the students who were still waiting.

The Constable soon withdrew, leaving Joyce and the WPC to deal with the trolleys and, for the sake of something to do as well as out of sympathy with Joyce Yarwood, Harriet crossed the room to help with the pouring out and the handing round of cups and plates.

Her own reaction surprised her. She supposed she ought to feel not compassion but jealousy perhaps. She wasn't sure. After all, she and Joyce Yarwood had both been Jake's lovers. But it no longer seemed to matter. Everything, including Jake's death, seemed curiously distanced. And now that the initial shock had passed, she realised that, of the two of them, she was the better equipped emotionally to deal with Jake's death. Indeed, Joyce looked ghastly. Even though she had retreated behind that closed expression which she normally presented to the world, the rigidity of the facial muscles, especially along the jaw and round the lips, and the automatic gestures with which she lifted the heavy teapots gave her, Harriet thought, the appearance of the walking dead.

I did not love him as much as that, she conceded as, summoning up a smile for the woman, she carried cups of tea to the more elderly students who, exhausted by the lateness of the hour and the trauma of the evening's events, remained seated about the room, longing for bed.

Harriet felt wearied herself; certainly too stupefied to respond when both Kay and Steve offered their services, merely indicating the trolleys wordlessly and letting them get on with it. Nor could she summon up any reaction when Bernard entered the room, seeking her out to complain *sotto voce* that he had been turned out – yes, actually turned out – of his study by that Chief Inspector who, in Bernard's opinion, was taking far too much on himself while at the same time doing absolutely nothing to expedite the inquiry.

But events were moving. Shortly afterwards a plain-clothes

116

detective came into the common room to read out names from a list and two by two people began to leave. Presumably the task of interviewing everybody had begun.

Boyce arrived a few minutes later to summon Murray who had been sitting by himself, well away from Bernard who also seemed to prefer to keep his distance and who had taken his cup of tea to his usual presidential position under Miss Poulson's portrait where he stood, looking so aloof and unapproachable that no one dared come near him.

With Murray's departure, Harriet realised her own summons would not be long in coming and, within twenty minutes, Boyce had returned with Murray, looking jaunty and bright-eyed with malice, an expression which quickly faded when the Sergeant told him to wait, the Chief Inspector might want to question him again, at which he flung himself down in a chair as pettishly as a thwarted child.

By this time, the occupants of the room had begun to thin out. Most of the elderly students had already gone, leaving only a few, Steve Mayhew and Kay Ratcliff among them, to witness the Sergeant's advance across the room towards her chair.

'If you could spare a few minutes, Miss,' he said, bending down to speak to her in a low voice, 'the Chief Inspector'd like to talk to you.'

It was a polite euphemism, Harriet realised. A few minutes would hardly be long enough to cover all the information Finch would want from her, not just about the discovery of Jake's body but about her relationship with him as well. As she rose to her feet and crossed the room in the Sergeant's wake, she was aware of both Steve's and Kay's eyes on her, trying to catch her glance and smile to signal sympathy.

But I don't need it, Harriet told herself.

Her mind was made up. She would answer the Chief Inspector's questions fully and frankly. The time for equivocation was over. Besides, she felt too exhausted to dissemble and dreaded now not so much the revelation of her relationship with Jake as having to describe in detail the discovery of his body and to relive that experience which she had so far managed to banish to the back of her thoughts.

In the event, the interview began easily enough. Finch took her through an account of her actions earlier in the evening, only

117

occasionally stopping her to ask a question but in so cheerful and friendly a manner that she began to relax herself. He was sitting in Bernard's chair, one arm over the back of it, legs crossed, the Sergeant, who was taking notes, out of sight somewhere behind her, so that, instead of a cross-examination, it was more like a chat between the two of them.

But she was not foolish enough to discount his intelligence entirely. Before the first part of the interview was over, he had established two facts which could be to her detriment: that she had known Jake was going to the hall that evening and that she had been alone in her room from twenty to nine until the time she had offered to go and look for Jake on Bernard's behalf.

'Why, Miss Wade?' Finch asked with a smile.

Why, indeed?

Harriet came to a sudden decision. She was damned if she was going to allow the Chief Inspector to repeat the question he had asked her earlier that evening and which she had then success-fully evaded: How well had she known Jake?

Chin up, her eyes on Finch's face, she replied, 'I wanted the opportunity to speak to Jake alone. It's not easy during the day when the students are around. You see, Chief Inspector, Jake and I had an affair during last summer's course and, although as far as I was concerned it was over, Jake seemed to think he could pick it up where we'd left off. I wanted to make quite clear to him that he was wasting his time.'

'But you went with Steve Mayhew to look for Jake,' Finch pointed out, slipping easily into the use of Christian names as if they were all friends together.

'He was coming out of the television room as I crossed the hall and suggested he came with me,' Harriet explained. 'As I'd already turned down an invitation earlier to go for a walk with him, it seemed unkind to refuse him a second time.'

'I see,' Finch replied. 'Go on.'

He saw a great deal more than the simple two-word phrase suggested, Harriet suspected; not just Steve's interest in her and her reluctance to encourage him but possibly also her relief that Steve's presence would postpone any confrontation with Jake, which she herself had been half-aware of at the time, and she wondered if after all her decision to end the affair with Jake had

118

been as firmly resolved as she had imagined. And perhaps Finch guessed that, too.

But there was no opportunity to speculate further on her past motives. Finch was taking her through the search of the hall and the backstage area.

'The door at the far end of the passage was unlocked and also ajar,' she concluded. 'It seemed natural to assume Jake might have gone out by that way but as it led nowhere in particular except to the swimming-pool, I suggested we went there to look for him.'

To her relief, Finch seemed to accept this explanation for all he said was, 'And it was then you found the body?'

'Yes; at least, it was Steve who noticed it first. It was lying close to the edge. I thought it was just a shadow. Steve dived in and between us we managed to lift the body out. Steve tried mouth to mouth resuscitation but it was no use. Jake was dead.'

'And who suggested it might be murder?' Finch asked with the same casual air. 'You or Steve Mayhew?'

'I suppose Bernard told you that?' Harriet demanded. When Finch remained silent, she continued, 'I think Steve suggested it first when he saw the wound on the side of Jake's head. He said it couldn't have been done accidentally. I wasn't convinced until I saw the sprig of rosemary in Jake's hand.'

'Ah, the rosemary!' Finch said softly. 'Now what made you think *that* was significant, Miss Wade?'

'*Hamlet* – the scene after Hamlet has murdered Ophelia's father, Polonius. Ophelia has gone mad and is handing out herbs and flowers to Claudius and the Queen. She says something like: "There's rosemary; that's for remembrance." I can't remember the rest of the quotation.' Turning, she indicated the glass-fronted bookcases which lined the right-hand wall and which contained editions of the classics, uniformly bound in brown leather with the titles and names of the authors stamped in gold on the spines. 'There may be a copy of the play in one of those.'

With Finch's help, she searched the shelves and found the volume containing Shakespeare's tragedies, handing it to him open at the right quotation.

He read it out loud as if it were unfamiliar to him although his final remark suggested that he knew the play.

'"There's rosemary; that's for remembrance; pray you, love,

119

remember; and there is pansies, that's for thoughts." But Ophelia wasn't murdered, was she, Miss Wade? She committed suicide.'

'She drowned herself. And Jake was found in the pool. It seemed significant, especially as he was holding the rosemary in his hand. I felt it was deliberate.'

'His death or the fact that he was holding a piece of that particular herb?'

'Both.'

The Chief Inspector repeated the words 'I see,' but more thoughtfully this time as if her comments had convinced him of an aspect of the case which he had not considered before although the question that followed was brisk and practical. 'Do you know if there's a rosemary bush anywhere near the swimming-pool?'

'No; not near the pool. There's a herb garden at the far end of the stable block though, where I assume rosemary could be found.'

'And that's some distance away?'

'Yes. It's behind the main building, near the kitchen garden.'

She made the reference to the kitchen garden without thinking and could have bitten her tongue out as soon as she said it, assuming Finch would pick it up and begin to question her about Joyce Yarwood and what she knew of the affair between her and Jake. But, to her surprise, Finch seemed more interested in quite another aspect of her remark.

'Ah, the kitchen garden!' he commented with the same soft intonation he had used earlier when referring to the rosemary. 'Who's in charge of looking after the grounds?'

'George Burton.'

'Tell me about him.'

'But what do you want to know?'

'Anything.'

Harriet hesitated. The Chief Inspector's interest in Burton seemed inconsequential, of no relevance to Jake's death. But evidently of importance to Finch who was leaning back in his chair, looking genial and only mildly concerned which made her immediately suspect that it was of some significance.

But what possible connection could there be between Burton and Jake?

She answered slowly, choosing her comments with care.

'He's in his fifties, I suppose; a quiet man; widowed, I believe. At least, he lives alone.'

'Where?'

'In what used to be the gatehouse at the end of the drive. But I don't see . . .'

Finch had risen to his feet and was holding out a hand.

'Thank you, Miss Wade. You've been most helpful. Detective Sergeant Boyce will take you back to the common room although, if you prefer, you can go to bed. I shan't need to question you again this evening.'

His dismissal of her was obvious but she was determined not to accept it too meekly. As she got up from her chair, she asked a question of her own which had been on her mind all evening.

'What's happened about Frank Goodyear? Has he been found yet?'

Even so, the answer was too bland to tell her much.

'My men are looking for him,' Finch replied before remarking to the Sergeant,' I'll speak to Mr Mayhew next.'

So at least an official search was being made, Harriet thought, as, accompanied by Boyce, she returned to the common room, empty now apart from Steve Mayhew and Bernard, still standing below the portrait of Miss Poulson but looking not so much presidential as ill and exhausted.

It was for his sake she remained in the common room after Boyce had escorted Steve Mayhew from the room although she would have preferred to follow the Chief Inspector's advice and retire for the night, a suggestion she put to Bernard as she joined him at the fireplace.

'Why don't you go to bed, Bernard? The police have already questioned you and there's nothing else you can do tonight.'

'I can't,' he told her. 'I have to see this thing through to the end.'

'But it could take hours yet.'

In answer, he pressed two fingers against the bridge of his nose, a gesture which expressed utter fatigue. Then he said, expressing what she guessed was his greatest concern, 'The scandal could finish the summer school. You realise that? If any word of it gets into the newspapers, it'll be the end of everything.'

But why was it so important to him? Harriet wondered. He had so many other successful aspects to his career, his lecturing, his reviews, his broadcasting. Why did the possible demise of the Morton Grange summer school matter, as it so obviously did?

As if in answer to her unspoken question, he added, glancing up at the benignly smiling portrait on the wall, 'Tradition's important, you know, especially academic excellence. Passing on the torch of learning to the next generation. It was a lesson I learnt at school and at Oxford and I've never forgotten it. Think of it, Harriet! The flame being handed on down the centuries – Aristotle to Hegel; Aeschylus to Shakespeare and on to Milton and Shelley and Eliot . . .' He broke off his litany to add abruptly, 'Yes, you're quite right. There is nothing more I can do. I think I shall take up your suggestion and go to my room although I shan't sleep. I have the notes for my lecture tomorrow morning to check through.'

And with that, he walked with a heavy tread towards the door where he paused to add, 'Turn out the lights, won't you?' before finally leaving.

So that's how he saw himself, Harriet thought; as a torchbearer in some cultural Olympics; or perhaps as a Prometheus stealing the eternal fire of knowledge from the gods. But here in Morton Grange? she asked herself. It was hardly the Academy at Athens. And did he really imagine that students like Leon, or come to that Miss Eversham or the lugubrious man, worthy and eager through they might be, were fit comparisons to Plato seated at the feet of Socrates?

It might have been amusing if Bernard didn't regard it with such obvious and passionate sincerity.

But he had shown no real concern, she realised, over Jake's death nor for the living Frank Goodyear who was still missing and whose continuing absence prompted her to cross the room and draw aside one of the curtains to look out at the dark garden.

It was still raining although not as heavily as before and, through the raindrops collected on the glass, she had a refracted view of the scene outside – a high moon, looking cold and remote, riding above the clearing cloud banks and turning them milky. In its pale glow, the trees and shrubbery were clearly visible now, making the distant lights in the assembly hall seem far-off and less brilliant.

But there was no sign of any living person moving about the

grounds. The whole place seemed deserted, laid out for only the moon's secret observation.

Dropping the curtain back into place, Harriet went towards the door, turning off the lights as she left.

The hall beyond seemed as deserted as the garden; no one moving; no sound of footsteps; the front door closed and the upper gallery in darkness apart from a light in one of the corridors which threw angular shadows across the passageway leading to the east wing.

As she approached the door to her own room, one of these shadows moved in the half-light and she stopped in sudden alarm as a hand came into contact with her arm, remembering the shadow which had been Jake and the touch of his flesh against hers. But this was warm and alive. It moved and it spoke.

'Are you all right, Harriet?' a voice asked.

'Oh, God, Kay!' she said. 'What in hell are you doing here?'

'I was worried about you. I've got a bottle of whisky in my room. Would you like some?'

It was absurd! Harriet thought. A mad, bad dream. First Jake offering me gin and now Kay and her bloody whisky. Midnight feasts in the dorm and whispered secrets in the darkness, all girls together. She didn't know whether to laugh or cry.

Instead, she replied with a primness she hadn't thought herself capable of, 'No, thank you, Kay. It's very kind of you but I think I'll go straight to bed.'

Closing the door of her bedroom behind her, she waited, holding herself erect and rigid until the soft pad of footsteps had passed on down the corridor.

It was only then that she wept, letting herself fall sideways on to the bed and gathering the pillow up into her arms although who or what she was holding in such a passionate and desperate embrace even she was not certain. It was neither Kay nor Steve. And, she realised as she hugged it close, it was certainly not Jake either.

13

Finch had intended that the interview with Steve Mayhew should be as brief as possible at this stage. It was now nearly half-past one in the morning and the investigation was by no means complete. Apart from checking up how the search was progressing at the swimming-pool, there were several other areas that Finch was eager to examine, including the assembly hall and the herb garden once he had found its exact location. The rest of the inquiry – a full-scale search of the grounds and the interview with Burton as well as a more detailed examination of Joyce Yarwood and Mayhew himself – would have to wait until the following morning.

As it happened, the interview with Mayhew was even shorter than Finch had anticipated. No sooner had he established the fact that, during the relevant times between half-past eight, even before Nolan had left the common room for the hall, and roughly eleven o'clock when Mayhew and Harriet Wade had discovered the body, Mayhew had been watching international athletics on television together with six or seven witnesses, thus giving him an alibi, than there came a knock at the door.

Boyce, who had gone outside to see who the caller was, returned within a few minutes, requesting the presence of the Chief Inspector in a tone of voice so carefully formal and official and so rarely used that Finch was warned that, whatever the nature of the interruption, it was of some importance.

Excusing himself from Mayhew, he joined Boyce in the corridor where he was waiting in company with the uniformed Sergeant, Harker, whom Stapleton had delegated to lead the small team of men searching for Frank Goodyear. By the expression on their faces, Finch could tell that the news was not good.

'We've found him, sir. But I'm afraid he's dead,' Harker explained.

'Where?' Finch demanded.

'In one of the lock-up garages. He's in a car, his I assume, with the engine left running.'

'Suicide?'

It seemed the most likely explanation.

'I don't think so, sir, but you'll see for yourself.'

His tone of voice, respectful but non-committal, suggested that, as a mere Sergeant, he had no intention of sticking his neck out by giving a Detective Chief Inspector his opinion of the facts.

But the facts were evident as Finch saw for himself when, having told Mayhew that the interview was postponed for the time being and he could go to bed, Finch, together with Boyce, followed Harker to the back of the main building.

Their route took them along the drive, passing the hall, the chapel and the swimming-pool, where the halogen lights were still shining behind the yew hedges, and continued on past the service area behind the kitchen quarters where a branch of it led off towards the yard, before swinging round in an arc towards another opening in a high brick wall beyond which lay a second, larger, cobblestoned yard.

The rain had cleared and the moon had risen, giving sufficient light for Finch to establish a clear idea of the layout.

The yard, oblong in shape, was lined on both its long sides by one-storey garages, converted from the original loose-boxes, and fitted with up-and-over metal doors although the central section of the block to his right was two-storeyed, housing, he assumed, the caretaker's flat which Harriet Wade had referred to earlier and which carried, in addition to its upper floor, a white-painted clock tower. Seeing it, he realised that the back wall of this part of the garage block must form one of the walls of the service yard which lay behind it and which he had noticed in his brief inspection during the interview with Joyce Yarwood.

Both the shorter ends of the stable-yard contained openings, the gateway through which they had entered and, at the far end, a wooden door which, he assumed, remembering another of Harriet Wade's comments, must lead into the herb garden which she had said was behind the stable block.

But his attention was not fixed on these details although he took them in with a few rapid glances as he and Boyce, accompanied by Sergeant Harker, crossed the cobblestones towards two uniformed men who were standing at one of the garages, mid-way down on the left-hand side, the door of which had been swung open.

The Constables stood to one side, and Harker also remained behind, as Finch and Boyce edged their way into the garage past a Morris Minor 1000 to peer into the open window on the driver's side.

Frank Goodyear, at least Finch assumed it was the missing student, was sitting behind the wheel, head slumped forward so that his forehead was resting on its rim, leaving nothing visible of his features except the top of his head with its thinning grey hair.

But other evidence was apparent. A ventilator grille in the back wall had been blocked up with a pad of sacking and, not visible but just as palpable, was the heavy atmosphere of carbon monoxide still hanging thick in the air despite the open door and which forced them into a hasty retreat as soon as Finch had reached in through the open window and, placing two fingers by the man's ear, had felt the coldness of the skin.

But it was not a suicide as Finch discovered when he and Boyce had emerged into the clean, night air.

'We found these, sir,' Harker said, pointing to a pile of sacks which had been hurriedly bundled up at one side of the garage. 'They were stuffed along the bottom of the door but on the outside, so he couldn't have killed himself, could he? I mean . . .'

He broke off, still anxious, it seemed, not to teach the Detective Chief Inspector his business although the implications were obvious. Someone other than the victim had placed the sacks in position and that allowed for only one interpretation – murder.

Once Boyce had been dispatched to telephone for the local doctor to confirm death, although this was a mere formality, and to alert McCullum, the police photographer, and the scene of crime officers, Finch obtained a statement from Harker on the discovery of the body.

The uniformed men, Harker explained, had begun at the front of the main building, fanning out on either side of the two wings, and it had been he himself, together with one of the Constables, who had eventually searched the stable-yard where they had been alerted by the sound of a car engine and by the sight of the sacks along the bottom of the garage door. Concerned that the missing man was inside and that he might still be alive, Harker

126

had kicked away the sacks, opened the garage door and gone in although, once he realised the man was dead, he had touched nothing else apart from turning off the ignition before leaving the scene to inform the Chief Inspector.

The time? He had checked his watch as he left the yard and it had been exactly 13.19.

So roughly two hours had elapsed between the discovery of Nolan's body and Goodyear's, long enough if the two crimes were connected, and Finch suspected that they were, for Goodyear to die of carbon monoxide poisoning although Finch suspected that he had died even earlier than that. The garage was low-ceilinged and only large enough to take a car with a few feet to spare, and with both sources of ventilation, the grille and the bottom of the door, sealed off, death could have occurred within half an hour or less.

It was a conclusion which Pardoe confirmed when, three-quarters of an hour later, the small, irascible figure of the police pathologist, more bad-tempered than usual at having been summoned from his bed, examined the body and then withdrew into the yard to confer with the Chief Inspector.

'In a place this size, I've known it take no more than ten or fifteen minutes. You realise,' he added snappily, 'that there's bruising on the left temple? Not nearly so deep or extensive as the injury on the other body in the pool but sufficient to break the skin.'

It was said in an accusatory voice as if both deaths had been specially contrived by the Chief Inspector in order to discommode Pardoe personally and deprive him of his night's rest.

'But not the cause of death?' Finch asked, anxious to have this point clarified.

Pardoe gave him a pitying look.

'The man died of asphyxia due to the inhalation of carbon monoxide. The petechial haemorrhages in the eyes and skin as well as the congestion of the veins prove that. Classic symptoms. But I suppose you couldn't see much of the face,' Pardoe replied, relenting a little. 'The wound on the temple could have knocked him unconscious though. I'll confirm all of that at the post-mortem as well as the time of death although at a rough guess he's been dead for at least four hours. You can move the body when you like. I've finished with it for the time being.'

And with that, he stumped over to his car which was parked in the yard opening and drove away.

It was a quarter to three in the morning before the body was finally removed from the car and the last piece of evidence came to light. As it was gently eased out from behind the wheel on to the waiting sheet of black polythene, the head and hands bagged, in readiness for the SOCOs to tape the clothing, Davies, one of the officers, retrieved a small object which had lain hidden under the dead man's feet and, placing it inside its own clear plastic envelope, brought it out into the yard for Finch and Boyce to examine.

'Some sort of flower,' Davies said with the air of a man no longer surprised at anything that might turn up at a murder scene.

Finch peered down at it with the aid of the powerful hand-held lamp which Davies was carrying.

It was a pansy, the blue and yellow petals crumpled and fragile.

As Davies carried it away, Finch said out loud almost before he realised he had spoken, '"Pansies, that's for thoughts."'

Boyce failed to make the connection.

'Thoughts?' he repeated.

'Just quoting, Tom.'

'Oh, from that play you and Miss Wade were reading.' Boyce sounded dismissive although he added more hopefully, 'Anybody in it die of CO poisoning?'

'No, although someone gets killed by a sword through an arras – a kind of curtain,' Finch explained hurriedly. 'But there are a couple of poisonings as well. Hamlet dies after being wounded with a poisoned rapier and his father is murdered by having hemlock poured in his ear while he's asleep.'

'Hemlock poured in his ear!' This time Boyce was merely derisive.

But Finch appeared not to hear. He had moved off up the yard towards the wooden door which he pushed open, remarking over his shoulder, 'Let's have a look at the herb garden.'

It was, he discovered, as he and Boyce stepped inside, a small square garden, almost entirely surrounded by walls apart from the door by which they had entered and another opening, closed off by a tall wrought-iron gate which was padlocked and beyond which lay a large vegetable plot as far as Finch could see when he peered through the bars.

The door from the stable-yard was therefore the only means of entry into the herb garden and would be easily accessible to anybody, staff and students alike, who knew of its existence.

It was, moreover, like the swimming-pool, hidden from view and, with its enclosed, secretive air, reminded him of the scene of Nolan's murder although there the comparison ended.

The smell of the place was different. There, at the pool, it had been the odour of chlorinated water mingled with the piney scent of the yew hedges. Here, it was warm, moist earth and the aromatic essences of the herbs, strongly fragrant in the nostrils after the rain.

He found the rosemary growing against the wall to the left of the wooden door, a wide-spreading, vigorous bush, covered with small, star-shaped blue flowers, its scent released as soon as he pinched a spray between his fingers.

And there is pansies, he added silently to himself.

They were close by at the foot of the rosemary bush, clustering in small, self-seeded clumps along the edge of the border, their flower heads closed.

Making no reference to the *Hamlet* connection, he merely drew Boyce's attention to them, remarking, 'We'll put a man on duty here, Tom. I don't want anyone trampling about the place until we've had a chance to search it. We'll get that done tomorrow in daylight.'

'And what now?' Boyce asked, following Finch as he tramped back into the yard where the SOCOs were still engrossed in their task of examining the interior of the car although the body, wrapped up like a roll of carpet inside its polythene sheet, had been moved to the back of the mortuary van.

It would have to be formally identified, of course, but not by Harriet Wade, Finch decided, even though Goodyear had been one of her students.

For several moments he watched the SOCOs, shoulders humped, as he made up his mind.

'I want Livesey here,' he told Boyce, 'Get him out of bed if you have to. He can make the ID. In the meantime, I'm going to take a quick look at the assembly hall.'

129

And before Boyce had time to reply, he had set off, walking rapidly out of the yard.

The hall was empty when he let himself in. More than empty, it seemed to Finch, but full all the same of that indefinable air of menace which some buildings seem to generate in the early hours of the morning as if resentful of any human intrusion.

The lights which blazed from the ceiling seemed to emphasise this quality, pouring down on the deserted expanse of the polished parquet floor and shining back from the sheets of plate glass so that the gardens beyond were invisible behind the walls of reflections.

Apart from a lectern, the stage, too, was bare; so also were the wings and the green-room beyond although, as Harriet Wade had done earlier in the evening, Finch opened doors, revealing empty dressing-rooms and lavatories before arriving at the exit at the end of a short passage.

As she had said, it was unlocked and seemed to lead, as he looked through the glass panel, to a broad path which continued on past the chapel towards the swimming-pool.

Standing there, Finch tried to imagine the sequence of events which had taken place. Nolan had intended clearing the stage but had evidently been interrupted in the task; the lectern left in the centre of the platform suggested this.

And then what had happened? Had someone persuaded him to leave the building by this side entrance and accompany him – or her, it could have been a woman – to the pool? Or had the encounter taken place at the pool in some pre-arranged assignation?

Either interpretation was possible. But two facts were evident to Finch. Firstly, the murder had been planned because Nolan's killer had arrived already equipped with the sprigs of rosemary which must have been present in the water at the time of Nolan's death. Otherwise he wouldn't, in his dying moments, have grasped so desperately at that fragile and useless lifeline. The second fact was as obvious as the first. The pool had been chosen deliberately as the scene of the murder. If not it would have taken place somewhere in the hall itself, either on the platform or, if that were considered too conspicuous, in the wings or backstage.

So the water had been significant and drowning the possible intended form of death, the blow on the head being merely a means of rendering Nolan unconscious before he fell or was toppled into the pool.

As for the *Hamlet* connection, that, too, seemed on the face of the evidence irresistible. The presence of the rosemary, the death by drowning, although Pardoe would have to confirm that at the post-mortem, both pointed to a direct link with the Shakespeare tragedy. But not entirely. In the play, the victim had been a girl, Ophelia, her death a suicide. In Nolan's case, the victim male and the death murder.

And in Goodyear's, the link was even weaker, despite the pansy found in the dead man's car. Not grasped in the hand, Finch reminded himself, unlike the rosemary gripped so fiercely between Nolan's fingers, but lying loose as if thrown in almost as an afterthought.

The means of murder had been different, too: death by carbon monoxide poisoning for which there was no parallel in the Shakespeare play although the injury to the left temple – not the right, as in Nolan's case – suggested that the two killings were linked and that the murderer had on both occasions chosen a similar mode of operation, first knocking the victim out by a blow on the side of the head before delivering the *coup de grâce*.

But why Goodyear?

According to Harriet Wade, and Finch was inclined to respect her judgement, Goodyear had been a quiet, unassuming man with no connection, that Finch could see, with Nolan. He hadn't even been in Nolan's tutorial group and yet he had been singled out as a victim.

Or had that second murder been unplanned?

Supposing Goodyear had witnessed, if not the murder itself, then the murderer on his or her way to the hall or the pool?

That line of reasoning would supply a motive. The killer would then be forced to eliminate Goodyear although quite where and when the confrontation had taken place was uncertain. Finch could form no clear picture in his mind of that particular sequence of events as he had done in Nolan's case.

He was interrupted in his reverie by the sudden appearance of the bulky reflection of Boyce looming up behind him in the glass panel.

'I've got hold of Livesey,' he announced. 'If you're ready, we'll get on with the identification, shall we? Then the body can be

shifted.' He added with that heavy curiosity that Finch sometimes found exasperating, 'Come to any conclusions?'

'No, not yet, Tom. It's too early. But we seem to have two
murders on our hands.'

Boyce was quick to pick up the equivocation.

'"Seem"? But there's no question about it, is there? Goodyear,
if it is him, couldn't have stuffed those sacks along the bottom of
the garage door from the outside. It has to be murder.'

Finch made no direct reply as they walked back across the stage
to the entrance door except to remark, 'We'll have to get the
experts to give this place a going-over as soon as they're finished
at the garage. As for the rest . . .'

He left it there. There was no point in running over aloud for
Boyce's benefit the catalogue of tasks which still had to be set in
hand before even the first stage in the inquiry could be considered
satisfactorily completed. As the Sergeant had said, their first
priority was to get the body identified and moved.

Instead, he continued, 'Where did you find Livesey?'

'Mooching about the entrance hall. Evidently he'd gone up to
his room but couldn't settle so he came downstairs. He's worried
about the place being properly locked up when we leave.'

Livesey's anxiety was apparent as soon as they entered
the stable-yard; also his exhaustion. He was standing by the
entrance, in company with two uniformed officers, shoulders
bowed, one hand clutching the collar of his silk dressing-gown
close to his throat although the night was warm. When Finch led
him forward, he moved with the shuffling gait of an old man to
peer into the back of the van where the body lay, the black
polythene in which it was wrapped turned back to reveal the face.

For a few seconds, he stood in silence, his face as closed and as
immobile as the dead man's. Then all he said was, 'Yes.'

'I must have a proper identification, Mr Livesey,' Finch told
him. 'Is that the body of Frank Goodyear?'

'Yes, it's Goodyear's,' Livesey said before turning away.

There were a great many other questions Finch wanted to ask
him but he felt disinclined to do so with Livesey in a state of
shock. They would have to wait until the following day. Instead,
he remarked as he escorted Livesey out of the yard, 'We've
finished interviewing for tonight, sir. I shall have to leave men on
duty at the garage and the pool. But as I shan't be needing your

132

help again until tomorrow morning, I suggest you go to bed as soon as you've given my Detective Sergeant Mr Goodyear's home address.'

'Yes,' Livesey repeated. It was an automatic response and Finch doubted if the man had heard a word of what he had said to him. He was about to say good-night and return to the yard to fetch Boyce when Livesey suddenly seized him by the arm in a fierce grip, drawing Finch so close to him that he could see the white rim to his lips where the saliva had dried.

Speaking rapidly, he asked, 'Will you have to make a statement to the press, Chief Inspector? Does that always happen in cases such as this?'

'Not necessarily,' Finch replied, trying to extricate himself from Livesey's grasp. 'I certainly shan't be issuing any statement until the next of kin have been informed.'

'You realise it could be the end of the summer school and everything I've worked for if any of this scandal gets into the newspapers?'

'I'm sorry, Mr Livesey,' Finch replied.

He meant it as a general commiseration, not only for what had happened but for any further personal or professional loss it might cause the man.

He began to walk away, leaving Livesey standing where he had left him, quite motionless, his head with its beaky, fastidious profile turning this way and that as if in stunned bewilderment, like a sleep-walker suddenly awakened who cannot understand where he is or how he arrived there.

For Bernard, it was a state of mind that continued throughout the next hour or so, for how long he had no idea. As in a dream, time had no meaning.

He was only aware that it was dawn before the police finally drove away, the headlamps of their cars looking puny and insignificant against the daylight that was beginning to break behind the trees.

The hall was now in darkness, its lights switched off, its oblong, prosaically functional shape slowly revealed as the sun lifted.

He stood watching it from his bedroom window, all he could see of the nightmare settings of the past events although the school chapel was also visible, a ray of light seeming to pick it out for particular emphasis and glittering on its gilded vane.

Bernard stared at it for a few seconds and then with a sudden gesture of rage or frustration or despair, he himself wasn't sure which, he dragged the curtains shut.

14

Despite the lateness of their departure, the police were back early the following morning, some to resume the search of the two scenes of crime by daylight, a smaller team under Barney to re-question those who had no alibi to cover the time of Nolan's death. This had been established provisionally between ten to nine when he had last been seen alive and roughly eleven o'clock when his body had been discovered although Pardoe's estimation that Nolan had been dead about two hours when he had examined the body shortly after midnight placed the timing at nearer ten o'clock than eleven.

As for Goodyear's murder, Finch was inclined to put it within the same time-scale but shortly after Nolan's for reasons which he explained at the conference held that morning at divisional headquarters and which he elaborated on for Boyce's benefit during the drive to Morton Grange.

'So you think Goodyear could have witnessed something suspicious and that's why he was killed?' Boyce asked.

'It seems the only feasible explanation for his murder,' Finch replied. 'Why else should anyone want to kill him? He seemed harmless enough. Besides, there are two pieces of evidence which link his death to Nolan's – the blow to the head and the pansy found in the car.'

'Oh, the *Hamlet* connection,' Boyce said disapprovingly as if such literary devices were an unnecessary and wilful complication to a simple theme of violent death. With unexpected perspicacity, he added, 'Is something bothering you?'

It was at moments like this that Finch most valued Boyce, not just as a professional colleague but as a friend. They had worked together for many years and, generally speaking, the Sergeant's contribution to a case was his tenacity at sticking to the facts, leaving the interpretation of them to the Chief Inspector which counteracted a tendency on Finch's part to allow theory to run ahead of the evidence.

But from time to time, as on this occasion, Boyce could show a sensitivity which was surprising.

'It's that blow to the head, Tom,' Finch admitted, humping his shoulders, a sign that he felt uneasy. 'You were at the post-mortem earlier this morning and you heard what Pardoe said. Nolan was struck down with considerable force, probably when he was kneeling or stooping down, presumably at the side of the swimming-pool. But even though the injury could have been fatal, he died from drowning.'

That fact had been established at the PM at seven o'clock that morning, an experience which Finch preferred not to recall in too graphic detail. Lack of sleep had added to the sense of unreality which such occasions always roused in him, as if he were taking part in some futuristic dream sequence in which stainless steel, rubber tubing and severed hands, encased in plastic, seen under bright, shadowless lights, formed the monstrous props. Thrusting these images aside, he continued, 'But the injury to Goodyear's temple wasn't nearly so deep and the weapon was different – not the iron bar Pardoe thinks was used on Nolan but something smaller with a rounded end. In fact, as Pardoe pointed out, it's doubtful the blow caused unconsciousness although that can't be ruled out.'

'Must have done,' Boyce said succinctly. 'At least, it must have knocked him out for long enough for the carbon monoxide to get to him. And in a garage that size, with a low ceiling and every air vent blocked up, it could have taken as little as five minutes before he was unconscious anyway from the CO. As for the change of weapon, I don't think that's all that important. Whoever killed Nolan could've chucked the iron bar away, supposing Pardoe's right and that's what was used, and then, realising that Goodyear had seen him, perhaps coming away from the pool, had to find something else to knock Goodyear out with.'

'In the car?' Finch persisted, voicing the other cause of his uneasiness. 'But how the hell did the murderer persuade Goodyear to go to the garage? Pardoe said that, apart from the

135

wound to the temple, there were no other injuries to the body so the killer can't have manhandled him there.'

Boyce shrugged. 'Pretended he had a gun? If he'd jabbed something into Goodyear's back, he'd've gone quietly. I know I would.'

'And then got into the car with Goodyear? Or, at least, leaned in the window on the passenger's side?' Finch mused, half to himself. 'The blow was to the left temple.'

'Could be.' Boyce sounded cheerfully indifferent. 'We'll probably only find out exactly what happened when we catch whoever did it. So remind me what's on the agenda for today,' he continued, deliberately changing the subject as if the Chief Inspector's doubts had been adequately dealt with.

Finch consulted the notes contained in the folder he held on his lap.

'Barney and his team are having another session with those who didn't have an alibi for yesterday evening – about eleven in all. I've told him to leave Murray and Livesey to us as well as Joyce Yarwood and Harriet Wade.'

'Arnott's not one of them?'

'So it seems. Barney checked with the two women students and they both agreed he was with them in the common room from just after supper until Livesey came in at about quarter past eleven to report that Nolan's body had been found. Which would make it impossible for him to have murdered Nolan.'

'Or Goodyear, come to that,' Boyce put in. 'Not if, as seems likely, Goodyear was killed soon after Nolan. What about Burton?'

'We'll question him ourselves. In fact, we'll get that done as soon as we arrive. Apart from the interviews, there's Goodyear's room to search. Wylie's in charge of that although I'd like to be there when he goes over it. And I want to take another look at Nolan's.'

This last decision was sheer curiosity on the Chief Inspector's part, an attempt to establish a link, however tenuous, with the victim. Not that Finch personally expected to find any evidence which would be useful to the investigation. Wylie, who was thorough, had gone over the room the previous night and he and his team had removed all the pertinent exhibits, including Nolan's address book, many of the addresses and phone numbers which it contained belonging to women. But no one called Rosemary as Finch had discovered when he had checked it himself.

Nor had there been any sign of the letter which Livesey had been searching for so desperately when Finch and Harriet Wade had surprised him in Nolan's room and which the Chief Inspector was beginning to suspect had been a piece of malicious invention on Nolan's part. Nolan, in fact, appeared to travel light and his room had contained little in the way of personal papers although Finch was hoping that a search of his Camden flat might produce more in the way of evidence.

They had passed through the village of Morton, a pretentious place full of antique shops and tea-rooms which no doubt drew their trade from the parents of the Morton Grange pupils, and were approaching the drive to the school itself when, seeing the gatehouse beside the entrance and remembering that Harriet Wade had told him that this was where Burton lived, Finch told the Sergeant to pull up in front of it.

'With a bit of luck,' he added, 'Burton may be at home.'

Their luck was in. Burton answered the door to their knock, inviting them inside with a jerk of his head.

'I usually have a tea-break about this time,' he told them in way of explanation although he did not add that normally it was taken in the kitchen at Morton Grange where, once the students' breakfasts had been cleared up and the dishwashers loaded, the kitchen staff gathered for tea and biscuits before preparations began for lunch. Rather grudgingly, Joyce Yarwood allowed Burton to join them. But that morning, having overheard the women gossiping about Nolan's death as well as Goodyear's, Burton had decided to absent himself, preferring not to come face to face with her.

He showed them into a small sitting-room which had once been comfortably if conventionally furnished with a three-piece suite which was too large for it and with a great deal of ornamental brasses, tarnished now through lack of polishing. The same bachelor's carelessness – or widower's in Burton's case – was evident in the clothes and newspapers strewn on the chairs and the bills and letters stuffed behind the ornaments on the mantelshelf above the fireplace in front of which Burton had taken up his stand with a defensive air.

He was a stocky man; in his fifties, Finch estimated, and not bad-looking but with a dour, heavy quality about him; physically strong as the broad chest and shoulders indicated although ill at ease with his own strength and oddly bashful with a habit of ducking his head before speaking as if unwilling to meet their eyes.

In view of his awkwardness, Finch began casually.

'You can probably guess why we're here, Mr Burton. We're inquiring into the deaths of Mr Nolan and Mr Goodyear which involves questioning everybody at Morton Grange, staff and students alike. Would you mind answering a few questions about your own movements yesterday evening?'

'I was here,' Burton said gruffly.

'All evening?'

'Yes. I knocked off work about six and came back to the house to get myself something to eat.'

'Are you telling me that you didn't leave the house at all?' Finch persisted and, as Burton hesitated, he went on, 'Look, I ought to tell you that you were seen crossing the lawn at the front of Morton Grange at about quarter to nine last night and then walking off in the direction of the assembly hall.'

'Who by?' Burton demanded.

'I'm afraid I can't give you the name but our witness was quite sure it was you.'

For several seconds, Burton remained silent as if pondering the implications of Finch's last comment or perhaps thinking over his reply, his face turned away so that all the Chief Inspector could see was his profile, ducked down so far that his chin appeared to be resting on his chest. Then he said, 'It isn't any good lying, is it? Yes, I did go out but not to the school hall whatever that witness of yours told you. I went and stood in the yard behind the kitchen.'

'Why?' Finch asked him although he thought he could guess the reason.

'To see her,' Burton replied after another long silence. 'Joyce Yarwood. The women who work in the kitchen are usually gone by a quarter to nine.'

'Did you speak to her?'

'No.'

138

'Then why . . . ?' Boyce began but was cut short by a look from the Chief Inspector who resumed the questioning.

'You just wanted to look at her, wasn't that it, Mr Burton?'

'Yes, that's all,' Burton agreed, his face still turned away from them.

'Was she alone?'

'Yes; she was clearing up the last of the supper things, putting saucepans away. I didn't stop long in the yard.'

Something in Burton's manner prompted Finch to ask, 'Why was that?'

'Someone switched on the lights in the assembly hall and, although I knew I couldn't be seen, I decided to clear off.'

'What time was this?'

Burton shrugged.

'I don't know. Before nine, anyway.'

'It was Mr Nolan in the hall. Did you happen to see him?'

'I didn't see anybody. I cut straight back here across the lawn.'

'You didn't notice anybody in the grounds or coming out of the main building?'

'I've just told you, I didn't see Nolan or anyone else.'

'But you knew Mr Nolan, of course.'

It was a statement rather than a question to which Burton responded with a slight movement of the shoulders which Finch took to be agreement.

'And did you also know that he and Miss Yarwood had been meeting each other?'

This time Burton's answer was immediate and unequivocal. 'No, I bloody well didn't!' he replied with a positiveness that wasn't entirely convincing.

'He knew all right,' Finch commented when, the interview with Burton having been concluded, he and Boyce returned to the car.

'Which would give him a motive,' Boyce pointed out. 'And he had the opportunity as well. He's admitted he was in the service yard. It's only a few minutes' walk from there to the hall. He could easily have nipped across there, persuaded Nolan to go with him to the swimming-pool . . .'

'How?' Finch demanded.

'I don't know. Said there'd been an accident. Pretended he had a message from Joyce Yarwood. But whatever excuse he used,

139

he then bashed Nolan over the head and either pushed him or let him fall into the water.'

'And then, realising Goodyear had seen him with Nolan, murdered him as well?' Finch completed the scenario for him, adding with the air of playing devil's advocate, 'But what about the *Hamlet* connection, Tom? The rosemary in the water? Burton didn't strike me as being a literary type and I can't see why the play should have any significance for him even if he knew it.'

'Perhaps it doesn't have any significance. I wasn't sold on the *Hamlet* idea from the start. It's possible the bloody stuff was chucked into the water by someone else, hours before the murder took place, and Nolan just happened to grab hold of a bit of it.'

'Then who threw it in? No one's admitted it. And besides, you're forgetting the pansy in Goodyear's car. There has to be a connection. And why the swimming-pool, Tom? If Burton murdered Nolan, why didn't he simply bash him over the head somewhere in the hall?' Finch asked, voicing out loud the thoughts that had occurred to him the previous evening. 'No, I'm convinced that whoever murdered Nolan intended it to be a death by drowning, for what reason God alone knows, but when we've discovered that we'll be a damn sight nearer to solving the case.'

They had drawn up in front of Morton Grange as he had been speaking and he took the opportunity to cut short the argument by adding, 'Come on, Tom. Let's have a look at Goodyear's room.'

Knowing Boyce, he would go on disputing the point, growing more stubborn as Finch responded with theories of his own; counterproductive as far as the investigation was concerned. It was better, he decided, to keep an open mind and channel Boyce's energies into a more practical outlet.

But Goodyear's room, like Nolan's, contained nothing in the way of useful evidence; less surprising in his case as his stay at Morton Grange was to have been for a week only and he was unlikely to bring much with him in the way of personal possessions.

The room, in the west wing and overlooking the back of the building with a view of the swimming-pool, had already been photographed and fingerprinted and, as Finch and Boyce entered, Wylie and a couple of plain-clothes Detective Constables were in the act of searching the chest of drawers and the small fitted wardrobe. Neither contained anything except clothes while the drawer in the desk-cum-dressing-table was empty apart from a half-finished essay and a photocopy of Piero della Francesca's portrait of the Duchess of Urbino, the sight of which, as he picked it up, gave Finch a jolt of sudden pain and pleasure. He remembered seeing that same pure profile with its high, pale forehead and elegant nose in one of Marion Greave's books on Renaissance art. Replacing it face down, he closed the drawer, shutting off all other memories which it might evoke of the evening when he and Marion had sat in front of the open book which lay between them on the low table and of her face, also in profile, with the ironic tilt to the corners of her eyes, the light from the lamps shining on her dark hair.

But that was over. So, too, was the examination of the room and they had come up with even less information than had been supplied by Goodyear's clothing, searched earlier that morning, which had at least yielded a wallet even if the contents had proved to be nothing more interesting than a cheque book and card, a driving licence and a ticket for Luton public library.

'I want to check on his background with Livesey,' Finch remarked as he and Boyce withdrew, leaving the plain-clothes men to pack up Goodyear's possessions into plastic bags.

The local police who had called round at Goodyear's home address in Luton had found the house empty and locked up, while none of the neighbours had been able to supply details about next of kin. It seemed Goodyear had moved to the area only six months earlier and very little was known about him.

'You'll want to look round his place?' Boyce asked, following Finch into the corridor.

'At some point,' Finch agreed, 'although Nolan's will be our first priority. I want to make some inquiries as well at that theatre he was involved with.'

They had reached the semicircular gallery landing at the head of the stairs where, breaking off his remarks to Boyce, Finch turned unexpectedly to the left under an archway and along a passage which led towards the back of the main building, passing down some steps and round a corner to a second much smaller landing at the rear of the upper floor. Here he paused at the top of a narrow flight of stairs, cocking his head to listen to the faint

141

sound of women's voices and the rattle of china which came up from the kitchen below.

'Service stairs,' he commented to Boyce who had been hurrying to catch up with him.

'So?' Boyce asked, unimpressed. 'It leads down to that little vestibule outside the kitchen. Joyce Yarwood must have used it yesterday evening when she came upstairs to get ready for her date with Nolan.'

'And not just Joyce Yarwood,' Finch pointed out. 'Anyone could have slipped downstairs this way without being seen and gone straight out by the back door into the service yard. From there, it's only a few minutes' walk to the hall or the garages. We'll get Marsh to fingerprint the rail.' Turning away, he added, 'Come on, Tom. Let's find Livesey. I want to ask him about Goodyear. I also want to interview Mrs Grayson. It seems she may have had something going with Nolan and she was one of those on the list without an alibi.'

15

Bernard saw them through the glass panel in the door coming along the corridor towards the music-room which, because the Chief Inspector had requisitioned his study, he had been forced to use as a temporary tutorial room. It had also been necessary to divide up Jake's students between the three remaining tutors, himself, Harriet Wade and Ron Arnott, an arrangement which Arnott had objected to strongly and which some of the students had only accepted under protest. Two or three of them had even approached him over breakfast that morning, threatening to leave and demanding to know what measures would be taken for the reimbursement of their fees.

Leon, too, was another problem, although it was his continuing presence rather than his threatened withdrawal which caused Bernard's chagrin. Because Leon might be needed for further questioning by the police, Bernard had been forced to withdraw his expulsion and allow him to remain at Morton Grange. It had also seemed to Bernard expedient to re-admit him into his tutorial class where he could keep a better watch on Leon's activities. But the suspicion of being implicated in two murders had done nothing to chasten him or modify his attitude. Every time Bernard looked up from his notes on Eliot's *The Waste Land*, he seemed to meet Leon's glance, amused and malicious.

Cocky little beast, Bernard thought, allowing himself a rare lapse into the vernacular.

The arrival of the Chief Inspector and his Sergeant was almost a relief and Bernard took the opportunity to cut short the tutorial, dismissing the class twenty minutes before the gong was due to be rung for lunch.

In the event, Finch wanted merely to check on Goodyear's background. It appeared there had been some difficulty in tracing Goodyear's next of kin, a problem Bernard could do nothing to help solve. The registration form for students required a home address and telephone number only, information which Bernard had already passed on to the Detective Sergeant the night before after the discovery of Goodyear's body, although, out of a desire to appear co-operative, Bernard accompanied them to the study – *his* study, he reminded himself, now occupied by a uniformed Constable who was manning the telephone – where he found the original form on which he had written the number of Goodyear's cheque and the bank on which it was drawn.

As Boyce copied out the details, Finch remarked that the Luton police would probably be able to make further inquiries through Goodyear's bank manager.

'And is that all you wanted to know?' Bernard asked as they emerged into the corridor.

He knew it was too much to hope that Finch would say 'yes' and go away, far, far away, taking his colleagues with him and leaving Bernard and Morton Grange in peace. The grounds were swarming with uniformed men. Passing a window, he had only to look out to see groups of them poking about in the shrubbery with sticks or standing around in twos or threes conferring with one another as if the place belonged to them. More guarded the hall, the swimming-pool and the garage block, allowing no one to enter.

But it seemed Finch was not about to leave. He had, he explained, more interviews to conduct, including one with Mrs Grayson which he was on his way to arrange. And nodding pleasantly to Bernard, the Chief Inspector and his Sergeant set off down the corridor towards Harriet Wade's tutorial room without so much as a by-your-leave.

It was, Bernard thought, watching their retreating figures, an imposition – a damned imposition.

Harriet Wade also regarded Finch's arrival with relief, more especially when she discovered that the reason for his appearance was not to question her further but to require the presence of Felicity Grayson in the study for interviewing, a prospect which seemed to cause the woman some alarm, to Harriet's secret satisfaction. It also removed her presence, a source of considerable exasperation to Harriet throughout the morning's seminars, from the tutorial group.

Although she had known Jake for less than two days and, as far as Harriet could ascertain, had never been more than his potential mistress, Felicity Grayson had nevertheless managed to squeeze out of his death as much dramatic potential as she might have done for a husband or a long-standing lover. Tearful and sullen by turn, she had sat throughout the tutorial sessions in the very centre of the half-circle of chairs where Harriet's glance was most likely to fall on her, hair disarranged, eye make-up streaked, the image of distraught bereavement.

Or, thought Harriet, her mind running on quotations from *Hamlet*, Hecuba, the 'mobled queen', whatever that phrase might mean, whose grief is described in the players' scene as moving the gods to tears.

But not me, Harriet thought as Felicity Grayson was escorted from the room, adding a wry misquotation of Hamlet's comment on the same scene: 'What's Hecuba to me; or me to Hecuba?'

What's Felicity Grayson to me? she asked herself. Or come to that even Jake, whose death seemed more distanced from her than ever? No, if she mourned anyone at all it was Frank Goodyear, that quiet, friendly, kindly man whom she remembered buoyant with happiness on that first afternoon when she had shown him up to his room and whose murder seemed so much more a waste of human life.

The interview with Mrs Grayson was more protracted than Finch had anticipated, due entirely to Mrs Grayson's tendency to

144

dissolve into tears as each question was put to her. It was a grief-stricken performance which Finch viewed with scepticism across the width of Bernard's desk although his face betrayed nothing more than a patient and sympathetic understanding.

The gong sounded for lunch soon after it began and Finch offered to break off the questioning but Felicity Grayson refused, insisting she was far too distressed to eat, forcing him to plough on with the interview.

At the end of three-quarters of an hour, he had managed to wring out of her enough information to establish the following facts – she knew Jake had intended going to the assembly hall and had been present when Bernard had handed over the keys to him in the common room. She had, in fact, offered to accompany him but he had turned the suggestion down, largely, Finch suspected, because Nolan had already fixed up a meeting with Joyce Yarwood later that evening.

Jake had then left the common room at about ten to nine, Felicity Grayson remaining behind to talk to one or two others for another half an hour or so, eventually going up to her room at approximately half-past nine where she had written several letters and done some personal laundry – underwear, Finch guessed, although she was coy about its exact nature – before going to one of the bathrooms further along the corridor to take a shower. It was there that Harriet Wade had discovered her when she had come looking for those students and members of staff who were missing when everyone had assembled in the common room after the discovery of Jake's body.

She knew nothing, she assured Finch, eyes brimming, of either Jake's murder or Frank Goodyear's.

But she'd had the opportunity, as Boyce pointed out when, the interview over, Felicity Grayson had left the study, her tear-soaked handkerchief pressed to her lips.

Finch, who had gone to stand hump-shouldered at the window, stared out at the view. In daylight, the scene looked much less dramatic and sinister than it had the previous night when the trees and buildings had been highlighted by the flashes of sheet lightning. Now it lay resplendent under the bright July sunlight with that secure, expansive repose of an English landscaped garden, tended lawns stretching out towards the distant woods, trees and shrubbery carefully composed into formal groups or occasionally, like the great cedar trees, allowed to stand majestically alone, the outlines of the buildings softened by the summer foliage. Even the yew hedges surrounding the swimming-pool seemed nothing more than an elegant decoration, an example of the topiarist's skill, echoing in their rectangular, architectural shapes the tall oblong of the chapel tower and the horizontal cube of the assembly hall.

It was difficult to believe that two murders had taken place in such a setting although, even as he watched, Finch could make out in the distance the figures of the uniformed men as they moved across those lawns and under those cedars, widening the search outwards from the scenes of the crimes.

'Well, what do you think?' Boyce was asking a little impatiently, his comment having elicited no response from the Chief Inspector. 'Don't you agree Mrs Grayson could have had the opportunity?'

Finch roused himself, turning away from the window back towards the room.

'Yes, I suppose she could, Tom, but I can't see she had sufficient motive. She'd known Nolan for only a couple of days and, even if she fancied him, there wasn't time for a grand passion to develop between the pair of them.'

In view of Boyce's scepticism about the *Hamlet* connection, he omitted to add that he couldn't see how the rosemary, nor come to that the pansy in Goodyear's car, had any significance if Mrs Grayson had carried out the murders. Like Burton, she had not struck him as a particularly literary type for whom the Shakespeare tragedy would have such relevance. All the same, it was too slender a piece of negative evidence on which to dismiss her entirely as a suspect, a point he made out loud to Boyce although he did not voice his real doubts concerning the case against her.

'But I suppose we'll still have to bear her in mind. She may have had a motive which we haven't found out about yet.'

'So we're left with four definite suspects,' Boyce said, ticking off the names on his fingers. 'Livesey, Murray, Harriet Wade and Joyce Yarwood, all of them with opportunity and an obvious motive. And two which are a bit iffy – Burton and the Grayson woman, although I'm inclined to put Burton in the first category. Then there's still the eleven who Barney and his team interviewed yesterday and who haven't got an alibi. When are you going to question them?'

'Later this afternoon,' Finch replied without much enthusiasm, a reaction which was confirmed when, one by one throughout the next two hours, they filed into Bernard's study. They were all either elderly or middle-aged and not one of them, as far as Finch could establish, had any connection with Nolan or Goodyear or any motive for murdering either of them. All the same, he and Boyce went through the motions, noting names and addresses and writing down a variety of statements on the movements of each individual which ranged from the taking of baths to solitary reading or writing in bedrooms, all unwitnessed, and, in the case of one – Harriet's anonymous lugubrious man who became identified, in Boyce's notebook, at least, as a Mr Stanley Morris, of Church Crescent, Streatham – a solitary game of chess played with a handbook of advanced moves which had lasted from quarter to nine to half-past ten.

The process also involved the soothing of ruffled feelings which varied with each individual and which encompassed, despite Finch's assurances that the interviews were a mere formality, the whole spectrum of human emotion from acute anxiety on the part of one elderly spinster who trembled visibly throughout the questioning, as if expecting Boyce to produce a pair of handcuffs from his jacket pocket at any moment, to enraged indignation on the part of Morris who threatened to write not only to his MP but to the editor of the *Daily Telegraph* as well.

'And that's that,' Finch announced when the study door had closed on the last of them although it was far from all over. Each statement would have to be typed up, filed and entered; perhaps even followed up at some later stage in the investigation.

But not yet, thank God.

Getting up from Bernard's desk, Finch stretched and looked at his watch. It was seven o'clock; too late now to interview Joyce Yarwood who would no doubt be involved with the preparation of the students' evening meal. Her interview would have to wait again for another day. Besides, he was tired of the routine of questioning. It was time for a change of pace and direction. The inquiry was beginning to become engulfed in written statements.

'We'll go up to London tomorrow, Tom,' he announced. 'I want to have a look at Nolan's flat and that theatre company he

147

was involved with. When we're back at the office, remind me to give the local Inspector in Nolan's district a ring to let him know we're coming. After that, I suggest we knock off for the day.'

'Doing anything special this evening?' Boyce asked in that casual, off-hand voice which warned the Chief Inspector that, if he said 'no', Boyce would immediately follow it up with an invitation to supper.

'Yes, I've got something fixed up,' he said vaguely. It was a lie and he busied himself by collecting up papers and putting them away in his folder in order not to meet the Sergeant's eyes.

In fact, he had made no arrangements for the evening apart from writing to Marion Greave. He had received a letter from her three days earlier, one of her friendly, non-committal letters, passing on her news which included a holiday soon to be taken on Crete with a colleague at the Leeds hospital where she now worked. But whether the colleague was male or female she hadn't specified.

He couldn't ask. It was none of his business. Nor had he any right to feel hurt that she had chosen to spend her leave abroad with someone else rather than him. All the same, it hadn't prevented that hollow sense of loss from opening up again somewhere in the region of his heart.

He would reply to her letter, he had decided, wishing her a good trip and ending as he always did 'Affectionately, Jack,' the nearest he dared come to telling her that his feelings for her had not changed.

And after that – what? He wasn't sure. A bath and an early night, perhaps, to catch up on the sleep he had missed the previous evening?

Boyce was saying, 'Only if you're at a loose end, you're more than welcome to come round to our place for a meal.'

'Thanks, Tom,' Finch replied. He genuinely meant it.

As he said it, he made up his mind.

He'd read *Hamlet*. It was years since he had studied it; not since his school-days, in fact.

It was a small enough decision and yet one which gave him great satisfaction nevertheless. The evening had been resolved, the pattern chosen and, despite it all, as he and Boyce went out to the car, he found himself looking forward to the hours ahead.

16

Nolan's flat in Huntley Street, Camden was above an antique shop specialising in pine furniture of the type Finch remembered from his own grandparents' home – wash-hand stands and heavy chests of drawers with white china handles, rejected as so much lumber once cheap veneers became available. Now, stripped of its yellowish-brown varnish, each item was priced at far more than his grandfather had earned in a year as a farm labourer.

Nolan's taste was less expensive. The flat, reached through a side door and up a flight of steep linoed stairs, was minimally furnished, a bachelor's pad of two rooms – a bed-sitter given over largely to sleeping, judging by the low divan, its bedclothes hastily bundled together, which took up most of the space, and a kitchen-cum-bathroom with a tiny electric cooker and a couple of cupboards squeezed in under the window while the bath and wash-basin occupied the opposite wall. Some socks dangled on a string over the bath.

The whole place smelt sour from two unwashed milk bottles which stood on the window-sill.

While Davies and Wylie, the two scene of crime officers, began the search of the bed-sitting-room, Finch hung back, studying the theatre posters sellotaped to the walls, their only decoration. They were printed in red and black on yellow paper, the house style preferred, it seemed, by Quartet, the theatre group Nolan was involved with, and all advertised a production in which Nolan himself had featured, either as actor, writer or producer. None of the names of the plays was familiar to Finch and none appeared to have any connection with *Hamlet*. Nor were any of the women's names featured on some of the posters Rosemary. There was an Angie Carr, author of *Urban Shadows*, a Melissa Craig who had produced one of Nolan's plays, *Conflict*, and a Mo Cunningham who could have been of either sex but whose name Finch nevertheless noted down as one worth inquiring about once the SOCOs were through with the search and he and Boyce

149

could move on to the next task of interviewing Nolan's associates at the Lion's Head.

The search of the bed-sitting-room was over in less than an hour; the one hanging cupboard contained a minimum of clothes, Nolan having taken most of his stuff with him to Morton Grange, Finch assumed. The only other piece of furniture, apart from a small table and a couple of chairs, was a sideboard which contained a half-bottle of gin, a dirty shirt, a few pieces of china and some typewritten copies of plays, dog-eared and heavily annotated with marginal comments. A scatter of personal papers was found in the two upper drawers along with cutlery, biros, a broken wristwatch and a packet of condoms.

Gathering up the papers, Finch seated himself at the small flap table as the SOCOs moved into the kitchen, dividing the collection up between himself and Boyce. His own pile yielded nothing useful, only bills, a picture postcard of Brighton sea-front from someone called Robin and some business correspondence.

Boyce's pile was almost as unproductive – more bills, some receipts for theatrical items, paint, fabric, hire of costumes, clipped together and which Nolan had presumably saved in order to claim as expenses, and three letters from Robin in Brighton, complaining of Nolan's lack of communication and significant only in their highly personal contents which suggested that Nolan's sexual interests were not confined solely to women.

But nothing from a Rosemary. And no letter, suicidal or otherwise, from Michael Bryant which made Finch suspect that Nolan's threatened exposure of Livesey had been based on a fiction.

Which did nothing, as Finch pointed out to Boyce, to clear Livesey of suspicion of Nolan's murder. Livesey couldn't have had any knowledge that the letter didn't exist.

There was also an impression which Finch kept to himself as the papers were sealed into plastic bags and labelled; nothing tangible, nothing that could be produced in a court of law as an exhibit but nevertheless important to his own interpretation of Nolan as victim. Sexually he had been active. The names were already beginning to cluster – Harriet Wade, Joyce Yarwood, Felicity Grayson, even though seduction hadn't apparently taken place in her case. And then there were Leon Murray and Robin

150

from Brighton and God knows who else beside whose connection with Nolan hadn't yet been established.

Had there also been a Rosemary? If there had, there was nothing to show, no letter, no photograph, not even a name in his address book.

Physically, Nolan had travelled light. His room in Morton Grange had suggested it; so, too, did his flat. It was basic, containing little more than was needed for a day-to-day existence, a bed, a couple of chairs, enough china and cutlery for one with allowance for perhaps an occasional overnight visitor. Finch had the impression that Nolan's real life was lived elsewhere, in bars and cafés or in other people's rooms, such as Robin's flat in Brighton where according to the letters, Nolan had spent a couple of weeks earlier in the summer.

It was also his impression that Nolan had kept his emotional luggage to a minimum as well, abandoning all past relationships along with any mementoes or souvenirs which might clutter up the present.

Was that what had happened to Rosemary? Had she been discarded as so much impedimenta which was no longer wanted on the voyage?

Hamlet had rejected Ophelia, he remembered. 'Get thee to a nunnery!'

But was it apt? Hardly in Nolan's case. He was no Hamlet. There were no sexual hang-ups there as far as Finch could judge.

So perhaps Boyce was right after all and the *Hamlet* connection was nothing more than a blind alley. But Finch wasn't prepared to abandon it quite yet.

If Marion Greave had still been living in Chelmsford, he would have made it an excuse to call on her in order to discuss the play with her and its possible relevance to the current cases. But she had gone and, although he regretted the lost opportunity of ever sitting again in her lamplit drawing-room, he knew he would have to learn eventually to come to terms with the past.

And if he needed anyone's literary advice, there was Harriet Wade. Talk to her again, he told himself as, getting up from the table, he moved across to the kitchen-bathroom and stuck his head round the door.

The SOCOs were making a thorough job of searching it. Wylie was poking about under the bath while Davies had emptied the cupboards of their assorted contents – saucepans, tins of food, a squeezed-out tube of toothpaste – and was stirring through a jar of coffee granules with a spoon.

'Nothing?'

'Nothing.'

Although one of them had forced open the sash window a couple of inches at the top, the odour of sour milk mixed with the aroma of coffee was overwhelming and Finch hurriedly withdrew his head.

'Let's get going,' he told Boyce.

Outside, Huntley Street smelt of warm dust, petrol fumes and hot charcoaled lamb from the Greek café on the corner.

The Lion's Head was a few doors further down – handy for Nolan, as Boyce pointed out. It was a carefully preserved Victorian public house with green tiles and engraved glass on the outside, its interior as genuine and at the same time as faked as the stripped pine and all the other bygones for sale in the shops they had passed on their way to it. From the marble-topped tables and mahogany and polished brass bar to the china beer handles and the barman's ankle-length white apron, it was a monument to the drinking habits of the past.

Boyce seemed to like it, though. He was looking about him, eagerly snuffing up the atmosphere although it was probably only the smell of beer which had set him off.

'Later,' Finch promised him.

First they had work to do.

The barman directed them to a door at the back where a staircase led from an inner vestibule to an upper room, the setting for Quartet's theatrical activities.

After the turn-of-the-century splendours of the bar downstairs, the room seemed stark and yet oddly claustrophobic. It was large but low-ceilinged and painted entirely with matt black emulsion so that entering it was like going into a huge darkened hole, an impression which not even the working lights, shining down from a metal gantry, also painted black, nor the dusty sunlight filtering in through a window on the opposite wall could dispel.

Bentwood chairs were clustered informally, some round tables covered with black and white gingham cloths, some in haphazard rows, the intention being to make the setting seem as spontaneous as possible – an intimate café cabaret or street theatre moved indoors.

All the chairs were turned to face a low platform at the far end of the room where a small, plump girl wearing jeans and a baggy brown sweater was arguing loudly with a young, fair-haired man, similarly dressed, who occupied centre stage and who, for all Finch knew, might have been rehearsing a scene from Nolan's *Conflict*.

'For God's sake, Humphrey!' the girl was shouting. 'Can't you get anything right? I told you last week I wanted *three* sets of yellow oilskins and a bass drum. So where the hell are they? We open in three days' time.'

In her anger, her large, round spectacles had slid down her nose, giving her the appearance of a vituperative owl. As Finch and Boyce came clumping in over the bare floorboards, she swung round to direct some of her anger at them, Humphrey taking the opportunity to slip away between the black-out curtains which draped the stage.

'And who are you?' she demanded.

'Police,' said Finch equably, flourishing his ID card.

'Oh, God!' the girl said with weary resignation, stepping down off the platform. 'What now? If you're checking up on our licence . . .'

'I'm afraid it's more serious than that,' Finch told her. 'It's a murder investigation.'

'Murder? Whose? Oh, not Barbie's! Tell me it's not Barbie's! How in the hell can I open without a leading lady? Please God make it a bit player or someone from backstage.'

'It's Jake Nolan,' Finch said, interrupting the half-humorous appeal which was not intended to be taken seriously. The name had an immediate sobering effect. Sitting down abruptly at one of the tables, she pushed up her glasses and stared at him through their huge round lenses.

'*Jake!* You're joking, of course.'

'I'm afraid not.'

'But where? How?'

'At Morton Grange School. He was found drowned although we believe his death wasn't accidental.'

It was all the information he was prepared to give her and he was relieved that she accepted it without further question.

153

Lighting a cigarette from a crumpled packet she took from her jeans pocket, she blew smoke in Finch's direction and said with a brisk, no-nonsense efficiency, 'What do you want to know?'

'Anything you can tell me about his background here. His contacts, friends, anyone close to him.'

She waved the hand holding the cigarette towards the stage.

'You can see our set-up. We're a professional group doing lunch-time and evening performances mainly here although we sometimes take a production to whatever festivals are on, Edinburgh, Bath, anywhere there's a fringe. Four of us are permanent, Jake, Humphrey, Vince and myself. That's why we call ourselves Quartet. I'm Mo Cunningham, by the way.'

It was a name already familiar to the Chief Inspector from the posters in Nolan's flat and settled the identity of one person at least on the list he had compiled.

'Vince is in charge of lighting and sound,' she continued. 'He'll be in later this morning. Humph who you've seen,' indicating the curtains through which the chastened Humphrey had disappeared, 'organises props and the backstage generally. He's usually okay but he's having boy-friend trouble at the moment. Jake and I are, *were*,' she corrected herself, the owl-like stare she had fixed on Finch wavering for a few seconds, 'supposed to be responsible for everything else, production, stage-management, advertising – you name it. I've even sold tickets at the door. Jake was also our writer-in-residence.' She put a humorous emphasis on the last words but was quick to dispel any false impressions. 'He was good, though. He knew his stuff. We took his *Phoenix Rising* to Edinburgh the year before last where it was a sell-out. We even got a mention in the *Guardian*. The rest, the actors and actresses and any extra backstage staff, are taken on as we need them. We haven't got the money for a full-time company.'

'Any actresses Jake was particularly friendly with?' Finch asked, only mildly interested. But Mo Cunningham wasn't fooled.

'I gather from that you know about Jake's reputation for sleeping around? Yes, there were quite a few and not just actresses either. I suppose you'll want their names?' Raising her voice, she shouted 'Humph!' several times and when the young man's head finally appeared between the curtains, she called

154

across to him, 'Be a sweetie and fetch me the card-index file from the office. You know the one I mean?'

Humphrey evidently did for he disappeared from sight to return shortly afterwards carrying a long, narrow box-file, full of cards arranged in alphabetical order, which he dumped on the table, announcing, 'If you want anything else, you'll have to fetch it yourself. I shall be on the phone to Jamie about those bloody oilskins and bass drum you asked for. And don't forget we have a performance in just over an hour.'

And with a look of disgust at Finch and Boyce, he returned backstage.

'Oh, God, yes!' Mo Cunningham exclaimed. She began scrabbling through the file, removing cards which she passed to Boyce so that he could note down the details. There were at least twenty and not all of them contained women's names as Finch discovered when he read a few at random from the pile. But there was no Rosemary.

The question would have to be asked although he slipped it in as an offhand comment in a more general line of inquiry.

'Is that the lot?'

It was meant ironically but she took it seriously.

'All that I know about. There could be others although Jake never made a secret of who he was sleeping with.'

'Anyone called Rosemary, by any chance?'

Boyce's pen paused for a second before continuing its steady progress across the page of his notebook.

'Rosemary? No, I don't think so.'

Finch got out his own notebook.

'What about these people. Angie Carr?'

'Yes, Jake had an affair with her but that was over two years ago. She's in the States now, I think.'

'Melissa Craig?'

'No, definitely not. Her tastes didn't run to men.'

'And the rest of the permanent company? What about them?'

'Humph and Vince? You must be joking! Vince is only interested in dimmers and tweakers. He has a wife in Finchley but even she comes a poor third. As for Humph, he's totally faithful to Jamie despite the lover's tiff. They're probably making it up this very minute over the phone.'

'And yourself?'

She took off her glasses. Without them, her plump, plain face looked curiously out of focus, the myopic eyes fixed on him with a pale, unseeing stare.

'You must be . . .'

'No, I'm not joking, Miss Cunningham,' Finch told her gently.

She was silent for a moment before, putting on her glasses, she said, 'Jake had other fish to fry. And so have I, Chief Inspector.' She tapped briskly on the man's watch strapped to her wrist. 'We've got a performance to put on shortly. What else do you want to know?'

A great deal more, Finch commented silently to himself but nothing that was likely to be of use to the investigation. His interest in her was entirely personal. She had loved Jake Nolan; he was convinced of that. He was also certain that there had never been an affair between them. Indeed, Nolan had probably never been aware of the depth of her feelings towards him, so successfully had she kept them hidden under the image of the fat girl, professional chum and fellow partner, reliable, hard-working but definitely not bed-worthy.

He turned to the next page in his notebook as if reading off the name and merely adding it to a list of possible contacts.

'And Leon Murray?'

Her reaction was immediate.

'Oh, Leon! That ghastly little toad! God knows where Jake dredged him up from. He was hanging about here last autumn, making a damned nuisance of himself. Humph threatened to leave on a couple of occasions. Even Vince lost his temper and it usually takes a major power failure to do that.'

'Wasn't Murray supposed to be financing a production?'

'Yes, he was; Max Stein's *Iron Soldiers*. Do you know it? No? Well, it was set in pre-war Nazi Germany. In fact, Stein had to be smuggled out of the country into Switzerland after it was banned. Jake had this marvellous idea of updating it to represent the struggle of the people against any reactionary forces with Schneider, the Nazi police chief, dressed in army combat uniform and masked dancers miming some of the action. Vince had worked out some incredible lighting effects. In the bar scene, the dancers were going to be dressed in black body stockings with this grotesque black and white make-up and a single spotlight picking them out one by one. It would have been fantastic. I know Jake was hoping to take it to the Bath Festival.'

'But nothing came of it? I gather Leon withdrew his backing.'

'Did Leon tell you that? Well, it's a lie. We paid him off to get rid of him. He wanted to run things his way although what he knew about staging a production could have been written down on the back of a beer-mat. He was always quarrelling with everyone, Jake in particular. So in the end we decided to cut our losses even if it meant the production went down the pan. It was a shame, though. We'd got Alec Hunt lined up to play Schneider and a marvellous girl who was doing the choreography.'

'Girl?' Finch asked, pricking up his ears.

'Oh, God, what was her name? Humph!' At the shouted appeal, Humphrey again stuck his head through the curtains. 'Who was that choreographer Jake found for *Iron Soldiers*? Wasn't it Liz somebody or other?'

'Patti Rayner,' Humphrey told her. His disembodied head retreated from sight only to re-emerge a few seconds later. 'By the way, I've got that bass drum for you and Jamie's chasing up the oilskins. And would you please hurry it up? I want to start setting the stage in exactly *five minutes*.'

And with that warning, the curtain fell back into place.

'Sorry, Chief Inspector,' Mo Cunningham said. It was meant as a general apology for the lack of time, for Humphrey's impatience and for the absence of any information on Patti Rayner. As Humphrey had been speaking, she had flicked quickly through the index file and, with a shrug of her plump shoulders, indicated there was nothing. 'Sorry,' she said again. 'Jake lined her up and he wasn't all that careful about making out cards. He probably wrote her name and address down on a bit of paper which was thrown away when the production was ditched. If you like, I could ask around.'

'No, don't bother,' Finch told her. They had enough names in Boyce's notebook. One more was neither here nor there. And, if necessary, he could take up Mo Cunningham's offer to make further inquiries about Patti Rayner at some later stage.

As he got to his feet to thank her, Humph re-emerged on stage, this time pushing an upright piano from the wings, while at the same time a man in heavy horn-rimmed glasses and a short-sleeved shirt, Vince most probably, entered by the rear door and,

157

after staring at them for a few moments hands on hips, began pointedly to draw the heavy black curtains over the window, cutting out the dusty sunlight and plunging the room into further gloom.

It was time to go.

Downstairs, the bar had filled up, some of the customers spilling out into the street with their glasses and sandwiches where a few white plastic chairs and tables gave a touch of Paris to the noise and dust of Huntley Street. A group was monopolising the bar, the actors and actresses who were taking part in the current production, Finch guessed from their conversation, and he had to push past them to get served with two pints of bitter. By the time he had paid for them, the group had begun to disperse towards the rear door which led to the upper room.

Carrying the glasses, he edged his way back to where Boyce was waiting.

'Want to see the production?' he bellowed at the Sergeant. Although they were standing only inches from each other, normal conversation was impossible above the din of voices.

Boyce shrugged and pulled a face, indicating his lack of enthusiasm.

'Some other time then,' Finch yelled, adding at the top of his voice, 'Drink up, Tom. We'll find somewhere quieter to eat.'

All the same, he looked back with regret when, at the sound of a bell ringing above the bar, the sign that the production was about to start, many of the customers, some still carrying their drinks, began moving towards the rear door as he and Boyce made their own exit into the street.

They ate in the Greek café a few doors further down, in a small back room to the sound of taped bouzouki music and the heavy churning of a ceiling fan which stirred the air to the consistency of warm soup. Swags of dusty plastic vine leaves and bunches of grapes hung on the walls, like relics of some long-ago bacchanalia which had surged briefly in and out before going on to find a more festive setting.

They ordered moussaka, Boyce, who would have preferred pie and chips, with reluctance, and when the waiter had taken their order and left, he got out his notebook and put it down on the table where it lay like a reproach.

158

'That was a bit of a waste of time,' he remarked.

He was referring to the search of Nolan's flat as well as the interview with Mo Cunningham and Finch could see his point. After all, what had they come up with apart from a list of names and addresses which were unlikely to have any connection with the investigation?

'I mean,' Boyce went on, rubbing it in as he voiced the same objections out loud, 'whoever committed the murders must have been someone from Morton Grange. No one from outside could have known Nolan was going to the assembly hall that evening, let alone where the garages were. Agreed?'

Nor where the rosemary bush was located, Finch added silently as he nodded in accord with Boyce's argument.

'So we scrub this little lot, do we?' Boyce went on, opening the notebook and flashing the page of names briefly in the Chief Inspector's direction before stowing it away again in his inside pocket.

Finch could see that point as well. They had too few officers on the case already to spare any of them for the task of chasing up a dozen or so actors and actresses whom Nolan might have bedded in the past.

All the same, he wasn't prepared to write off that aspect of the investigation quite yet.

'For the time being,' he replied, 'although we may need to follow them up later.'

'All right. Suit yourself.' Boyce let that one go without too much argument. 'So what now?'

A hell of a lot, Finch thought wryly. Although much had already been accomplished in the way of interviews and investigation at the scenes of the crimes, more still waited to be done, including follow-up sessions with the major suspects, a detailed examination of the forensic evidence and a full study of the layout of Morton Grange itself with its several exits and entrances, all of which needed to be carefully planned. It was his job to co-ordinate those inquiries and organise the teams of men, at the same time keeping all the threads of the inquiry firmly in his control.

And that was part of the trouble. Some of the threads didn't seem to connect.

Take Goodyear's murder. If he had been killed simply because

159

he had witnessed Nolan's murder, why had the pansy been placed in his car?

He was given a few moments' grace before the necessity of replying by the arrival of the waiter with their moussaka which the Sergeant examined with deep suspicion before picking up his knife and fork.

As the waiter departed, Finch made up his mind.

Boyce was right. All the threads led back to Morton Grange.

'We start re-interviewing tomorrow,' he announced.

17

There was a small group of reporters and photographers waiting at the gates of Morton Grange the following morning and not just from the local press either. Finch knew the *Weekly Chronicle* and the *Essex Review* men well, having dealt with them on many occasions over the years. But along with Whittaker and Rowe and their cameramen, there were other unknown faces belonging to London journalists, he suspected.

'But who the hell tipped them off?' he said to Boyce as the uniformed PC on duty swung the gates open and their car sped away up the drive before the pack could close in.

His own statement to the press, issued for the first time that morning, had been deliberately low-key and unsensational, merely reporting the discovery of a body in the swimming-pool at Morton Grange School and adding that, although the death was possibly accidental, the police were making further inquiries. No mention had been made of Goodyear's murder and not even Nolan had been named. Although Nolan's next of kin, a sister in Exeter, had been traced through Nolan's address book, the Luton police had so far not been able to contact any of Goodyear's family and were still trying to chase up leads through his bank and the solicitor who had handled the purchase of his house six months earlier.

As for the press, the name of Morton Grange School was prestigious enough in the county to attract the local newsmen even to a supposedly accidental death. But the London dailies? Hardly. There had to be a tip-off.

'Murray?' Boyce suggested.

It was the same name which had occurred to Finch. Murray had good reason to bear a grudge against Livesey and what better means of paying off an old score than by making sure the summer school's reputation was damaged by newspaper reports of a double murder?

Bernard had also come to the same conclusion. The telephone in the entrance hall had been ringing constantly since eight o'clock that morning with requests for confirmation of a report that there had been two murders at Morton Grange, inquiries which Bernard had at first parried with a bland 'No comment', although after the fifth such call, he had resorted to the simpler expedient of leaving the telephone off the hook.

It was obvious to him that Murray was responsible. It smacked of the kind of vindictiveness of which Murray was perfectly capable although in the first teaching session of that morning on Philip Larkin's poetry, Bernard seeing no reason why he should adapt his teaching schedule to accommodate Nolan's drama students who had joined his group, Leon had been unexpectedly subdued, the model student as, head bent over his notebook, he assiduously scribbled away.

Pose, Bernard decided, letting his glance rest with considerable disfavour on that golden cap of hair.

He himself had taken refuge in his pedagogic role. Cold, distant, hands clasped behind his back as if under an academic gown, the transatlantic geniality quite forgotten, he rattled off his Larkin lecture from the elevated position of the music-room dais, his back firmly turned on the view through the long windows of the school assembly hall and the policeman still on duty at its entrance.

It was the only way he knew how to cope not only with the students whose mutinous whispers were becoming daily more apparent but also with his own apprehensions about the future.

The Morton Grange summer school was doomed. Objectively, he was aware of this fact. Indeed, the best and easiest solution would be to cancel all future bookings, return the fees of those students already present and declare the courses closed. But part of him rebelled against such a decision. It would be a defeat, the ruination of everything he had worked for and the thought of it filled him with a rare but deep rage – at Murray whom he blamed for this latest blow to the summer school's reputation and even against Nolan and Goodyear whose murders had set the whole train of devastation in motion.

His mood was not improved when, the gong having sounded for the mid-morning break, he was informed by Arnott, whom he met in the doorway of the common room, that the arrival of the coffee would be delayed.

'That Chief Inspector chap's interviewing Joyce Yarwood,' Arnott told him, 'so the Wade woman's gone to fetch the trolley herself from the kitchen.'

'But it's preposterous!' Bernard fumed *sotto voce*, forced to speak softly in order that the students who were milling about the hall shouldn't overhear him. 'Why wasn't I informed that Finch was here? And how can I be expected to run this place efficiently when the staff aren't available for duty?'

As he said it, he saw a small, pleased smile touch the corners of Arnott's mouth and it suddenly occurred to Bernard that it wasn't only Murray who was capable of that act of malice in inform- ing the press. Arnott was just as vindictive. In fact, he would be in a better position than Murray not only to be aware of his, Bernard's, fear of adverse publicity but also of the fact that Goodyear's death was being treated as murder by the police.

He came to a decision.

'I'm calling a meeting for half-past six,' he announced. 'We'll hold it in your tutorial room, Ronald, as my study is still out of commission. Please inform Harriet Wade.'

And brushing past Arnott, he went ahead of him into the common room where, waving a dismissive hand at those stu- dents who had the temerity to try to question him, he took up his position under Miss Poulson's portrait to await the arrival of the trolley.

Finch interviewed Joyce Yarwood in her bed-sitting-room, partly because, unlike the kitchen which was occupied by rest of the domestic staff, it was quiet and private and partly out of curiosity to see something of her personal background.

There was another motive as well. He wanted to check the

162

route from her room to the downstairs lobby where the back door opened into the yard and to establish how long it would have taken her or anyone else to leave the building by that exit. Boyce had orders to confirm the timing.

Her bed-sitting-room was large and sunny, with a bathroom and a small kitchen opening off it and a view through one sash window across the service and stable-yards towards the walled herb garden. Another pair of windows looked out over the grounds behind the west wing in the direction of the school chapel and the swimming-pool although the assembly hall was too far to the left to make it possible to see either its entrance doors or the path leading to it, only a section of its long roof-to-ground windows.

The furniture in the room was pleasant but nondescript; not, he imagined, her own personal property. The bed, the chest of drawers, the small writing-table under one of the windows had the same bland look of the furniture in Nolan's and Goodyear's bedrooms – solid, plain beech of a contemporary appearance, one degree better than utilitarian but designed all the same to last. An oblong coffee table and two Windsor-type armchairs with cushioned seats and backs, drawn up in front of a fireplace, boarded up and fitted with an electric fire, constituted the sitting-room area.

Apart from a pot of African violets on the table and a small display of family photographs and ornaments on the mantel-shelf, there were few signs that Joyce Yarwood had attempted to impose the stamp of her personality on the room, an impression heightened by its excessive tidiness and the absence of any clothes or make-up, or even books and magazines littering the surfaces.

They sat round the coffee table, Finch and Joyce Yarwood in the two armchairs, Boyce on the straight-backed chair which he had turned round from its place in front of the writing-table.

Finch said, 'I'm sorry to have to question you again, Miss Yarwood, but I need a more detailed statement than the one we took the other night.'

'Yes, of course, I understand,' she replied. She sat quite still in the chair, knees and ankles together in the regulation pose of a candidate being interviewed for a job, her face politely non-committal although Finch detected in the faint trembling of that long upper lip some of the emotion which she must have been feeling.

'About your relationship with Mr Nolan,' he continued.

As he said it, he wondered what on earth Nolan had seen in her. She seemed to typify the potential old maid, her virginity slowly drying up into sterile middle age. But perhaps it was this very lack of experience which Nolan had found attractive. There was nothing like gratitude for flattering a man's ego and she must have seized eagerly on his attentions.

'We were lovers,' she said simply.

'Since when?'

'The summer three years ago.'

The answer surprised him. He hadn't imagined her affair with Nolan had been so long-standing.

'You met here at Morton Grange?'

'Yes. He suggested we went for a walk one evening. After that, we used to meet in the grounds, well away from the school buildings. But the last two years he'd come up to my room. He'd let me know which evening by passing me a message or a note, like the one he gave me at supper-time on the night he died. He'd make some excuse to get away from the common room and then walk round by the service yard to the lobby door.'

'The one downstairs by the kitchen?'

She nodded in agreement before continuing, 'I'd wait in the kitchen to make sure it was safe for him to come in. If it wasn't, I'd stand at the window by the sink. He'd know then that someone else was about and he'd go away and try again later. He could see the window from the entrance into the service yard. If it was all right, he'd let himself in by the lobby door and go straight up to my room by the back stairs. I'd listen for him coming and follow him upstairs a few minutes later.'

'Did anyone in Morton Grange know of your relationship with him?'

She hesitated before replying. 'Not on the teaching staff; at least, not until recently when I think Harriet Wade guessed the truth. But I'm fairly sure George Burton, the gardener, had known about it since last summer.'

Finch left it there. It was not his business to tell her that Burton had indeed known and had been keeping a watch on her most evenings from the service yard. From the manner in which she spoke of Burton, he guessed that she knew about Burton's feelings for her and that they were unwelcome.

Instead, he asked, 'Did you ever meet Mr Nolan in London?'

He thought he could guess that answer, too.

'No,' she replied. 'He didn't want me to. He wouldn't even give me his address so that I could write to him. He preferred not to be tied down to a permanent relationship.'

I bet he did, Finch thought. It must have suited Nolan very well to have a mistress ready and available at Morton Grange for his summer visits with no strings and no responsibilities attached to their affair.

'But you knew he had other women?' he asked.

He saw the long upper lip stretch and tremble.

'Yes,' was all she said.

'Including Miss Wade?'

It seemed cruel to continue. The lip was still pulled taut, stretching the mouth into a parody of a smile. But he had to know. If she were guilty, motive had to be proved.

'Yes,' she repeated.

He moved on briskly to the last part of the interview, a confirmation of the first statement she had made.

'I just want to check your movements on the night Mr Nolan was murdered, Miss Yarwood. You said that after you received the note over supper, you came up here to get showered and changed at about half-past nine and then went back to the kitchen to wait for him to arrive at ten o'clock. But he didn't come. Is that correct?'

'Yes,' she agreed simply.

'Did you know he was going to the assembly hall that evening?'

'No, I didn't.'

But she could have seen that the lights were on in the assembly hall either from the service yard or from her bedroom window, Finch added to himself. And it wouldn't have taken much intelligence on her part to put two and two together and realise that it was Nolan who was in there. As drama tutor, he was the most likely person to be using the hall at that time in the evening.

He cocked an eyebrow at Boyce who took up the questioning about the other victim.

'Did you know Mr Goodyear?'

The change of interviewers seemed to distress her. For the first time she showed obvious signs of the emotion she must have been feeling under that passive exterior. While the long upper lip remained stretched in that parody of smile, the lower lip and chin began to tremble.

'I'd seen him in the dining-room when I'd served the meals.'

'You'd had no other contact with him?'

'No more than with any of the other students.'

'Thank you, Miss Yarwood,' Finch said in his official voice as he rose to his feet. 'That's all for the time being.'

Outside in the corridor, he held Boyce back by the arm, allowing Joyce Yarwood to go ahead of them down the service stairs before, with a gesture of his head to the Sergeant to follow, he set off in the other direction along the passageway, retracing the route they had taken two days earlier until they emerged finally on the circular gallery above the entrance hall where the two corridors leading to the east and west wings branched off to the left and right.

'Time it for me, will you, Tom?' Finch asked. 'Any of the students or staff who know the layout could have come out of one of the bedrooms in either of the wings and left the building through the lobby door at the back. That way, it'd be a much quicker route to the hall or the swimming-pool, or come to that, even the garages, than using the front door and going round by the west wing. But I want to know the exact timing.'

'Four minutes,' Boyce announced shortly afterwards when, having retraced their steps, they emerged from the lobby door into the service yard.

It took another two minutes to walk from the yard to the hall and approximately the same length of time to cover the distance from the yard to the garage block, give or take a few seconds, as Boyce pointed out.

The stable-yard was empty, the team of SOCOs and fingerprint experts having completed their search of it the previous day although the garage where Goodyear's body had been discovered was still sealed. From the yard, Finch led the way into the herb garden in order to look at it again in daylight.

It was smaller than he had imagined from his brief examination of it by moonlight on the night of the murders. Then, the deep shadows cast by the walls had given it an air of mystery, the boundaries uncertain, melting away into the shadows.

Now, with the sunlight flooding in, Finch saw that it was square and trim, the beds divided by stone paths. A wooden bench stood against the wall at the far end while over to his left was the tall wrought-iron gate which gave access into the kitchen garden which lay beyond.

He paused again by the rosemary bush as he had done on that first night, pinching a tip of it between his fingers before bending down to examine the small clumps of pansies which grew along the edge of the border, their flower-heads open this time with their blue and yellow petals turned towards the sun.

Boyce waited beside him, impatient to get down to discussing the case.

'Do you think she could have done it?' he asked.

Finch straightened up. He seemed bemused by the heat of the enclosed garden and the heavy, aromatic air.

'Joyce Yarwood? It's possible. She certainly had motive and opportunity and, if she caught Nolan by surprise, I can imagine her finding the strength to give him that blow on the side of the head. But Goodyear? I can't *see* her carrying out that murder, Tom.'

He meant it literally. As he and Boyce had walked from the swimming-pool to the stable-yard, timing the distance, he had tried to imagine Joyce Yarwood returning by the same route with Goodyear, forcing him to go with her before striking that second blow as he sat, presumably passive, in the driving seat of his car.

'Unless,' he continued, completing the train of thought out loud, 'there's some other explanation.'

'For Goodyear's murder? But the two murders are linked. They have to be. What motive is there for Goodyear's unless he witnessed Nolan's? Otherwise the two crimes don't make sense.'

'You're probably right,' Finch said, appearing to agree as he set off towards the stable-yard.

'Where to now?' Boyce demanded, hurrying to catch up with him.

'I want to have another talk with Harriet Wade,' Finch announced. 'But I'd prefer to speak to her alone this time, Tom; make it more of a chat than an interview. Besides, we'll need a statement from Mayhew about the discovery of Nolan's body. So I'll leave you to deal with that while I talk to her.'

It was near enough to the truth to satisfy Boyce who shrugged as much as to say he didn't mind either way. There was, however, another motive behind the Chief Inspector's suggestion. He had sat up to the early hours the other morning re-reading *Hamlet* and was anxious to discuss the play with someone whose judgement he could rely on but without Boyce being present, whose scepticism about the *Hamlet* connection would make it heavy going. In the past, he might have talked it over with Marion Greave. In her absence, there was no one else to turn to except Harriet Wade.

Joyce Yarwood reached the lobby at the foot of the service stairs where she paused, her hand on the kitchen door. Behind it, she could hear the voices of the women and the clatter of saucepans and china as they prepared lunch for the students.

It was her world, the only place in which she felt totally at ease, and yet she hesitated to enter it, dreading the glances of the women, Mrs Soames and Mrs Foy and Shirley who would look up as soon as she walked in. She knew she could not face them; not yet.

Instead, she opened the lobby door and crossed the service yard, intending to walk along the drive in the direction of the swimming-pool.

There was no one about. The students were in their classes and the policeman who had been on duty at the pool had gone.

She had no clear idea herself why she had decided to come. At first, her only intention had been to postpone for a few minutes the necessity of returning to the kitchen before she had collected her thoughts and controlled the inner trembling which at times during the interview with Finch had been so strong that she had stared down in surprise at her own hands, clasped quietly in her lap, as if at a stranger's.

But, as she turned out of the yard, the high yew hedges round the pool seemed to dominate her view, blocking out every other feature of the gardens, and she was suddenly overwhelmed by the thought that it was there that he had died.

And I didn't even say goodbye to him, she thought absurdly.

The image of him lying dead was as vivid as if she had witnessed it – his face upturned, his hands open, palms uppermost, as he had so often lain in bed, replete and lazily smiling.

She had hardly reached the entrance to the yard when she saw Burton approaching from the opposite direction, coming from the kitchen garden, a basket on his arm.

'If you've come for those tomatoes you wanted,' he said to her, 'I've got them here.'

He was standing four-square in the drive, blocking her way and watching her with that look of such intense concentration that it was almost like a scowl.

She said hurriedly, 'Yes, thank you. I'll take them.'

He handed over the basket, adding with quick concern , 'Are you all right?'

'Of course,' she replied.

'Well, you don't look it. If there's anything I can do . . .'

'There's nothing.'

'No,' he agreed. 'I didn't think there would be. But if you ever want anything, anything at all, you only have to ask.'

His presence gave her no other option but to turn back into the service yard although, as she walked away, she felt her distress turn to anger.

Damn him! Damn him! Would he never leave her alone? Was he always going to be there spoiling even her most private moments?

But at least her anger gave her the courage to face the women.

Dumping the basket of tomatoes on the preparation table, she announced loudly to Mrs Soames, 'You deal with those. I'm going to open the hatch in the dining-room,' before marching off, head held high, ignoring their astonished and curious glances.

18

When the message was brought to her that Detective Chief Inspector Finch wanted to interview her again, Harriet Wade dismissed her tutorial class even though there was at least a quarter of an hour before the gong was due to be sounded for lunch. She was past caring whether Bernard would disapprove or not. The summer school was breaking up anyway and it was only Bernard's stubbornness in refusing to admit defeat which kept the place going although Morton Grange itself seemed un-touched by the double tragedy.

The thought occurred to her when, having met Finch in the entrance hall, she suggested that they walk in the gardens rather than remain indoors.

'Unless it's an official interview?' she added.

'No, it's more of a chat,' Finch replied easily.

She chose the lawn in front of the main building where a marble bench stood beside a formal rosebed; not exactly the same place where she and Jake had talked on that first afternoon although the view of Morton Grange was similar. As she sat down, she looked across again at its façade, serenely beautiful in the clear, bright sunshine, its many windows glittering, the long elegant line of the white stone parapet along its roof standing out against the unblemished cerulean blue of the sky.

It was the perfect setting for some eighteenth-century love affair, she thought, of scented billets-doux and silk skirts rustling across the lawns; not for murder. And neither, she realised, for the kind of surreptitious fornication which she and Jake had carried out under that same roof.

But she no longer wished to remember any of that although she suspected that Finch, damn him, intended questioning her about it.

She was aware that he was watching her with much the same close yet apparently casual observation with which he had scru-tinised her on that first evening when he had followed her upstairs, missing nothing of either her appearance or her demeanour, a realisation which put her immediately on the defensive.

'So what did you want to chat about?' she asked, determined to be the first to open the interview.

But if she had hoped to disconcert him, she was disappointed.

'About you and Jake,' he replied equably, dropping into first-name terms which was, she realised, part of his technique, intended to disarm. 'Did you ever meet him in London after your affair with him last summer?'

'No; I gave him my phone number as he wasn't on the phone at his flat. He said he'd ring me and we'd meet for drink but he didn't get in touch.'

'And you didn't try to contact him?'

170

'No, although I thought of writing to him once or twice at the theatre he was involved with. But I didn't want to seem too eager to keep up the affair. I felt it was over anyway. Jake wasn't the type to go in for permanent relationships.'

'Did you mind?'

'Did I mind?' She repeated the words with a strange objective curiosity as if examining not her own reactions but someone else's. 'Yes, I suppose I did, at least to begin with. I felt let down as I suppose any woman would under the circumstances. And I was angry when he tried to start the relationship again this summer, especially when I realised he was already having an affair with Joyce Yarwood. I thought it was a damned nerve on his part. But not angry enough to kill him, Chief Inspector, if that's what you're thinking.'

It was exactly what Finch was thinking and it occurred to him that, out of the two women at Morton Grange who had been Nolan's lovers, it was Harriet Wade rather than Joyce Yarwood who possessed that single-mindedness of purpose to revenge herself on Nolan for his infidelity. She was cool and intelligent enough, too, to carry it out, even as far as going through the pretence of finding his body afterwards. And he wondered, as he glanced quickly at her profile which, with its straight nose and stubborn little chin, balanced by the heavy, coiled plait of dark gold hair, reminded him of a figure on a Greek vase, if she hadn't offered to go and look for Nolan in Bernard's place in order to make sure that he really was dead.

The *Hamlet* connection would have appealed to her as well. She had, he suspected, the type of mind to which such literary allusions would have been second nature.

Which brought him to one of the main purposes for the interview although he wasn't quite sure how to introduce the subject. As he put the next question, he was aware that, had he been able to discuss the play's relevance with Marion Greave, he could have been more direct in his approach. It was on occasions such as these that he missed that intellectual companionship which he had valued so much and which he had never found in any other woman.

'So you're not like Ophelia, Miss Wade, driven to despair because of a broken heart?

'I certainly wouldn't chuck myself in the river on his account nor go around handing out flowers,' she replied with deliberate facetiousness.

Finch picked up the reference so quickly that Harriet suspected that this was the whole point of the conversation.

'Madness. Is that one of the themes of the play would you say?'

'One of them.'

'And vengeance is another?'

'That, too. Shakespeare's *Hamlet* is supposed to have been based on an old revenge play. Do you know the quotation, "I am very proud, revengeful, ambitious"? But there are other themes as well – action and inaction, guilt, disillusionment, betrayal, sexual disgust. You can take your pick. But why do you ask? Are you looking for a motive?'

But he refused to be drawn, merely remarking, 'I suppose that's why it's still acted even after three hundred years,' before adding with another rapid change of subject, 'What else can you tell me about Frank Goodyear?'

'Very little more than I've already told you. He was a quiet, pleasant man; rather ordinary with nothing specially noticeable about him.' As Finch waited, head cocked, clearly expecting her to continue, she added, casting about for other details, however trivial, 'A slight Midlands accent; arrived early on Sunday afternoon which was a little annoying.' Remembering that occasion when Frank Goodyear had surprised her in the hall, standing in front of the mirror with Jake's hands on her shoulders, she added quickly, 'He spoke about his car being difficult to start which was why he was anxious to get it under cover. Most of all, though, he seemed so happy to be here, oddly happy, in fact.'

'You noticed that in particular?'

'Yes; it struck me as rather strange at the time. Because he arrived before anyone else, I showed him up to his room. He kept saying, "Nice, nice" and looking about him like a child at Christmas. He seemed', and she remembered the word which had occurred to her at the time, 'buoyant.'

'Buoyant?'

Finch queried the word as if unsure of its relevance to Goodyear.

'Physically happy, actually bouncing on his toes as a small boy does when he's been given an extra-special treat.'

Whether or not it had any significance to Finch's inquiries it

172

was impossible to tell. As he stood up to indicate the interview was over, he said nothing more except to thank her formally before escorting her across the lawn towards the main entrance. Here he left her and walked across to the car where his Sergeant was already waiting.

Harriet stood on the steps watching as the car drove away.

She had no idea how well or badly the interview had gone. Finch let so little of his real feeling appear on the surface. And that, she felt, with a novelist's eye for character, was probably the most distinctive feature about him. He was essentially a private man, for whom that bland and equable exterior served as a convenient mask although, underneath it, she could discern a capacity for deep emotion, even passion.

Was he married? Probably not, judging by that solitary air about him of a man who preferred his own company. But whether married or single, she was convinced that he would love only once and that the commitment would be absolute.

Not like Jake. For him, love was merely a pleasurable pastime, in which the only person to be hurt was any woman fool enough to try to play the game for keeps.

As the car disappeared from sight behind the trees and she turned away to enter the building, she caught herself thinking that, given the choice, she would prefer Finch's kind of love any day, a reaction which surprised even herself by its unexpected conviction.

Bernard met her just inside the entrance. The gong had been rung for lunch a few minutes before and the entrance hall was crowded with students from both Bernard's and Ron Arnott's tutorial classes, making their way towards the dining-room.

Bernard drew her to one side.

'Where on earth have you been, Harriet?' he demanded.

'Talking to Chief Inspector Finch.'

'And where is he now?'

'Gone, I assume,' Harriet replied. 'The last I saw of him, he was driving off in his car.'

Bernard seemed considerably put out.

'Damn! I wanted to speak to him about the press. You realise there's a whole posse of them waiting at the gates? And the telephone hasn't stopped ringing all morning. I've been forced to leave it off the hook. Someone must have informed them.'

'You're not suggesting Finch himself is behind it?'

'Good Lord, no!' Bernard was quite certain of this. 'The last thing he'd welcome is a pack of newspapermen breathing down his neck. I simply wanted to ask his advice on how to deal with them although I think I know who's responsible.'

'Leon?' suggested Harriet. It seemed the obvious answer.

Bernard did not reply directly. Instead, he gave her an oblique glance, secretive yet conspiratorial.

'Possibly. But Leon's not the only one who would take pleasure in seeing my reputation suffer.' Breaking off suddenly, as if introducing an entirely new subject, he added, 'By the way, did Arnott tell you about the meeting I've called for half-past six this evening?'

'Yes; he did mention it.'

'Then please make sure you're present,' Bernard said before hurrying off in the direction of the dining-room.

So, Harriet thought, lingering in the hall, Bernard thinks Arnott could have tipped off the press. It hadn't been difficult to follow Bernard's mental processes nor the link he had subconsciously made between the suspected informer and Arnott's name, even though he might not have been aware of it himself.

And Bernard could be right. Arnott was just as capable of such a calculated piece of malice as Leon and probably had stronger reasons to wish for Bernard's humiliation.

She was filled with a sudden disgust. God, how petty and spiteful it all was! Goodyear and Jake were both dead and yet Bernard seemed more concerned about his reputation while Arnott couldn't resist the temptation to pay off old scores.

What price humanity now? she thought angrily. And what in the hell happened to forgiveness and loving kindness?

Finch was silent as the car drew away down the drive, turning over in his mind the implications of the two interviews he had conducted that morning. As far as the investigation was concerned, the interview with Joyce Yarwood had produced the most useful evidence – that it was possible for anyone to enter or leave the main building unseen by using the lobby door and the service stairs, as Jake Nolan had done during his affair with Joyce Yarwood, a method of exit and entry which could have been used by three of the suspects, Harriet Wade, Leon Murray or Felicity Grayson although the evidence against her was flimsy to say the least.

But it was Harriet Wade's statement which stuck in his mind, two remarks in particular, more for their use of language than for any other reason.

One was a quotation from *Hamlet*: 'I am very proud, revengeful, ambitious.'

If, as she had suggested so perceptively, he was looking for a motive, what better reason was there for murder than any one of those? Or even all three?

Her other remark about Goodyear had also struck a chord in his mind. Goodyear had been, she had said, 'buoyant' with happiness.

'Buoyant'. It was a good word, bringing to mind a clear picture of the living Goodyear, not the huddled body in the car, crouched over the steering-wheel.

Boyce was saying, 'We'd better have the windows up as we go through the gates otherwise we're going to find one of those bloody reporters sticking his head in.'

As he wound up the window on his side, Finch came to a sudden decision.

'I want to look at Goodyear's house in Luton, Tom. Once we've picked up the keys from headquarters, we'll go straight over there.'

'Suits me,' Boyce replied with a shrug, adding as they slowed down to turn out of the gates, 'Look at the stupid sods! It'd serve them right if one of them got run over.'

He blew his horn with angry satisfaction as the car edged through the crowd of newspapermen, larger than when they had first arrived and now numbering among its members a couple of television crews, forcing them to fall back as the car accelerated away.

19

Goodyear's house in Eaton Road was one of a street of similar houses, built by the same property developer in the 1910s, respectable, solid, with square bay windows upstairs and down and small front gardens. His, number twenty-seven, was distinguished only by the four standard rose trees which lined the short path of red and black quarry tiles to the front door.

Finch put Goodyear's Yale key in the lock and, turning it, let himself and the Sergeant in. Beyond was a narrow hall with two doors leading off it and a third at the far end, all closed. A staircase went up on the left, the treads covered with the same burgundy-coloured fitted carpet that was on the floor.

The place smelt warm and stuffy, with a faint medicinal tang behind it of lavatory disinfectant.

'What are we looking for?' Boyce asked.

'Anything,' Finch replied.

For the moment though, he seemed content merely to open doors and stick his head inside rooms, a sitting-room to the front, dining-room at the back with a kitchen next to it, all tidy and conventionally furnished, the kitchen immaculate in blue and white and sparkling with cleanliness like one of those TV adverts after the housewife has used the brand cleaning product.

From there, he tramped upstairs and began the same routine again, revealing bedrooms – the front one, evidently unused, containing the best suite of furniture in figured walnut with a pink eiderdown on the double bed. The small bedroom was unfurnished except for a folding bed against one wall and some cardboard boxes of books, still unpacked.

Goodyear slept in the middle bedroom, over the dining-room, where a sash window gave a view of the back garden, mostly lawn with narrow flower borders on each side leading down to a shed at the bottom, so small it looked like a creosoted sentry box.

The room was as conventionally furnished as the rest of the

house with a single bed and a matching wardrobe, chest of drawers and bedside cabinet in light oak.

Unlike the other rooms, it bore some stamp of Goodyear's personality. A paperback edition of Hardy's *Under the Greenwood Tree* lay on the bedside cabinet while on top of the chest was a framed wedding photograph which, because of his sister's re-marriage, prompted Finch to cross the room and examine it before turning his attention to the drawers. Goodyear looked back at him, a younger Goodyear but nevertheless recognisable as the same man who had lain in the body sheet at the back of the mortuary van.

It was a pleasant, ordinary face, smiling a little self-consciously into the camera, hair carefully combed, a peach-coloured car-nation in his buttonhole matching the bride's bouquet and the bridesmaids' dresses – a wedding as undistinguished and as unremarkable in its own way as the three-piece suite in the sitting-room downstairs and yet Finch found himself staring down at it for longer than was strictly necessary. He was struck by the poignancy of such photographs which in their grouping, the smiles and the flowers, were designed to capture a specific moment of happiness, dressed up for, posed for, intended to be kept and cherished.

But Goodyear was dead. So presumably was his wife. The thin film of dust over the glass seemed to emphasise this fact and, prompted by God knows what emotion, he wiped the front of the photograph with the sleeve of his jacket before replacing it on top of the chest and beginning the search.

The folder was in the middle drawer, tucked under some pullovers which Goodyear had not needed to take with him to Morton Grange. Made of simulated leather, it was the type of large wallet with pockets in it designed to hold writing-paper and envelopes.

Inside it, tucked into the larger of the two pockets, was a photographer's envelope of stiff paper containing snapshots and, behind it, too big to be included, a studio portrait of a young girl mounted on deckled card.

Finch carried the wallet over to the bed, Boyce breaking off his search of the wardrobe to join him as the Chief Inspector lifted the flap of the envelope and tipped its contents on to the quilt. The snapshots were all of the same girl in the studio portrait, taken at various stages throughout her life from a baby in a pram through childhood and adolescence to young womanhood, plump-faced in the earlier shots and fining down over the years to thinner, more angular features but still recognisable as the same person in the widely spaced dark eyes and narrow chin. And recognisable, too, as Goodyear's daughter; or, if not his daughter, then some close blood relation.

It was Boyce who found the newspaper cuttings. Finch was studying the studio portrait in which the likeness to Goodyear in the wedding photograph was even more apparent – the same light brown hair and shy, rather self-conscious smile; not pretty but attractive in much the same way as Goodyear must have been appealing to Harriet Wade for a friendly ordinariness about the features.

'Nothing else in there?' Boyce was asking, up-ending the wallet and giving it a shake.

The cuttings fell out of the smaller pocket, folded in half and held together with a paper clip which Finch removed before flattening out the strips of newspaper.

The largest of the three, dated Friday, November 4th of the previous year, occupied five inches of print spread over two columns under the headline TRAGIC DEATH OF LOCAL GIRL and read:

> Depression following the loss of her job led local girl, Rosemary Goodyear, to take her own life, an inquest at Helstone was told this week.
>
> The body of Miss Goodyear, aged 23, of Willowbank Drive, Helstone, was found floating in the canal near Willis Street on Sunday, October 2nd by old-age pensioners Mr and Mrs E. Haines who were walking their dog along the tow-path.
>
> Father of the deceased, Mr Frank Goodyear, manager of the Helstone branch of the Midlands and County Building Society, told the court that his daughter, who had recently returned to the family home, had been depressed after losing her job in London.
>
> 'Her work meant everything to her,' he said. 'Since coming home, she had been in very low spirits.'
>
> Letters left by Miss Goodyear expressed her unhappiness and her sense of failure.
>
> Pathologist Dr David Rowe stated that death was due to drowning.

Recording a verdict that she took her own life, Coroner Dr Arthur Colby said it was a tragic loss of a young life.

Handing the cutting over to Boyce who had been trying to read it over his shoulder, Finch waited, holding the other two unread in his hand, for the Sergeant's inevitable reaction. It came moments later.

'*Rosemary!* And she was Goodyear's daughter . . .'

'And she committed suicide by drowning.' Finch completed the sentence for him in a flat, dry voice which merely stated the facts. 'But we need a hell of lot more evidence before we can start linking her death with Nolan's murder, Tom. We don't know if she'd ever met him.'

'But the rosemary found in the swimming-pool! There bloody has to be a connection.'

It was much the same conclusion that Finch himself had come to. The two deaths had to be associated in some way. That much was clear. But how? The rest of it – Goodyear's murder, the pansy found in his car, the seeming references to *Hamlet* – all of these made less sense than they had before although, as the thought occurred to him, he felt there was a shape which flickered briefly just beyond the periphery of conscious thought, like a shadow seen from the corner of one's eye before it darted away.

'We'll go to Helstone,' he announced.

'All right by me,' Boyce replied, 'if I knew where it was.'

He found it in the road map when, having locked up Goodyear's house behind them, he and Finch went out to the car. It was marked as being on the outskirts of Nottingham, close to the M1, making it a straight run through on the motorway as Boyce pointed out, starting the car.

Finch was silent for most of the journey, spending part of the time reading the two smaller cuttings which he had only glanced at so far, one being a short account of the discovery of the body in the canal, the other, slightly longer, covering the funeral with a list of mourners, pathetically few, and what were referred to as 'floral tributes'.

Having read them and glanced again at the photographs, Finch sat holding the wallet in his lap, staring out as the anonymous landscape reeled backwards past him – wheatfields, cows grazing in a meadow, a distant view of a village cut off suddenly as an

179

embankment rose and sped across his line of vision, the concrete stanchions of a fly-over bridge casting a bar of shadow into the car before they raced out of it into the sun again. And always the glaring surface of the motorway in front of them, devoured, it seemed, by their wheels.

The slip road for Helstone began in the same nondescript landscape – pylons straddling a field and factory chimneys in the distance. Then the outskirts of the place took over. A round-about, a petrol station, a row of pebble-dashed semis marked the suburbs before the road narrowed and they were driving down a street of small shops and terraced houses with glimpses down side turnings of factories or mills and the same tall stacks which they had seen on the horizon poking up above the huddled slate roofs.

Boyce had radioed in to divisional headquarters in Chelmsford before they had set off, requesting details of the exact location of the local police station in Helstone and for the Inspector in charge to be informed of their arrival.

It was in a side-street off the main square, a handsome building of red brick with sash windows and three steps up to the front door which suggested that at one time it had been the town residence of some local dignitary, a solicitor, perhaps, or a doctor, before the smoke and dirt of the industrial revolution had driven its occupants out into the suburbs.

Inspector Dutton's ground-floor office bore out this impression with its shabby marble fireplace, boarded in, and its high ceiling ornamented with a central rosette of plaster leaves. But there the comparison ended. The filing cabinets and the hanging fluor-escent lighting tubes were entirely modern. So, too, was Inspec-tor Dutton himself, a lean, sharp-faced officer with the air of a man in a hurry, who announced as soon as they were shown in, 'I got the message from your divisional headquarters that you were coming about the Goodyear case and I've looked up the file for you.'

The buff-coloured folder lay on the desk but Dutton made no attempt to open it, referring instead to a typewritten sheet of paper immediately in front of him, the contents of which he read out at a rattling speed, barely giving Boyce time to take notes of what was obviously a résumé of the known facts – the date the body was discovered, location, age and address of the victim, much of which Finch had already gleaned for himself from the newspaper cuttings.

He felt suddenly exasperated by Dutton's attitude, seeing him as merely a policeman on the professional make for whom the tragedy meant nothing more than some pieces of paper in a manila folder. A girl had killed herself; two other people had died, presumably in consequence, and yet he could refer to the case as the 'Goodyear suicide' as if it were merely a statistic.

He broke in abruptly. 'That's enough. I want to know about the girl – what she was like, why she killed herself, what her father's feelings were.'

He was aware of the effect his interruption had on the others – Boyce glancing up from his notebook, surprised and yet pleased that the Chief Inspector's impatience was being directed at someone else for a change, Dutton's face expressing a look of shamefaced consternation which made him appear younger and more vulnerable.

In his turn, Finch felt ashamed that he had used his rank to put the man in his place. For Dutton's zeal was, he suspected, not merely motivated by the desire to get on nor to impress a superior officer by his efficiency but possibly for subtler reasons which could have included a sense of his own inadequacy at dealing with tragedy. Finch had known other police officers like him. On occasions he himself reacted in the same way. You distanced yourself either by reducing it to what could be shut up inside a folder or by turning the whole stupid, bloody mess into a macabre joke you could laugh at over drinks in the police club bar.

He said, 'How far is this canal where she was found? Can we walk there?'

'Yes, sir. It's only about ten minutes away.'

'Then let's get going,' Finch told him. 'You can fill me in with the details on the way.'

They set off along the road away from the town centre and into an area of small side turnings lined with terrace houses which stretched out in diminishing perspectives of narrow façades, a front door with one window down, two up, squeezed so tightly together that, at the end of the vista, the doorsteps and window-ledges seemed to run in one continuous line. And yet, despite the grim, impersonal setting, there were touches of individuality – a bright blue door here, a geranium on a window-sill there, a

181

glimpse through an open door of a living-room with a flowered carpet and a mirror over a fireplace.

'Goodyear didn't live here?' Finch asked.

He was walking ahead with Dutton, leaving Boyce to follow behind. Somehow he couldn't imagine Goodyear in these streets.

'No, sir. He lived on the Ashley estate. That's on the far side of town. It's a posher area, built since the war. Nice gardens. Near the golf course.'

He spoke with the wistful manner of a man who himself aspired to a house on the same estate with a view over the links.

'Did you know him?'

'Goodyear? Not personally and not until after the case when I had to interview him.'

'How did he take it?'

'Badly. It seems his wife had died a couple of years earlier and the girl was his only child. I heard later he'd taken early retirement, sold the house and moved somewhere down south but I don't know where.'

'Luton,' Finch told him.

'Oh, really?' Dutton sounded only mildly interested. 'Had relatives there, had he?'

Finch was spared the trouble of having to explain that it appeared Goodyear had other motives for moving south by Dutton's next remark.

'The canal's down here, sir.'

He had paused in front of an alley opening that ran between two of the terrace houses, only wide enough for one person, and down which he turned, Finch and Boyce falling in behind.

The alley emerged on to a broad footpath which ran beside the canal, enclosed on the near bank by the high yard walls of the houses which backed on to it and, on the opposite bank, by the tall façades of derelict buildings, warehouses by the look of them although they could have been factories, their tiers of broken windows reflected in the water which lay as sluggish as oil, scarcely stirring the rubbish and the clumps of whitish foam which scabbed its surface.

A little further along, an iron footbridge spanned the canal and, over to the right, a tall factory chimney poked up above a confusion of angled slate roofs and lower chimneys against which the clean blue sky seemed incongruous.

God, what a place to choose to die! Finch thought as, hands stuffed in pockets and shoulders hunched, he stood on the tow-path and looked about him. Everywhere lay desolation and decay – rust, soot, slime, shattered glass and broken bricks, the trampled earth the colour and texture of dirty concrete. Even the plant life, such as it was, seemed stunted, starved blades of grass struggling up through the scattered rubble and a few scrawny elder trees growing here and there along the bank, their lower branches ripped off.

Inspector Dutton said quickly as if in answer to Finch's criticism although the Chief Inspector hadn't opened his mouth, 'It's a tip, isn't it? But we're hoping to get it cleaned up under the Community Service Scheme.'

'We're.' That word made all the difference. It spoke of Dutton's sense of belonging to this community, of his shame at its decline but underneath that, the feeling of civic pride which had prompted the city fathers in the days of its prosperity to erect that turreted town hall they had passed in the main square.

'Why?' he demanded and, when Dutton appeared not to follow, he continued, 'Why kill herself and why here?'

'The usual story – she was a couple of months pregnant according to the path report and the man didn't want to marry her. That much was clear from the letter she left behind for her father. There was another for the coroner. She'd lost her job as well. I suppose she felt it was all hopeless. They often do. Perhaps that's why she came here.' He kicked out at a beer can that lay on the path, sending it rattling towards the canal bank where it teetered for a few seconds before falling in. 'It was early on a Sunday morning. Her father said he didn't hear her leave the house. When she didn't come down for breakfast, he wasn't too worried. He thought she was having a lie-in. She'd been depressed and on edge ever since she'd come back from London but he didn't know she was pregnant. At about eleven o'clock, he went up to her room and found it empty and the letters on the bedside table. But by then it was too late. She'd already been fished out of the canal and a PC was on his way to the house to tell him. It shook up the couple who found her – Mr and Mrs Haines; elderly pair, out walking the dog. The wife's still on tablets because of it. I see the husband out and about in the streets

183

sometimes, on his way to the post office in Hulton Road to collect his pension.'

Finch heard him out in silence, postponing the questions he was fretting to ask, caught up by Dutton's story which was told in the same matter-of-fact, serviceable language which Dutton probably used in all his personal conversations, however intimate. At the same time, he was struck by how many people's lives had been affected by Rosemary Goodyear's suicide.

When Dutton had finished, Finch was silent for a few seconds, letting the story have its own dying fall. Then he asked, 'What was her job?'

The answer was what he had expected.

'Something to do with the theatre in London.'

'As an actress?'

'No, modern ballet, I think. She'd won a scholarship to some school of dance and drama in London and stayed on there working at various theatres until, as I said, she got the push and came home.'

'Did she use her own name?'

'I can't help you there. She's down in the file as Rosemary Goodyear.'

'No mention of Patti Rayner?'

Dutton looked dubious.

'Her second name was Patricia. Maybe Rayner was her mother's maiden name. That's what these theatre people do sometimes, isn't it? Make up a new name for themselves?'

Dutton was probably right about the mother's maiden name. It was a detail that could be checked out later. But at the moment, Finch had more pressing concerns on his mind.

The shape was beginning to form, still too nebulous for him to put a name to it although he thought he could grasp at a motive. What was it Hamlet had said? 'I am very proud, revengeful and ambitious.'

Any one of those would do.

In the meantime, the evidence had to be checked, the connection made.

He glanced at his watch. It was nearly quarter past five, too early yet to catch Mo Cunningham at the Lion's Head but he could stop off at a service station on the drive to London and telephone her to arrange an interview.

They met in a tiny backstage office within earshot of the evening performance which was going on a mere ten yards away behind the black curtains and within sight of a harassed-looking Humph who could be glimpsed through the glass panel in the door, standing at a trestle table waiting to hand out props and pieces of additional costume as the performers came off stage.

Mo Cunningham sat on the only chair with Finch and Boyce standing behind her as she looked at the photograph of Rosemary Goodyear which the Chief Inspector had just handed to her.

'Yes, that's her,' she said. 'That's Patti Rayner.'

'You're sure?'

'Of course I'm sure. Christ, we worked together on *Iron Soldiers* for nearly two months before Leon started to play silly buggers and the production was given the chop. Then, as I told you, she left because we couldn't afford to keep her on.'

'So Leon Murray knew her?'

'He must have done. He was always hanging about during rehearsals.'

'When did she go?'

'As soon as we decided to get shot of Leon and give him his money back. That was about the end of September. We'd started work on the production in the first week as soon as Jake got back from the summer school. He arranged for her to join the company. He'd seen some choreography she'd done at the Edinburgh fringe and liked her work. But it was me who had to tell her to go.'

She smiled as she said it although there was bitterness in her voice.

'She was pregnant,' Finch told her.

'By Jake? It follows.' Mo Cunningham shrugged her plump shoulders. 'What happened to her? An abortion?'

'She committed suicide.'

Mo Cunningham took off her glasses.

'Oh, Christ,' she said.

Finch took the photograph from her and returned it to the wallet before adding in his formal voice, 'There's a couple more questions I want to ask you, Miss Cunningham. Have you noticed anyone taking a particular interest in the place, turning up regularly in the audience, for example, or asking about Nolan after Patti Rayner left, say from about October of last year?'

185

'Not especially. I don't see much of the audience. I'm usually backstage. But no one's been hanging around or asking about Jake to my knowledge. As for phone calls, Jake would be rung up quite often – he wasn't on the phone at his flat – but none of those were anything out of the ordinary as far as I know.'

It seemed an impasse. But that was impossible. There had to be a way through.

He put his last question.

'Is there any way someone could have found out that Jake was a tutor at Morton Grange?'

Her answer was immediate.

'Oh, easily. Jake always put up a poster in the bar downstairs advertising the summer school with the names of the tutors and details of the courses on it. Anyone could have seen it who came in for a drink.'

It was as simple as that.

20

The meeting at half-past six that evening was held in Arnott's tutorial room which was not nearly as comfortable nor as intimate as Bernard's study. There was no sherry either and the absence of the decanter and glasses seemed to set the mood even before Bernard entered, uncharacteristically late, and strode up the length of the room to Arnott's desk.

It was like being back at school, Harriet thought, she and Arnott sitting at the students' tables, Bernard at the desk, looking down disapprovingly at a folder in front of him as if about to return their below-standard essays.

She looked sideways at Arnott, not really expecting him to share her amusement. He had chosen a seat several places away from her and was sitting hunched up on the plastic chair which wasn't quite wide enough for his thighs, elbows on table, staring morosely at Bernard who, having placed the open folder precisely in the centre of the desk, scraped his own chair forward and sat down.

The lesson was about to begin.

'I have convened this meeting,' Bernard announced, 'in order to discuss with you the short-term future of Morton Grange summer school. Several students have already approached me requesting to withdraw and asking for reimbursement of their fees. I have their names here,' he added, tapping the topmost sheet of paper in front of him with an ominous finger as if it were a list of prisoners for the gallows. 'If anyone makes similar inquiries of either of you, I'd be grateful if you passed their names on to me so that I can speak to them personally. In the case of the drama students, I can see no other option than returning at least part of their fees as that particular course is no longer operational . . .'

'What about next week?' Arnott broke in to ask. 'Who's going to run the drama course then?'

'I was coming to that,' Bernard told him coldly. 'I made arrangements this afternoon for another tutor to take over the course temporarily for a fortnight. After that, I shall have to make further inquiries about a more suitable replacement.'

'So you're not going to ditch the whole thing?'

'"Ditch"?' Bernard picked up the word as fastidiously as if it had been some unsavoury morsel. 'No, certainly not, Ronald. Morton Grange summer school will continue despite the problems we are currently facing. Which brings me to my main reason for calling this meeting – publicity. Someone, I don't at the moment know who, although I have my suspicions, has been in touch with the press. I cannot stress the importance of discretion too strongly. Irreparable damage could be done to the reputation of Morton Grange if the newspapers publish the details of the recent events which have taken place here. I trust I can rely on your loyalty.'

It was an appeal for their joint co-operation in adversity, all three of them pulling together with the good old Dunkirk spirit although, as he spoke, Bernard's glance rested on Arnott. It was so embarrassingly pointed that Harriet did not dare to look in Arnott's direction to see his reaction.

The next moment, Bernard had cleared his throat and began winding up the meeting with a proposal that he addressed all the students the following morning after breakfast and that he expected both of them as tutors to be present promptly at nine o'clock, a warning which was again addressed specifically at Arnott who was frequently late and could be seen snatching a cup of coffee at the last moment from the trolley before Mrs Soames wheeled it away.

The meeting over, Harriet went upstairs to her room to await the supper gong. She wanted no further contact with either Bernard or Arnott. Nor indeed with any of the students although it was impossible to keep entirely aloof during the evening meal even though she waited for ten minutes before joining the others so that she could choose where to sit.

She picked a table which was occupied by some of the older students, including the lugubrious man. Carrying her tray over to the empty place, she was aware that Steve had risen to his feet at a far table to signal a free seat there. She was aware, too, that as she kept her eyes on her tray, he had sat down again, looking abashed.

She couldn't help it. The low-spirited mood which had affected her earlier still persisted, not helped by the conversation at the table in which the lugubrious man was playing a major part.

'It's outrageous,' he was saying. 'I certainly didn't enrol here expecting to be interviewed by the police. Legally, I think we're entitled to a full repayment of fees . . .'

He had the grace to break off as Harriet joined them and the talk shifted to less controversial topics, initiated by Miss Eversham, but it remained stilted, like conversation after a funeral, everyone trying too hard to be social and to avoid any reference to the subject in the forefront of all their minds.

Harriet added her pennyworth, listening to herself speaking in a sprightly voice about the *roman fleuve* and its literary significance, the topic of the next morning's seminar, before excusing herself from the table as soon as she decently could.

As she carried her plates back to the hatch, she congratulated herself on having escaped so lightly. Steve had gone. There was no sign either of Bernard who she suspected had taken his tray upstairs to eat his supper in the privacy of his own room. Arnott was there, however, hunched up over his plate at an empty table but he made no attempt to raise his head as she passed.

And then, just as she moved away from the hatch, a voice, Kay's, said, 'Hello, Harriet. How are you?'

The tone was light and pleasant; nothing more. In the few seconds it took Harriet to turn round, she decided she would respond. What had she to lose by it? Kay would be leaving in a few days' time. Besides, she could hardly ignore the woman and walk away.

All the same, she replied in mock cockney, itself a means of avoiding any real contact, 'All right. Mustn't grumble.'

Kay fell into step beside her, her thin, clever face looking concerned.

'I haven't had a chance yet to say how sorry I am about Jake Nolan and Frank Goodyear. Frank was in your tutorial class, wasn't he? I liked him a lot.'

'You knew him?' Harriet asked, surprised.

She hadn't imagined Kay would have singled him out for particular attention. Frank hadn't seemed Kay's type. But perhaps she was doing Kay an injustice by such a conclusion.

'I talked to him once or twice, the last time on the afternoon before he died. I met him wandering about the gardens on his own. He said he'd been to look at the chapel but it was locked so he couldn't get in.'

'Did he say anything else?' Harriet asked. It suddenly seemed ridiculously important for her to know the details of that chance encounter, as if, by seeing it through Kay's eyes, she could imagine for herself something of Frank's last hours. Unlike Jake, he seemed to have made so little impact on anyone, including herself. And now he was dead and it appeared no one mourned his passing.

'We talked a little about Morton Grange. He said how beautiful the place was. He seemed so happy to be here.'

'Happy? Yes, he was happy,' Harriet replied.

She was touched that Kay should have recognised this quality about him; touched, too, that as they reached the hall, Kay, as if knowing that she would prefer to be alone, added, 'I'm going up to my room. But if there's anything I can do at any time, Harriet, please ask,' before turning away to walk up the stairs.

It was said sincerely but with no particular emphasis, letting the offer of further contact lie for Harriet to pick up or not as she chose and, as she let herself out of the front door, Harriet felt her spirits lift a little with relief and with gratitude at Kay's sensitivity.

It was a warm, still evening. The sun had dipped down behind the chapel tower and she followed the drive towards it, thinking that Frank Goodyear must have come this way on his last afternoon. But the walk was not intended as a sentimental

189

journey, merely an opportunity to be alone and, before she reached the path which led to the chapel, she struck off across the grass towards the distant belt of trees which marked the far boundary of the grounds.

It was real woodland, she discovered as she entered it; not the carefully maintained shrubbery and ornamental landscape of the rest of the grounds, and this, too, was a relief.

Morton Grange was no longer visible either. As she reached the far edge of the wood and climbed over a low iron fence into a wheatfield, she glanced back over her shoulder and could see nothing of it, not even the line of its roof nor the crenellations of the chapel tower.

It was like running away, Harriet thought, remembering a similar experience in her childhood when she had escaped from an hour of hated piano practice, jumping the ditch at the bottom of the garden and running along the side of a hedge, knowing that somewhere behind her but unheard her mother would be calling her name.

She began to run now, filled with the same wild and yet fearful exultation, rejoicing in the freedom which, because it was only temporary, seemed all the more exhilarating.

In the common room, Leon Murray helped himself to coffee and stood for a few moments by the trolley, sizing up those present. The group by one of the windows seemed the best option. It was composed of the more outspoken of the middle-aged students, including a lugubrious-looking man from Harriet Wade's tutorial group who appeared to be in charge of the gathering.

Snatches of their conversation drifted across the room above the sound of other voices.

'. . . quite disgraceful . . .'

'Bernard has no right . . .'

'I really think someone ought to . . .'

Brushing the flick of blond hair back from his forehead, Leon sauntered across the room and stood smiling down at them, one hand on the back of a vacant armchair.

'Would you mind awfully if I joined you?' he asked at his most youthful and charming. 'I couldn't help overhearing what you said and I do so agree. I'd like to make a suggestion, if I may.'

As he sat down, he could see the hostility in their faces vying with an eagerness to accept him as a recruit into their ranks.

'You see,' he continued, 'I feel I know Bernard rather well, having had my own little disagreement with him and I really do think the democratic approach is the right one.'

'I don't follow you,' the lugubrious man said heavily. He seemed annoyed that Murray should have strolled in and practically taken over what had been *his* meeting.

'A petition,' Leon explained. 'If you could get everyone's signatures, then Bernard would have to accept the majority opinion. It's just a suggestion, of course, but personally I'd be willing to sign if someone else drew it up. I'm afraid I'm quite hopeless at organisation.'

He looked appealingly at the lugubrious man, drawing everyone else's eyes to him as well, and then sat back smiling at their response.

'What an excellent idea!'

'Bernard would be forced to take notice . . .'

'Wouldn't you organise it, Mr Morris?'

By the time Leon had drunk his coffee, not only had the lugubrious man produced a sheet of file paper and drawn up its heading but the petition was already circulating round the group of chairs, Leon adding his own signature with a particularly triumphant little flourish of black ink under his surname.

George Burton took the newspaper into the sitting-room of the gatehouse and tried to settle down to read it. But his eyes kept glancing up from the pages to the clock on the mantelpiece.

It was half-past eight. Soon the kitchen staff would be leaving and Joyce would be alone.

He imagined her passing to and fro in front of the lighted windows, an image so sharp and bright that it seemed more real than the printed words in front of him.

But he wouldn't go. Not this evening or ever again. That was a madness he had to overcome. It was finished. Done with.

All the same, he kept lifting his eyes to the clock, watching the hand creep closer to the quarter-hour.

At ten to nine, he thrust the paper behind him and, getting up abruptly from the chair, let himself out by the back door.

It was one of those quiet evenings, not a breath of wind, the trees standing motionless, the setting sun lighting up the sky with great horizontal bands of colour behind the west wing of Morton Grange.

Turning his back on it, he set off in the opposite direction, hands deep in his pockets, walking rapidly away under the trees to put as much distance as he could between himself and those lighted windows which still seemed to draw him like a memory from childhood of coming home.

Joyce Yarwood stood at the kitchen window and watched Soames' car drive past the entrance to the service yard and disappear from sight, taking Mrs Soames and the other women with it.

As soon as it had gone, she took off her overall coat and let herself out of the kitchen door.

It was getting dusk and there was no one about, the students being either in the common room or in their bedrooms. There was no sign either of George Burton although she walked quickly, fearful that he might appear at any moment round the corner of the stable block as he had done the previous afternoon, forcing her to return before she had carried out her mission.

It was darker inside the yew hedges than she had anticipated, having only visited the pool in daylight before to swim there in her off-duty hours. The air seemed heavy, giving the place an enclosed, secretive atmosphere. Even the water lay motionless, the surface immaculate, reflecting back a great sheet of sky still bloomed with the last peach and orange light from the sunset.

She walked a few paces forward, hearing the sound of her footsteps strike back from the paving stones.

It was like being in church, she thought; the echoing silence, the sense of space around her, the air spiced, not with incense but with the scent of yew while the water stretched out before her like a huge horizontal stained-glass window framed in stone.

She approached the edge and on a sudden impulse knelt down, leaning foward to peer into the water. Her face looked back at her, startling her by its appearance. Disembodied, it seemed to float just below the surface as if it were she who was lying there and only the ghost of her remained kneeling on the paving stones.

How easy it would be to slip in! To lie as he had done, lapped in the water and to drift away, oblivious of everything except the sky above her deepening into night.

Bernard waited until it was getting dark before returning his supper tray to the kitchen, anxious to avoid the kitchen staff who he estimated would go home at about nine o'clock once the clearing up was done. Joyce Yarwood would still be on duty but he did not mind encountering her so much. She would not stare at him in quite the same vulgar manner as the other women. In fact, when he had approached her earlier that evening with the request that he took his supper upstairs as he felt unwell, she had made no comment, merely fetching a tray and placing his dishes and cutlery on it.

His ill-health was simply an excuse to be alone although he was genuinely aware of a pressure behind the eyes which if not exactly a headache made him reluctant to face the noise of voices and rattling china in the dining-room.

He went down by the back stairs, a route he rarely used but which had the advantage of taking him directly to the kitchen without having to cross the main hall where he might be waylaid by one of the students pressing him for a decision about the future of the courses and the repayment of fees.

The staircase led down to a small vestibule with the door to the kitchen on his left but when he knocked and entered, he was surprised to find the room empty and no sign of Joyce Yarwood although all the lights were on and her overall coat was lying across a corner of the preparation table.

It was obvious she had left in a hurry and, standing there with his tray, Bernard felt a sharp sense of alarm.

The kitchen seemed so dreadfully empty; ominously so in the harsh white strip lighting. It reminded him of the night Nolan had been murdered and of the lights left blazing in the empty assembly hall.

Had something happed to her? Should he go and look for her? Or was he allowing his imagination to run away with him? She could, after all, be upstairs in her room.

Setting down his tray on the edge of the draining-board beside a rack of saucepans and some kitchen knives left to drain, he came to a compromise.

He would carry out his original intention of going to his study to fetch the copies of Eliot's *Murder in the Cathedral*, the subject of his lecture the following morning and itself a compromise in order to appease the drama students. On his way back, he would check the kitchen again and if Joyce Yarwood still wasn't there or in her room, he would appeal for help from Harriet Wade and one or two of the more sensible students and initiate a search although he hoped to God it wouldn't be necessary.

Closing the kitchen door behind him, he set off along the passage which led from the vestibule past the dining-room and which, after a sharp right-hand turn, took him to his study.

It was exactly as he had left it before that damned man Finch had requisitioned it. The long brocade curtains were drawn back from the window, revealing a view of the twilit garden, and, on the far side of the lawn, the assembly hall, school chapel and swimming-pool were lined up across the vista as they had appeared on the night of Nolan's murder, except this time the hall was in darkness.

All the same, it was too painful a reminder and Bernard's first thought as he entered was to cross the study and draw the curtains shut.

As he stood at the window, holding the heavy folds in his hands, he heard the door open and someone come into the room behind him.

Annoyed by this unexpected visitor, he looked briefly over his shoulder.

'Oh, it's you,' he said. 'What do you want?'

Harriet re-entered the grounds of Morton Grange behind the kitchen garden, having circled round by the fields which lay beyond the perimeter fence.

It was an area she was unfamiliar with and it surprised her by its size. The part nearest to the boundary was given over to an orchard of old, twisted trees growing haphazardly in long grass but still productive, judging by the quantity of fruit hanging on them. In turn, these gave way to neat rows of newer, bushier varieties. Then came a line of netting cages for soft fruit, followed by long cordons of blackberries and raspberries before the garden opened up into vegetable plots, smelling of warm, cultivated earth in the dusky air.

A broad, central, grassy path dissected the beds, leading straight on to the back of the stable block, Harriet realised. It was a part of Morton Grange that she had avoided since Frank Goodyear's body had been discovered there and, unwilling to approach too near, she took a narrower side path which turned off past a greenhouse, its panes dimly reflecting the sky and the darkening trees, following it to the point where it joined the main drive as it swung round by the service yard.

She noticed there were lights on in the kitchen and, as she walked on past the swimming-pool towards the chapel, another light sprang up suddenly in the darkened façade of the ground floor of the main building.

It was Bernard's study. She glanced towards it, her attention caught by the unexpected oblong of brightness.

And there was the figure of Bernard himself, outlined against the window, arms outstretched in the act of drawing the curtains together but with his head turned away as if he were speaking to some unseen person in the room behind him.

The next second, the curtains closed and the little scene, so briefly glimpsed, was gone.

Without giving it further thought, Harriet continued on to the side door at the corner of the west wing by the common room and, having let herself in, turned along the corridor towards the main hall which, thank God, was empty, allowing her to escape unnoticed up the stairs to her room.

21

When Bernard failed to appear at breakfast the following morning by a quarter to nine, Harriet's first reaction was one of annoyance. After all the stress he had laid at the meeting the previous evening on the need for Arnott and herself to be in the dining-room promptly at nine o'clock for his address to the students, it seemed to her particularly exasperating that Bernard should choose that very morning to be late himself. She assumed he had overslept, remembering that he had arrived late for the staff meeting, looking tired and peevish.

By five to nine, her impatience had changed to alarm. Some of the students had already finished breakfast and were beginning to move towards the hatch to return plates and cutlery before leaving the dining-room. It occurred to her that perhaps she ought to make an announcement herself, asking them to wait for Bernard's arrival, but she hesitated to do so.

Supposing something had happened to him?

It was crazy, of course. Nothing had happened to him. Any moment he would come bustling in, annoyed at being late and annoyed with her as well for having made such a fuss.

She could imagine his pained comment. 'But, my dear Harriet, surely you realised I had simply been delayed for a few minutes?'

At five past nine, she made up her mind. She would go and look for him. Classes began at half-past which gave her plenty of time to search the obvious places such as his bedroom and tutorial room.

She began her inquiries discreetly of Joyce Yarwood, waiting until no one else was at the hatch before asking, 'Have you seen Bernard this morning?'

'No, I haven't,' Joyce Yarwood replied. 'Perhaps he's ill. He asked for his supper on a tray last night because he wasn't feeling very well.'

She looked ill herself, her face pale and taut with dark patches under her eyes like black thumb marks.

Harriet thanked her and walked away, feeling relieved. Bernard was unwell. It was the obvious explanation although it occurred to her that if he were too ill to take his classes that morning, it would add considerably to the problems they already faced in organising the tutorial groups. A lecture in the common room to the whole thirty of them seemed the only solution and she supposed she would have to give it. She couldn't imagine Ron Arnott offering his services.

She went upstairs by the back staircase which was nearer the dining-room and made her search for Bernard less public. There was no point in advertising his non-appearance before she had spoken to him herself and arrangements had been made between them to cover his absence.

His room was empty. She knocked, waited and knocked again before finally opening the door and entering. The shock of finding no one there, the bed not even slept in, brought her up short.

Turning quickly and with an increasing sense of urgency, she closed the door behind her and set off down the main staircase this time, walking briskly and ignoring the students who had begun to gather in the hall before dispersing for their tutorials.

The music-room which Bernard was using as a temporary tutorial room was empty, too. Without needing to open the door, she could see through the glass panel that Bernard wasn't there either. Nor was he in the common room. As she closed that door behind her and stood hesitating outside it, wondering where to try next, she was reminded of the search she and Finch had made of the building for Frank Goodyear on the night Jake was murdered. And God, think of how that had ended!

You are becoming hysterical, she told herself severely. Bernard is perfectly all right. There is some quite logical explanation for his absence.

As the thought crossed her mind, she remembered suddenly the brief glimpse she had caught of him the previous evening standing at the study window as she returned from her walk and felt an immediate sense of relief.

Of course! How stupid of her not to think of it before. He'd be in his study. Although Finch had taken it over for his own use, Bernard still kept his books and papers there. It was perfectly feasible that he had gone to collect something he needed, such as notes, for his morning's tutorials although, at the same time, a small voice of logic demanded, then why hadn't he arrived in time to address the students and why wasn't his bed slept in?

The study was in semi-darkness, the curtains still drawn across the windows so that, as she entered, she had to switch on the overhead lights in order to see. At first, the room seemed empty, too, and she was about to turn back towards the door when she noticed that one of the curtains was not properly in place, the heavy brocade bulging forward on the rings, allowing small, half-moons of daylight to seep in along the top of the pole.

Approaching the desk, she saw why. Some large, bundled *thing* lay on the floor behind the curtain, huddled close to the wall below the sill and dragging the folds of the fabric outwards. But a bundle that had a recognisable shape and from which a dark stain had seeped across the parquet floor to touch the handle of a knife which lay, blade towards her, on the edge of the carpet.

Harriet retreated quickly to the far side of the desk, astonished by her lack of surprise or panic. The huddled shape was Bernard's body. That much was obvious. In fact, she thought, picking up the telephone receiver and dialling 999, the whole situation, considered in her present state of delayed shock which she also recognised with the same sense of distanced objectivity, seemed to have its own crazy logic.

'Indeed, this counsellor
Is now most still, most secret and most grave.'

Hamlet's words to Gertrude after he had run Polonius through with his sword as he hid behind the arras.

Replace 'arras' with 'curtain' and it made perfect sense, she thought, as she listened to her voice saying with brisk competence, 'My name is Harriet Wade. I want to report another murder at Morton Grange School.'

The call came as Finch was in the middle of a meeting in his office at divisional headquarters with Boyce and Pardoe, the pathologist. It was not a full-scale conference. Finch wanted to be more sure of his ground before he suggested this new approach to the inquiry to the other officers involved. But once Pardoe had confirmed at least one possible interpretation of the evidence, he would feel confident enough to go ahead.

Pardoe was saying, 'I haven't yet had a report back from the lab, but yes, what you suggest is possible. The wound on Goodyear's temple could have been . . .'

At this point, the telephone rang and Finch picked up the receiver. He listened in silence, aware that the other two were watching him, Boyce still looking sceptical at the theory the Chief Inspector had just put forward, Pardoe annoyed that he had been interrupted in mid-sentence.

Finch replaced the receiver carefully on its cradle before announcing, 'There's been another murder at Morton Grange.'

It gave him an unexpected sense of satisfaction to see their expressions change, Boyce's to astonished disbelief, Pardoe's to stupefaction.

'Whose?' Boyce asked.

'Livesey's,' Finch told him, reaching round to the back of his chair for his jacket, adding to Pardoe, 'Do you want to come with us or would you prefer to use your own car?'

'Mine,' Pardoe said but with none of his usual belligerence. 'You'll be kept busy for the rest of the day and I shall want to get on with the post-mortem. Any idea how he died?'

'No,' Finch replied, already half-way through the door. 'But we'll find out soon enough when we get there.'

It was a stabbing. McCullum and the scene of crime officers were already there by the time the Chief Inspector and the Sergeant drove up and parked in front of the main doors of Morton Grange.

The body, still wrapped up in the curtain, was in the process of being photographed by McCullum when they entered the study, closely followed by Pardoe who had arrived seconds later and who stepped gingerly round the desk to lift back the curtain once McCullum had withdrawn.

The fabric was unmarked, Finch noticed, except for the blood which had stained the bottom edge. No slits, no tears in the brocade although the weapon, a long black-handled cook's knife, lay on the carpet close to the pool of blood which had run across the floor.

Livesey's body was huddled up near it, knees drawn up, the head, its silvery hair dark with blood, bent forward, stretching the neck taut and exposing the inch-long wound just below the ear.

'One clean blow,' Pardoe announced, bending forward to examine it although, judging by the quantity of blood, 'clean' was hardly the epithet Finch himself would have chosen to describe it. 'Severed the carotid artery. Whoever did it was either very lucky or knew exactly what he was doing.'

It was luck, Finch commented to himself although that, too, was an unfortunate choice of word under the circumstances.

'Who found him?' he asked of Wylie who, in white coverall and boots, was marking out the position of the body in chalk on the parquet.

'One of the tutors, sir. A young woman – Harriet Wade. She let us in when we arrived; said she'd wait for you in her tutorial room. We've got a good set of prints, by the way, on the knife. Looks like one from a kitchen set. Whoever used it, didn't bother to wipe it afterwards.'

Finch leaned forward to peer at it over the top of the desk. The fingerprints were clearly visible in the aluminium powder with which it had been dusted. He thought he recognised it, too, or one very like it, recalling the evening when he had first interviewed Joyce Yarwood in the kitchen. There had been a set of knives with similar black handles on a wall-rack by the stoves.

He retreated to the door, beckoning Boyce to follow with a jerk of his head.

'We'll talk to Harriet Wade first,' he told the Sergeant.

Although he was convinced he knew the identity of the murderer, a few more facts had to be established before he could make the arrest. What before had been mere speculation, a new interpretation of the evidence, had moved beyond theory into tragic reality in the few hours since his return from Helstone.

But what could he have done to prevent Livesey's murder?

Nothing, he told himself. This last death was totally unforeseen. He had imagined it had all finished with Goodyear's. Livesey's murder was a macabre postscript, a signing off in blood which no one could have anticipated. At least, he hoped to God he was right and that the sequence of killing was now ended although he found the quotation from *Hamlet* still running through his head as he and Boyce crossed the hall where a few students stood silently about as if in a state of shock.

'I am very proud, revengeful, ambitious.'

Harriet Wade was waiting for them in her tutorial room, wearing the same numbed expression Finch had seen on the faces of the students, hands clasped together on the top of her desk as if waiting to begin a seminar although, as they entered, he doubted if she registered their arrival.

He said, 'I'm sorry, Miss Wade,' realising, as he drew up a chair and sat down facing her, how absurdly inadequate the words were. 'I'm afraid I'm going to have to ask you a few questions.'

She appeared not to hear him but to be listening instead to her own thoughts as she spoke.

'I saw him last night. He was drawing the curtains in the study. He had his head turned away from the window as if someone had just come into the room. That's when he was killed, wasn't it?'

'What time was this?' Finch asked.

She shook her head as if trying to clear her mind.

'I'm not sure. About half-past nine, perhaps. I'd gone out for a walk and it was getting dark as I came back. I saw the light go on in Bernard's study and then he came to the window. I didn't see any more. Then this morning, when he didn't appear in the dining-room to talk to the students as he'd arranged, I went to look for him.'

She began to shudder, her hands going up to her shoulders as if to control the spasms, her head bowed between her arms so that Finch could see only the top of her head with its thick coil of wheat-coloured hair.

He was about to apologise and withdraw, postponing the interview until she had recovered a little from the shock of finding the body, when she suddenly raised her face to look at him across the desk.

'He was stabbed through the curtain, wasn't he? Like Polonius?' She laughed shakily, the note cracking on the point of tears. 'What did you find this time, Chief Inspector? More rosemary? Or was it rue, the herb of grace o' Sundays? "Oh, you must wear your rue with a difference."'

'Miss Wade,' Finch broke in, 'there is no *Hamlet* connection.'

He felt rather than saw the reaction on the part of Boyce who had tactfully seated himself to the left of them, beyond their line of vision. It was an almost imperceptible stiffening of his attitude, a drawing together of himself as much as to say, 'You see, I was right after all.'

I should have bloody well listened to him, Finch thought. Or taken his courage in both hands and phoned Marion Greave as he had been tempted to do several times during the investigation.

But he was gratified to see that his statement had some effect on Harriet Wade who suddenly looked more alert and attentive.

'No connection? But there has to be! The rosemary in the pool . . .'

'It referred to a girl's name, that's all.'

201

'And Frank Goodyear's murder?'

Finch let that one pass, apart from remarking, 'That was part of a deliberate attempt to link both deaths to the play.'

She was silent for several seconds as she took in the information. Then she said, 'I'm sorry. I didn't mean to mislead you. When I saw the rosemary in Jake's hand, I was convinced it was a reference to *Hamlet*. And then, when you asked about the theme, that seemed to connect as well with a reason for their murders.'

'We were both misled,' Finch assured her. 'That was the whole point. It was intended to confuse the investigation. And the theme wasn't so wrong after all. Revenge was one of the motives.'

And pride. And ambition. But, given the universality of Shakespeare's imagination, was this so very surprising?

She had recovered sufficiently for him to ask the question which was one of the main purposes of the interview.

'I shall have to talk to one or two others. Have you any idea where I might find Mr Arnott?'

'Ron? No, I don't know where he is. I don't think he was at breakfast. At least, I didn't notice him but he's often late. In fact, I haven't seen him all morning. Why do you want to see him? He can't have anything to do with Bernard's death. Even though you say there's no *Hamlet* connection, the other two murders must be linked, mustn't they? And Ron had an alibi for those.'

Finch said in an easy, pleasant manner, 'Yes, of course he had, Miss Wade. All the same, I have to check on everyone's movements if only for elimination. I also thought Mr Arnott might be able to help us fill in the details of what Mr Livesey was doing yesterday evening. You said you saw him at about half-past nine at the study window as you came back from your walk. I wondered if Mr Arnott might have talked to him earlier than that.'

She seemed a little appeased by his answer although she was still watching him warily, Finch noticed, as she replied.

'Yes, I see. Well, I don't know if Ron can help you. We were both at the meeting Bernard called at half-past six yesterday evening. He wanted to discuss the interest the press seems to be taking and also to arrange to speak to the students this morning. Ron was at supper later although Bernard wasn't. Joyce Yarwood said he took his tray up to his room. I haven't seen either of them since then, apart from catching that glimpse of Bernard at the study window.'

'So you haven't seen Mr Arnott since about half-past seven last night?'

'No, I haven't,' Harriet said.

Finch got to his feet, aware that her eyes were on him, following his every movement.

'Well, I expect we'll find him soon enough,' he told her, trying to sound casually reassuring.

She was too intelligent to be fooled.

'You think something may have happened to him, like Bernard and the others?' she cried. It was almost an accusation.

'I don't think anything of the sort, Miss Wade,' Finch replied although once he and Boyce had left the room and the door was closed behind them, he added, 'I only hope to God she isn't right.'

Boyce was about to reply when they saw a young, dark-haired woman coming towards them along the corridor carrying a tray on which were two cups of coffee, clearly on her way to Harriet Wade's room.

Her arrival relieved Finch of one anxiety. He had been considering sending for a WPC to sit with Harriet Wade until the last stages of the investigation were completed. The young woman would serve that duty.

The other and more urgent anxiety remained.

Where the hell *was* Ron Arnott?

'Come on, Tom,' he said to Boyce. 'We'll try his bedroom first.'

As soon as Finch and Boyce had left the room, Harriet got up from her chair and went to stand at the window where she rested her forehead against the cool glass.

Beyond the window, the gardens of Morton Grange lay serene and inviolate, stretched out peacefully in the sunlight under a blue sky faintly marbled with white cloud. And yet the view seemed to her curiously distanced and unreal, a painted backcloth which had no connection with the violent death which was taking place in front of it. Or was it the violence which was unreal? It was like waking after a particularly vivid dream when, in those first few seconds, she was uncertain which was the reality, the world of sleep which she had just left or the conscious one she had only at that moment entered.

She was even more unsure how to react when Kay knocked and entered with the tray, announcing briskly, 'It's break time. I thought you might like to have your coffee in here rather than with the others.'

Part of her was grateful for Kay's concern on her behalf but she would have preferred to be left alone. Anyone's presence, but especially Kay's, was an added burden, reminding her of the other world of responsibilities and duties and, in Kay's case, of relationships which she lacked the coherence to think about, let alone to decide what her response should be.

All the same, she felt obliged to ask, 'What's happening about the students?' although she was careful to keep her distance as Kay put the tray down on the desk.

'Steve Mayhew and I rounded them up and told them the classes are cancelled. They'll be having coffee now anyway so there's no real need for you to feel concerned about them.'

'Was Ron Arnott there?' Harriet asked, trying to keep her voice and manner normal so that Kay should not see her anxiety which, she felt, would make her vulnerable to this woman's strength. But she must have betrayed something of her real feelings for, as Kay brought her cup of coffee over to her at the window, she said quickly, 'No, he wasn't. In fact, I haven't seen him all morning. Why are you so worried about him, Harriet?'

'No reason. The police want to interview him, that's all.'

'They'll want to question everybody eventually, I imagine. But that isn't why you asked, is it?'

Feeling the tears begin to gather behind her eyelids, Harriet turned away, shaking her head at the cup of coffee Kay was holding out to her. Through the myopia of tears, the view seemed even further distanced, outlines undefined, colours blurred, the sky itself dissolving into a blue wash which ran down to meet the watery green of the trees.

Behind her, she was conscious of Kay standing silent waiting for her to answer and yet offering her the choice of either accepting or rejecting her.

It was Harriet's decision. She could herself remain silent in which case Kay would go away, making as her excuse some banal remark about Harriet preferring to be alone. Or she could take up the offer, confide in her and accept the possibility of a relationship.

Almost without being aware of having spoken, she heard herself saying, 'I think something may have happened to him.'

It was the same phrase she had used to Finch but Kay picked it up at once.

'What do you mean by "something"? Are you saying that you think he's been murdered?'

The word was so shocking that Harriet swung round to face her.

'I don't know!' she cried. 'I can't bear to think about it. I just feel he's involved in some way.'

'In the other murders?'

'No, not that. He can't be. He had an alibi for Jake and Frank's deaths. He was in the common room, talking to two of his students, when they were killed. And Finch agreed. But he's worried himself about him. I could see that even though he tried not to show it. I blame myself.'

'In God's name, for what, Harriet?'

'For not looking for him earlier. I should have done when I realised I hadn't seen him since last night but I just felt relieved that he wasn't around.'

Kay said brusquely, 'You didn't like him. I didn't like him either. But not liking somebody doesn't make you responsible for him.'

'No,' Harriet said.

It seemed to make sense and for the first time Harriet allowed the tears to fall although she brushed them angrily from her cheeks.

'Come,' Kay was saying. She had carried Harriet's cup over to the desk where her own was standing on the tray. 'Sit down and have your coffee. We may have to wait a long time.'

'We'. It was such a small word and yet it seemed to express, at least on Kay's part, an acceptance of their relationship and, after a moment's hesitation, Harriet joined her at the table.

22

Arnott was not in his bedroom nor in his tutorial room nor anywhere else in Morton Grange as far as Finch could discover.

He and Boyce moved fast, opening any doors that were unlocked and looking briefly round them, even trying, with the aid of two uniformed men who had been called in to help with the search, the more unlikely places such as the kitchen, cloakrooms and the other study bedrooms. But everywhere they had drawn a blank.

Which left the outbuildings and the grounds and there were bloody acres of those as Boyce pointed out gloomily when, after an unsuccessful search of the music-room and the ground-floor rooms in the west wing, they returned to the main entrance hall.

Finch stood with his shoulders hunched, looking out through the glass doors at the garden.

Boyce was right. For a full-scale search, he'd need about thirty extra men and that meant taking them off other duties. Besides, there was no guarantee that Arnott's life was in danger.

He came to a decision.

'We'll try the outbuildings first,' he announced. 'Then, if we come up with nothing, we'll have to extend the search to the grounds. You two,' addressing the uniformed men, 'take the garage block behind the main building. The Sergeant and I will deal with the new extensions by the west wing.'

As they moved off, Boyce asked, 'I take it by "extensions" you mean the swimming-pool as well.'

'I didn't like to mention it,' Finch replied. 'It seemed like tempting fate.'

He gave Boyce a wry look and they walked on in silence to the corner of the west wing where they struck off along the path towards the assembly hall.

It was locked and empty as Finch could see by merely looking in through the long windows while Boyce went to try the side door.

That, too, was locked, the Sergeant reported.

'Do you want to try the chapel?' he added.

Finch shrugged. It was a long shot but worth the twenty or so yards' walk between the two buildings. And once that had been checked out, there was only the pool left to search.

They struck off across the lawn, approaching the chapel through a bank of shrubbery which lined the broad path leading up to it, before ascending a flight of shallow stone steps towards the double doors which were set under an elaborately carved Victorian Gothic porch.

Finch waited, hands in pockets, as Boyce put the flat of his palm against one of the wooden leaves, ready to turn and walk away once Boyce had tested that it, too, was secured.

To the surprise of both of them, it opened, swinging back on its huge wrought-iron hinges and allowing them to step inside where they waited, letting their eyes adjust to the gloom after the brilliance of the sunshine outside.

Whoever had designed the chapel had evidently possessed a predilection for dark, polished oak which amounted almost to an obsession. It was everywhere, in the heavily vaulted roof, in the pews, in the pulpit, in the panelling which lined the choir, in the reredos itself.

Against this richly glistening background, colours and gilding seemed to float suspended, the stained glass of the exuberant east window, Christ in Glory with saints and angels adorned in ruby and sapphire and a galaxy of saffron haloes, hanging like a great up-ended jewel above the altar where the tall gilt cross and candlesticks glimmered with the rich splendour of a subterranean treasure-trove. Above the lectern, like the guardian of this Aladdin's cave, loomed a gilded eagle, wings outstretched, head reared ready to strike, while rows of brass candleholders, each with its small, white parchment shade, marched in a phalanx of glittering sentries, three deep, along both sides of the choir stalls.

If Arnott had not spoken, they might not have seen him. He was sitting in the choir stalls, hunched forward, his face as pale as one of the parchment shades.

'So you've found me,' he said.

With Boyce behind him, Finch began to walk quietly up the nave, his footsteps deadened by the long strip of dark matting which ran along the centre over the marble tiles. But they had gone only a few yards when Arnott called out, 'That's near enough. If you want me to talk, then keep your distance or you'll get no confession out of me.'

He meant it and Finch, with a nod at Boyce, sat down in one of the left-hand pews, the Sergeant joining him once he had pronounced the words of the official caution.

Arnott gave no sign that he had heard it. He was sitting some distance away, his face in profile, looking towards the opposite bank of choir stalls and, when he finally responded, it was as if he were addressing some unseen listener across the width of the chancel.

He spoke slowly, the flat, harsh voice by some acoustical quirk of the building echoing back from the vaulted roof and assuming a strange, disembodied resonance.

'I killed Livesey,' he said. 'But not the others. You believe that, don't you, Chief Inspector? If you try to pin those other deaths on me, I'll fight you through every court in the country.'

'I believe you,' Finch assured him. 'I know what happened between Goodyear and Nolan and I know why.'

There was no need to elaborate for Arnott's benefit although Finch could have continued with his explanation. Goodyear had planned Nolan's murder as a punishment for being the cause of his daughter's suicide. Already widowed and then, after her death, left childless, he must have set about her revenge quite dispassionately although 'revenge' was perhaps not the right word to use. Goodyear would have looked on it as a just retribution. All the same, whatever name you gave it, Goodyear had not rushed into it in the first agony of despair. He had even sold up his house and moved south in order to be nearer Nolan, tracing and following him to Morton Grange where he had waited for the right moment before finally acting. And his decision to murder Nolan had given him great satisfaction. Finch had Harriet Wade's evidence for that. He had been buoyant with happiness, she had said, like a child at Christmas. Or, in his case, a man with a mission.

His opportunity had come quickly, on only the second evening of the summer school course when Nolan had gone alone to the assembly hall. It wouldn't have been difficult for Goodyear to slip unseen out of the main building and follow him. What excuse he had made to persuade Nolan to go with him to the pool would

208

probably never be known. Had he said perhaps that there had been an accident? It was feasible. But whatever the reason Goodyear had given, Finch had no doubt that Nolan had gone willingly, not knowing that Goodyear was Patti Rayner's father.

The site for Nolan's murder must have already been chosen and, for Goodyear's purpose, the swimming-pool was ideal. His daughter had drowned herself; Nolan would die in the same way. The rosemary, too, must have already been picked and the weapon concealed somewhere near the pool, Finch suspected.

Once Nolan was there, the rest was easy. Goodyear had merely to coax Nolan close to the edge of the pool; simple enough if Nolan thought someone was in the water who needed rescuing. All Goodyear had to do then was to retrieve the weapon and strike him on the side of the head before pushing him or letting him topple into the pool where the sprigs of rosemary were already floating. They had been taken from the herb garden near the garages and, Finch believed, were not part of Goodyear's original plan but had been added because, having noticed the bush, he thought the rosemary a fitting tribute to his dead daughter.

And after that . . .

But Arnott was saying, 'If you know what happened, you'll know Goodyear committed suicide after he'd murdered Nolan.'

'Yes,' Finch agreed simply.

That, too, had been planned. He had Harriet Wade's evidence for that as well. She had said that, as soon as he arrived, Goodyear had been anxious to put his car under cover. In other words, he had made sure he secured one of the garages for his own use. And death by carbon monoxide poisoning was one of the classic means of suicide. In fact, when he had first heard of Goodyear's death, Finch's own initial assumption had been that he had killed himself. Every piece of evidence had pointed that way except for two.

Out loud, he asked, although he thought he already knew the answer, 'Why did you make it look like murder by putting the pansy in the car and moving the sacks to the outside of the garage door, Mr Arnott?'

Arnott turned his head to look at the Chief Inspector.

'If you know so bloody much, can't you guess?' he asked in a jeering voice.

'Revenge on Livesey?' Finch suggested.

'And why not?' Arnott countered. 'What the hell had he done for me? He could have given me a few decent reviews, pushed up my book sales. Instead he ignored me as if I was some tuppeny ha'penny scribbler not worth a damn. It was the same here at Morton Grange. When I was in the best-seller lists, nothing was too good for me. He sold his bloody summer school on my name alone. But as soon as the sales started to drop off, Livesey turned on me. It was done very cleverly. There was nothing crude about Bernard. But he still made his meaning clear. It began with petty criticisms. There had been complaints about my teaching. Would I try to make myself more agreeable to the students? And would I please make sure the written assignments were assessed on time? Then he brought that damned Wade woman in on the course. It was a deliberate insult! What the hell did she know about writing? She'd produced one novel – one! – and I'd spent a lifetime as a writer. But because she'd been well reviewed, Bernard was all over her. Miss bloody Wade could do nothing wrong.'

For a few moments, Arnott was silent, his face in profile once again as, hunched up in the choir stall, he brooded on the wrongs done to him.

'He intended dropping me from the course,' he continued. 'I could see that. Suddenly he was all sweetness and light. But he didn't fool me. He was softening me up for the push. Knowing him, it'd be by letter. Bernard hadn't the courage for a face-to-face showdown. That's when I decided to mess things up for him. One murder and a suicide was bad enough publicity. But two murders! That'd finish his precious summer school.'

'So you changed the evidence,' Finch put in, trying to draw Arnott back from the pit of his own bitterness. 'And it was very cleverly carried out, too, Mr Arnott. You certainly fooled me. As you had an alibi for Nolan's and Goodyear's deaths, you were in the clear.'

As a sop to Arnott's ego, it worked as Finch had intended. Arnott laughed, a humourless, self-satisfied chuckle which, re-verberating back from the vaulting, sounded insane. And quite possibly he was mad, Finch thought, although not crazy enough to plead insanity at his trial.

'Yes, it was ingenious, wasn't it?' Arnott agreed. 'It gave quite a nice little twist to the plot. After Nolan's body had been found and you lot had been sent for, Bernard called a meeting. He asked that Wade woman to get everyone togetner in the common room. Her again, you see. Not me. So I cleared off upstairs to my room. I could see from my bedroom window a bit of what was going on round the pool but not very clearly. I wanted a better view. Call it a writer's curiosity, if you like. I knew if I went to the yard by the kitchen, I'd be able to see more. It had started to rain by then so I took a coat and went down by the back stairs, let myself quietly out by the lobby door in case Joyce Yarwood was in the kitchen and walked across to the yard entrance. I was too far away from the pool for any of your men to notice me but, while I was standing there, I saw Joyce Yarwood come to the kitchen window and look out. I was afraid she might see me so I moved round the corner to the stable-yard.

'When I got there, I heard an engine running. It seemed odd that someone should have started up a car at that time of night, especially as all the garage doors were closed. When I went to look, I found Goodyear.'

'Already dead,' Finch stated.

'Of course, Chief Inspector.' Again that derisive note was in Arnott's voice. 'He was sitting behind the wheel but had fallen heavily across the passenger's seat, striking his head on the door handle on the far side. I lifted him up and, when I saw the bruise, the idea suddenly came to me. Nolan had been struck on the head. I knew that much from what Harriet Wade had said earlier. If I moved Goodyear's body so that it was lying over the steering-wheel, wiped any blood and hair off the handle and faked the other evidence, I could make it look like another murder. But I'd be in the clear. I had an alibi. As you so rightly said, it was a clever bit of thinking. I knew I'd touched the handle on the driver's door when I'd opened it so I wiped that clean as well and made sure I kept the handkerchief over my hand so I wouldn't leave any more prints. The window on Goodyear's side was already open. All I had to do was lift his hand through it and press the fingers against the handle to put his prints on it instead. I had to work fast as the place was full of exhaust fumes.

'The rest was easy. The herb garden was only a few yards away. At the meeting, the Wade woman had mentioned the rosemary Nolan had been holding in his hand and in fact it was I who suggested that *Hamlet* connection. Even Bernard hadn't the

211

sense to see the link. It was a false trail, of course, but added, I thought, a nice little literary flourish to Goodyear's supposed murder. At first, I was going to leave another sprig of rosemary in the car but then I noticed the pansies growing near the bush and it occurred to me that one of those would be an improvement. I can't remember the exact quotation. It's something about pansies being for thoughts, isn't it? It seemed more than apt. You'd have a hell of a lot of thinking to do when you found it.' He laughed again. 'So I picked one, chucked it into Goodyear's car and cleared off, taking the letter with me.'

'Letter?' Finch asked sharply.

'Goodyear's suicide note,' Arnott replied. He seemed annoyed at being interrupted in mid-flow. 'Didn't I mention it? It was lying on the passenger seat. Later I read it. In it, he gave an account of his reasons for murdering Nolan – how he'd got his daughter pregnant and then refused to marry her, telling her to get an abortion. Typical of Nolan; he had the morals of an alley cat. Anyway, it seemed she'd loved him; more fool her. But Goodyear was able to trace Nolan down here through that theatre company he belonged to and arrange his murder. I realised when I read it that there was no *Hamlet* connection. The rosemary was just a reference to his daughter's name. Not that it mattered. You and the Wade woman seemed convinced there was a link and it suited my purpose to add to it. I found it all rather amusing.'

But not so very wrong, after all, Finch thought. Revenge had been the motive behind both murders although he said nothing except to ask, 'What happened to the letter?'

'I burnt it,' Arnott said promptly. 'I wasn't going to be fool enough to keep it in case you searched my room.'

Finch let it pass. He could get a more detailed account of its contents from Arnott once he had been charged and taken to divisional headquarters although he could make a good guess at what it had contained. At the moment, he was more concerned with letting Arnott finish his statement.

'And then?' he prompted.

'Goodyear had already blocked up the air grille in the garage wall and laid the sacks along the bottom of the door, only on the inside, of course. I found them when I lifted the door up. All I had to do once I'd closed it down again was to put the sacks along the outside to make it look like another murder. I then went back to the house, dropping the iron bar which Goodyear had used to kill Nolan and which he'd also left in the car down one of the drains by the service yard. But I didn't go back by the lobby door. Knowing Joyce Yarwood was likely to be in the kitchen, I didn't want to risk it. Instead, I let myself in by the side entrance where the passage to the west wing joins the main corridor by the common room.'

'But my men must have started to search the grounds by then!' Finch protested.

It angered him that Arnott had had the bloody nerve to make his escape practically under their noses.

Arnott gave that humourless, chuckling laugh again.

'Yes, they were. I saw them. They were prodding about the bushes and flashing lights everywhere; too damned busy to notice me. I kept to the grass and there was plenty of shrubbery for cover. I simply let himself in, left my wet raincoat in one of the lockers in the cloakroom by the vestibule and went straight to my tutorial room which was next door where I sat down at my desk. I didn't dare go back upstairs to my room; I might have met someone on the way. By a bit of good luck, I had a folder of work in my desk drawer so, when you found me, to all intents and purposes I'd spent the evening there writing. Fooled you, didn't it, Chief Inspector? And your Sergeant?'

Finch was damned if he was going to admit as much for a second time although he noticed that Boyce lifted his head from his half-sitting, half-crouching position in the pew beside him where he was surreptitiously taking notes, as if resenting Arnott's derision.

'And then Livesey had to be murdered,' Finch said. 'Why, Mr Arnott? Hadn't he already been punished enough?'

It was an aspect of the case he couldn't even guess at. Up to that point, Arnott had been in the clear. With an alibi to prove his innocence of any implication in the other two deaths, why had he murdered Livesey? And why, having used his not inconsiderable ingenuity to falsify the evidence of Goodyear's suicide, had he not even bothered to wipe his prints off the knife?

There was a long silence before Arnott answered and when he did finally speak, his voice sounded even more muffled and disembodied than before. Peering forward into the shadows of

213

the choir, Finch saw that Arnott was now leaning forward, his face hidden in his hands.

'I'm not sure myself any more,' he replied, 'although at the time it all made sense. Yesterday evening before supper, he called a meeting to discuss publicity. Someone had evidently tipped off the press about the double murder. Bernard seemed to think I'd done it. As if I'd go to the bloody newspapers! He should have known better. They crucified me when my marriage broke up last year, phoning me up at all hours of the day and night, lying in wait for me outside the house, wanting to know all the sordid details. The gutter press had a bloody field day. Do you know what one of them had the gall to call me? "Former best-selling novelist". Former! And yet not one of them had printed a decent review of my books for the past five years although they'd fallen over themselves to interview me when *The Pool* was filmed and was top of the best-sellers. I remember thinking when Bernard hinted that I'd tipped them off: If that's what he thinks of me, then he ought to be bloody dead like Nolan and Goodyear. After that, it all seemed to happen as if . . .'

His voice trailed away.

'As if what?' Finch prompted.

'You're not a writer, Chief Inspector, otherwise you'd understand,' Arnott replied. 'It was as if Livesey's murder had already been plotted like the ending to a book. It wasn't so much a question of deciding what to do as acting out something that had already been written. After supper last night I went up to my room. I sat for a long time thinking about Livesey and how he deserved to die. At about half-past nine, I decided to have a bath. I opened my bedroom door and suddenly there he was! He was coming out of his bedroom, carrying a tray. I can't explain how I felt. It was as if, by thinking about him, I'd somehow managed to conjure him up like one of my characters. I followed him to the top of the service stairs where I waited while he left the tray in the kitchen. Then he came out and went along the corridor which leads past the dining-room. I remember thinking: He's going to his study. As soon as he'd disappeared round the corner, I went downstairs and into the kitchen. I wanted to check first that no one was there. He'd left the tray on the draining-board beside some kitchen knives. I remember picking one of them up, God knows why. I don't think I'd planned what was going to happen

214

next in any detail except there had to be a good, exciting climax like the fight scene at the end of *The Pool* when Deacon is knifed by Harry. My readers expect a dramatic ending.

'He was at the window, drawing the curtains, when I went in. He turned round and said, "Oh, it's you," his voice and expression full of contempt. No, not contempt,' Arnott corrected himself. 'It wasn't even that. He was simply dismissive as if I counted for nothing. You remember in *The Pool* that's why Deacon is murdered? He says to Harry, "You're rubbish," and turns his back on him. Harry thinks of all the times Deacon's treated him like dirt and picks up the bread knife. You remember that scene?'

He repeated the words eagerly as if anxious for Finch's reassurance, not only that he had read the book but that he understood Arnott's motivation.

'Yes,' the Chief Inspector replied. 'I remember.'

But it was not quite as Arnott himself would have wanted the scene to be recalled. In the novel, Harry had seized the knife which had been lying on the table. In Arnott's case, he had gone to Livesey's study with the weapon already in his hand. There was the difference.

Arnott was saying, 'He fell forward on to his knees. I can still see him. The blood was pouring out of his neck. And suddenly it wasn't like a book any more. It was real.' He shuddered, his voice dropping so low that Finch could barely hear him. 'All that blood!' Then unexpectedly his voice rose as he threw back his head and the laugh rang out again. 'If you want a quotation, Chief Inspector, what about this one? "Who would have thought the old man to have had so much blood in him?" Wrong play, though, isn't it? That's *Macbeth*, not *Hamlet*.'

'What happened next?' Finch asked. He was in no mood for any more literary references. It was time to force Arnott on to complete his statement.

The laugh broke off abruptly.

'I lifted the curtain over him to cover him up. I couldn't bear to look at him. I don't know what happened to the knife. I must have dropped it somewhere. But I remember taking the keys which were on the desk. I don't know why.'

Because they were symbols of Bernard's authority? Finch wondered but there was no time to speculate. Arnott was still

215

speaking, the voice harsher now, the sentences more broken as if he were tiring and losing coherence.

'I walked about the gardens for a long time – hours, it must have been. Then I unlocked the doors and came in here. It was getting light. I wanted somewhere to sit down. Odd that, isn't it? I haven't been inside a church for years, not even for my marriage. That was in a registry office. But a church is peaceful. You can think your thoughts. I'd considered killing myself but I couldn't decide how. Like Goodyear? Or should I drown myself in the pool as Nolan had died?'

Finch nodded although he doubted if Arnott or even Boyce noticed that small gesture of the head, acknowledging his own fears that Arnott might have taken his own life, completing the same pattern of murder followed by suicide which had marked the conclusion to the Nolan and Goodyear case.

'In the end,' Arnott was saying, 'I hadn't the courage. I'm dying anyway, of cancer of the bowel. Not very dramatic, is it, Chief Inspector? Hardly the ending I would have chosen for one of my characters but it'll serve its purpose. One death's as good as another. Either way, I'm finished so, if you want to take me, I'm ready for you.'

He stood up as Finch and Boyce approached, moving out of the choir stall to stand facing them, the altar and the east window behind him.

Boyce glanced inquiringly at Finch who looked up at the stained-glass window, depicting Christ in Glory. Then, with a gesture of his head, the Chief Inspector led the way down the nave towards the porch.

Even so, it was a curious place in which to charge a man. As Boyce stepped forward under the Gothic arch to speak the formal words of arrest, Finch waited, his eyes on the view of Morton Grange across the sunlit lawns. Bernard's study window was visible in the ground-floor façade while, to his left, he could see the dark yew hedges which surrounded the swimming-pool and, a little further off, above the roof-line, the white clock tower with its gold and blue dial which marked the stable-yard.

He was thinking that perhaps the choice of place for Arnott's arrest wasn't so very unsuitable after all.

23

It had not been Finch's intention to return to Morton Grange after Arnott's arrest although he had been vaguely aware that some unfinished business remained behind there without being quite certain of its exact nature. But, with Arnott in custody, the next two days were entirely taken up with preparing the report to go before the DPP, collating statements, checking exhibits and forensic reports, so that he barely had time to cook himself an evening meal, let alone put his mind to any other commitments apart from official paper-work. He even forgot on occasions to think about Marion Greave.

Her second letter came as a complete surprise, arriving so soon after the last which he had not yet answered, having postponed replying to it until he had found a little space in his life to consider how to react to her news that she would shortly be going abroad with a 'friend'.

He found the letter lying amongst other correspondence, mostly bills, on the front doormat as he came downstairs after showering and shaving. At first, he didn't notice it, picking it up with the rest of the envelopes which he sorted through quickly on his way to the kitchen to put the kettle and the electric toaster on for breakfast.

The familiar handwriting brought him up short. Neat, brisk, competent, it faced him from the front of the white envelope almost as if Marion Greave herself was looking back at him with that humorous, upward tilt to the corners of her eyes.

Still standing, he opened it and took out the letter, aware suddenly of how silent the house was now that his sister had left. He could hear the fridge in the corner humming quietly to itself and the rapid, staccato ticking of the alarm clock on his bedside table upstairs.

The letter was short, a mere two paragraphs, but even so he had to read it through twice before he was able to convince himself of its contents.

She was leaving for Crete in a week's time and would be away for a fortnight, returning on August 28th. As she would have a few days' leave in hand, she was proposing to spend them in London. If he was free, would he care to meet her? Knowing how busy he was, there was no need for him to write back; he could leave a message at her London hotel, the address and phone number of which followed.

Would he care to meet her!

Suddenly it no longer mattered whom she might be going abroad with. The day took on an entirely different shape and colour and dimension. It was as if everything about him expanded, filling him with a sense of new hopes and possibilities, of limitless horizons.

He was – yes, buoyant with happiness.

It was Harriet Wade's expression, he remembered, standing there with Marion's letter in his hand and it was because of this that he made up his mind to go back to Morton Grange but alone this time although, as he rang headquarters to tell them that he wouldn't be coming into the office until after lunch, he wasn't quite sure himself why he had made the decision.

Partly, it was in the nature of a celebration, a desire to break free of the mould and mark the day out by creating an entirely different pattern for himself. Partly, too, it was a desire to drive off somewhere into the country, itself a pleasure, taking Marion's letter with him to think about and exult over.

But also, he realised, as he put the receiver down, it was in the nature of a repayment, God alone knew why or for what. He was simply aware that he had a commitment to fulfil connected with Harriet Wade which, on its completion, would leave him free to enjoy his own happiness to the utmost.

Harriet Wade was packing when she heard the car draw up. She had cleared the table drawer of papers which she had spread out on the bed before sorting through them and deciding which to throw away.

Glancing out of the window, she saw the stocky figure of the Chief Inspector get out of the car and stand for a few moments in the drive, looking about him with that alert, cocked angle to his head which told her he was taking in every detail of his surroundings.

His arrival surprised her. She imagined that the police had finished with Morton Grange although the fact that he was alone suggested that he hadn't come on official business.

All the same, she felt uneasy as she went down the stairs to let him in, her disquiet increased by her awareness of how deserted the place was now that the students had left. Its emptiness oppressed her. All those vacant rooms! All those yards of silent corridors!

She met him in the doorway as he came up the steps towards her. He was smiling, to reassure her, she imagined, although she felt there was some other reason for his obvious happiness.

'It's all right,' he told her. 'I've simply called as a visitor to see how you are.'

'That's kind of you,' she said.

'Shall we walk?' he suggested. 'It's too nice a day to be indoors.'

She accepted the invitation with relief, glad to have the excuse to escape from Morton Grange.

As if by common consent, although neither of them had spoken, they strolled towards the great cedar trees and the banks of evergreens which marked the far end of the east wing, turning their backs on the assembly hall and the other buildings to the west of the main block.

'So you're managing all right?' Finch asked, as if picking up an earlier conversation.

She was touched by his concern about her and a certain awkwardness of manner as he put the question as if afraid of intruding on her privacy, a reticence on his part which she could understand. As she had realised before, he was an essentially private man himself.

'The last students left yesterday,' she told him. 'It was a relief in a way. At least I'm no longer responsible for them although the place seems very quiet now they've gone.'

'I'm sorry you've had to cope with it all on your own.'

'I haven't minded so much. It kept me busy. Besides, I shan't have to deal with everything. I've been in touch with Bernard's solicitor and accountant. They're arriving this afternoon for a meeting with the school governors when I imagine the final arrangements will be made to settle Bernard's affairs and close the summer school officially.' Unexpectedly, she added, 'Why did Ron kill Bernard?'

She had halted and turned to face him. It was one of the questions which so far she had been unable to answer for herself. The rest, Jake's murder and Frank's suicide, she felt she could understand.

'For much the same reasons that Hamlet gave,' Finch said. 'Pride, revenge, ambition. He felt Bernard didn't appreciate his talents sufficiently. He suspected, too, that Bernard intended sacking him as a course tutor. But mainly, it was an accumulation of years of bitterness and frustration which came to a head when Bernard accused him of tipping off the press. That's what really hurt his self-esteem.'

'Yes, I can understand that,' Harriet replied. 'At the time, when Bernard hinted it was Ron, I thought he might be right. Ron seemed capable of hitting back at Bernard in that way. But I didn't realise at the time, although I feel I should have done, that Ron wasn't really like that. He had a kind of integrity of his own which I should have recognised.'

'Perhaps,' Finch said, appearing to agree but omitting to add that Arnott's integrity wasn't quite as scrupulous as she imagined, remembering Arnott's confession and his bitterness against Harriet Wade herself.

But who was he to spoil her morning? Or, come to that, his own?

'So you think Leon could have been behind it?' he asked.

'Oh, I'm quite sure of that now,' she said.

They walked on in companionable silence, turning back at the far end of the lawn towards the house. Harriet was thinking how easy it was to be with him. He seemed to demand so little in the way of either conversation or response, content to be himself and to let her be herself, too. Not like Jake. And not, she realised, like Kay whose relationship with her, especially in the last few days, had become increasingly committed as if, after that encounter with her on the morning of Bernard's murder, Kay had some special ownership over her.

'You'll keep in touch with me, of course,' she had said the previous evening before driving away, gazing up at Harriet through the open driver's window of her car, willing her with her eyes to smile back and agree.

220

Looking sideways at Finch's profile, she thought how relaxed and undemanding he seemed, strolling along, hands in pockets, gazing about him at the trees and the formal rosebeds with those quick little interested glances of his which missed nothing, a man at peace with himself and his surroundings.

'And what about the others?' he asked suddenly, meeting her eyes. 'What's happening to them?'

It occurred to her that this was the reason behind his unexpected visit. Having entered their lives, he couldn't go away without reassuring himself of all their futures.

'I had a long talk yesterday with Joyce Yarwood,' she told him. 'She's leaving Morton Grange. In fact, she'll give in her notice at this afternoon's meeting with the governors. She said she'd like to go abroad; perhaps take up hotel management. George Burton's still here. I suppose he'll stay on. But once Joyce leaves . . .'

She left the rest of the sentence unfinished, unable to guess at his future apart from his loneliness.

'And you?' he asked finally.

They had reached the steps to the main entrance.

'Me? I'm not sure although I'll probably go away by myself for the rest of the summer. I might even start another novel. After that, who knows?' She shrugged and smiled. 'But I'll be all right. I'll survive.'

She spoke lightly. All the same, he believed her. She had the quality of a survivor about her.

He was about to say goodbye and walk away to his car when she added, 'Would you do something for me?'

'Of course,' he said, turning back quickly. 'What is it?'

'Would you let me know the date of Frank Goodyear's funeral? I'd like to go.'

'Ring me at my office in a couple of days' time,' he told her, giving her his card. 'I should know by then. We managed, by the way, to trace a couple of his relatives, a cousin and a brother-in-law on his wife's side of the family. Even so, I don't imagine there'll be many at the funeral.'

'He knew about the herb garden,' she continued. 'Yesterday, before he left, Steve Mayhew told me he remembered seeing Frank at the door that leads to it from the stable-yard on the afternoon before he killed Jake. He didn't go in as Steve was

221

already there. But I suppose he could have noticed the rosemary then and gone back later to pick it. It's a small point but I thought you might like to have it cleared up for the record.'

'Yes; for the record. It's important to have as many loose ends tied up as we can,' Finch agreed, smiling and seeming oddly pleased at such a trivial piece of information.

He nodded goodbye, giving her a final wave through the driver's window as the car accelerated away.

Harriet went back upstairs to finish her packing, sitting down on the bed to sort through the papers she had left there. Some were quickly disposed of – her lecture notes for the Morton Grange summer school, for example. Tearing them in halves and then into quarters, she dumped them in the waste-paper basket.

So was Kay's address. It took no more than a few seconds' thought before Harriet tore that, too, into small fragments.

But she hesitated over Steve's address. He had written it out for her the previous day before leaving, having made much the same request of her that she had made of Finch.

'If you can find out when Frank's funeral is, will you drop me a line? I'd like to go. He was a nice man.'

And tearing out a page from his diary, he had scribbled down his address and phone number.

She could hardly throw it away, could she? She felt she had entered into some kind of obligation to him, although as she folded the slip of paper in half and put it in her wallet with Finch's card, she would have preferred to make the break complete and to throw that away, too, along with all the other pieces from the past.